the
PLANET
MASTERS

ALLEN WOLD

ST. MARTIN'S • NEW YORK

Library of Congress Cataloging in Publication Data

Wold, Allen.
The planet masters.

I. Title.
PZ4.W85313Pl [PS3573.046] 813'.5'4 78-3997
ISBN 0-312-61398-9

 For information, write:
St. Martin's Press, Inc., 175 Fifth Ave., New York, N.Y. 10010.
Manufactured in the United States of America
Library of Congress Catalog Card Number: 78-3997

First Edition

PROAIRESIS

PROAIRESIS

It was the cleanest spaceport McCade had ever seen. He stood for a moment at the head of the landing ramp, looking around at the spotless concrete, the sparkling buildings, the clear sky. The *Dovetail* was the only ship on the apron, and there were no other people as far as he could see. But it was clean. He could imagine the cleaners coming out of some shed somewhere after the *Dovetail* left again, in two days, polishing away all signs of its ever having been there.

A breeze came from the west and brought with it the scent of trees and growing things. He knew the port, in the Red Dog district of Loger, was at the edge of the city, but to have no city smell at all was very strange. Every city he'd ever been in, on every world, had had a city smell. Maybe when the wind changed the true aroma of this place would return.

As he stood he saw a low, broad vehicle come out of one of the terminal buildings, all glass and chrome, and come floating centimeters above the ground toward the *Dovetail* in a graceful, unhurried curve. And then he felt a touch at his elbow.

"Everything all right?" the tall, graying man asked.

"So far, Captain," McCade answered. The shuttle car stopped, connected to the base of the ramp, and McCade and the Captain went down to the vehicle and got inside. There was no driver. It was fully automatic.

When they had gotten themselves comfortably seated, the car detached itself from the ramp and started smoothly back toward the terminal.

"Are you sure you don't want to come back with me?" Captain Toledo asked. It was plain that he was truly concerned.

"Quite sure," McCade said, watching the apron slide by.

"I won't be back for six months," Captain Toledo went on, "and as far as I know, nobody else stops here."

"That's quite all right," McCade said. The car slid into the terminal, one side opened up, and they were now at the edge of a large, comfortable waiting room. One whole wall of the room was a series of such cars, twenty in all, each with a capacity of fifty passengers. There was nobody else in sight.

"Is it always this empty?" McCade asked.

"Always. They don't get many visitors, and none of the residents ever goes traveling, which is good enough for me."

"You must find *some* profit in this trip."

"Oh, yes, I do," was all Toledo would admit.

They left the waiting room, where on any other world innumerable ticket counters would have displayed their colorful logos. Here, on Seltique, there was only one desk, no timetables, no fancy insignia, just one man, who looked like an executive. And who looked bored. He did not rise as McCade and Toledo neared.

"Captain Toledo," the man said. "Welcome back."

"Thank you. Here's the invoice for this shipment." He handed the well-dressed man a thick envelope, which the man dropped into a slot in his desk. Immediately another one rose up out of it.

"And here is your new invoice," the man said. "We'll have you unloaded by midmorning tomorrow, inspected by noon. If there's no need of extensive service, you should be ready to go by noon the next day."

"Very good," Toledo said and grinned. "I'll be at my usual place." He turned to McCade. "Noon the day after tomorrow," he said. "If your change your mind, be here before then."

"If I do," McCade said, "I will. Goodbye, Captain."

Toledo stood a moment longer, then with a scowl, turned and walked across the bright tiled floor to where the sign said "Public Road." McCade turned back to the man behind the desk.

"And you are?" the man asked.

"Larson McCade." He handed the man his papers and ticket. The man took them doubtfully, examined them resignedly, and returned them mechanically.

"They are in order," he said.

"Good. Where do I get my bags?"

The man pointed to a sign.

"Fine. And I'd like to confirm my hotel reservations." The man looked blank.

"I signalled ahead a week ago," McCade said, "and booked a suite at the Firesign. Would you check for me please?"

The man stared a moment longer, then looked down at his desk, touched a button to one side, and scanned the glowing panel.

"Ah," he said, "I'm sorry to have misunderstood. You desire transient accommodations. The Firesign is not equipped to take care of you, and therefore your reservation has been canceled."

“What do you mean, it can’t take care of me?”

“It is a place for romantic assignations, not living. Begging your pardon, sir, but you are an outsider, and I’d strongly recommend that you accompany Captain Toledo on his return flight.”

“Is cancelling my reservation your way of emphasizing that recommendation?” McCade asked.

The man looked up at him again, and after a moment smiled quite genuinely.

“No, sir,” he said. “But you are an outsider, and it’s understandable that certain aspects of our society here would be beyond your knowledge. We are not used to tourists, have no facilities for them, and really nothing for them to see.”

“Maybe so,” McCade said, “but I’ll give it a try anyway.”

The man just shrugged, grinned again, and lost interest in him.

“Excuse me,” McCade said. He was not flustered, he was too experienced for that.

“Yes?” the man said, looking up again.

"Even if I stay only two days,” McCade said, “I’ll need some place to sleep.”

“Oh, of course. I’m sorry.” The man touched another button on the desk. Again the screen lit up.

“Room . . .” the man began.

“Suite,” McCade corrected.

“Pardon. Suite for one, immediately,” the man said. “No credit.” There was a flicker of light in the panel.

“Cash in advance,” McCade said, flipping open a packet of blue-green vouchers with red scrolls and figures. The man was not impressed.

“We can accommodate you,” he said, “at the Morphy Chessica. Please understand, it is not what you might be accustomed to.”

McCade nodded, put the vouchers away, and went to the sign that said, “Luggage Pick-Up.” There were his bags, three of them, and a small case that must have been Toledo’s. McCade gripped the handle of the floating rack and drew it out after him. There were no porters. He was not used to doing things like this for himself, but that didn't matter. So far he was having no more trouble than he'd expected.

Towing the bags after him, he went through the door Toledo had left by, and found himself in a sort of arcade, roofed over with milk glass and open at either end, through which ran a shimmering belt some fifteen meters wide. There were no vehicles. For a moment he was at a loss and started to re-enter the terminal, but then took another look at the road surface. It was a molecular belt, one way, to the left.

"Morphy Chessica," he said out loud, and the road winked. He took his bags off the float, set them down on the twinkling belt, and as he stepped on himself, saw the luggage float going back into the terminal, under its own direction and power. Then the molecular film under his feet began to move, accelerating so slowly that his balance was not in the least disturbed.

He slid out of the arcade, and the belt joined a main road. Here there were people, moving in both directions, sliding effortlessly on the molecular belt which ran down the center of a tree-lined lawn. Buildings rose on both sides, widely spaced, landscaped with shrubs and flowers. It looked more like a middle-class business district than a portside area. He watched the people as he and his bags joined the moving way, and they, in turn, watched him.

He grinned. He knew what they were seeing. His looks had turned out to be one of his best assets. Because of them, no one ever took him seriously, and he liked it that way. It gave him an advantage. With a deeply cleft chin, full cheeks, a mouth that always quirked in an almost smile, broad forehead, big blue eyes, curly hair, he looked twenty instead of thirty-five, and a little bit silly. Somehow, people never thought that the style and fit of his clothes, which were always perfect, could possibly be a contradiction to his face. Until it was too late.

He rode northward for just a few blocks and stopped in front of a large tower. He took his bags from the belt and, leaving them on the lawn, walked up to the entrance.

There was no clerk in the lobby, just a specialized comcon keyed to voice.

"I called from the spaceport," he said.

"Do you have luggage?" a pleasantly modulated, neutral voice from the comcon asked.

"Outside," he answered. There was a ping. Then the voice said, "You are from off world?"

"That is correct."

"You will have to pay cash until you have established proper credit," the voice told him. A low cart appeared beside him with his bags on it. He took out his packet of vouchers, pulled two of them off, and laid them on the comcon. They were whisked away, and numbers appeared on the panel in front of him.

"This is your credit balance after deducting two days' lodging," the voice said.

McCade did not answer, but turned to the cart, which moved away across the lobby to a tiny cubicle. He followed it in. The door closed and a moment later opened again, and McCade followed the cart out of the cubicle down a broad, chair and potted-plant lined hall to a door. There was no number. There was no key. The door opened when he touched it, and he went inside. This time it was the cart which followed him.

It was a fairly decent suite, with a living room, a bedroom, a large bath, a study, and a kitchen-dinette. Nothing fancy by his standards, but certainly adequate.

The cart had deposited his baggage in the middle of the living room. He spent the next hour unpacking and putting things away. Then he sat at the comcon in the study and punched out the universal code for information.

"A directory, please," he said to the bright geometric pattern on the screen. There was a click. A door underneath the screen opened, and he took out a large, onionskin volume. Quickly, he thumbed through, punched another number, and this time a face appeared.

"May I have an atlas of the city?" he asked.

"Certainly," the attractive young woman said. She punched, his comcon clicked again, and he removed another volume. He switched off, but before the screen faded completely, some numbers flashed on. His credit balance. It had shrunk considerably. He took out his packet of vouchers and fed ten more blue-green bills into the appropriate slot.

Then he turned his attention to the directory. He knew nobody in Loger, but he had some names, names he'd heard as a boy, and he wanted to see if any of them still existed here, on a world that, though in the center of the Orion Limb of the galaxy, had been only sporadically visited for the last two thousand years. Everybody knew Seltique was here. It even figured in the history books. But the people of Seltique discouraged visitors, and nobody wanted to come here much anyway.

None of the names were in the directory. He turned to the back section, and found a haberdasher. One thing he had noticed on his trip from the spaceport, his clothes were badly out of style here. Though there was still effective and efficient non-physical communication between Seltique and the rest of the Limb, these people had gone their own way more than any other planet.

He dialed the haberdasher and ordered some clothes. The comcon took his measurements where he sat. As he waited for the haberdasher to prepare his clothes he looked up the Morphy Chessica in the directory. It was, he discovered, not a hotel at all, but a place advertised to provide comfortable living for people who had suffered a "demotion," whatever that was, and who, for obscure legal reasons, had to leave their own houses and could not immediately move into a new house. He closed the directory and ran over in his mind what he knew about this world.

Seltique was not exactly isolated, though little news came out of it. Much went in, he knew, but what these people did with it, no one could say. It was a shy world, caught alone in the middle of a crowd, afraid to reach out, afraid to go away. It saw and heard what went on elsewhere in the Limb, but contributed nothing. Not that it couldn't, McCade thought as the comcon pinged and he began to remove packages from the recess. Several things he'd seen so far today had impressed him as being highly desirable elsewhere—the luggage floater, the molecular road which was the best he'd seen anywhere, the cleanness of the air. Contrary to his expectations, even in the city proper, there was no city smell or city noise.

He removed the package of clothing. The comcon flashed his balance, and he fed it the rest of the voucher packet.

He turned to the atlas, orienting himself on the small-scale overall map. His hotel, as he continued to think of it, was at the western edge of the city of Loger. To the north, south, and east the city spread, divided into fifty-four districts. Red Dog was, he knew, the lowest-class district of all, as befitted a spaceport area. But if what he had seen of Red Dog so far was any indication of low-class, he could hardly wait to see some of the better districts.

Checking with the index at the back of his atlas, he located a number of spots of interest to him: the main offices of the Eight Brotherhoods, several libraries, museums, schools, major churches. He grinned softly as he familiarized himself with the layout of the city, and for a moment he looked very much the good-natured clown. But there was more in his eyes than humor.

Satisfied at last that he could not get seriously lost, he changed into some of his new clothes, carefully selected not to be at the peak of style, but a few steps below it. Still, he would do himself well. The fit was perfect, and if he had insisted on hot colors, what was it to anyone else? Then he left his suite, took the elevator down to the lobby, and went out into the street. People still noticed him, of course, but not as many, and their reactions were less pronounced. His face was still bright and foolish, but now he was one of them, not an outsider, and would be soon forgotten. He stepped on the belt, said, "Go," and just went.

He quickly passed out of Red Dog into Aragon to the north, across a river, under a bridge of some sort, into an area of comfortable homes on landscaped yards. He continued north into Rocky Point, where there were more high-rises, all beautiful. Then he veered east, cut across a corner of Regan and into Hadoth, where towers of enameled crystal rose to the clear sky. He skirted along the edge of another river, small and neat with manicured banks, across which was Whitefriar, where he had no business going as yet. North again, through Beach Harbor; east again across the tip of residential Newport, into Yarbrough, where the buildings were short but extensive; south towards Emeraud and its mini-estates, across a belt of Foxes, which followed no style, but with style, then further south through Rand, Duchane, St. Clair; west across Carmel, which reminded him of Chicago or Lorke, on to King's Lake with its huge lawns and Redkirk with its spires among the trees; south a bit to Bethim; further west through Chatham and Riverside; then north again and back into Red Dog. He was south of the spaceport now, and at the westernmost edge of the city of Loger. He had seen but a fraction of it. There were districts he had not yet glimpsed. Still, it was enough to give him a feeling for the place, though he had stayed out of the highest-class neighborhoods. As he understood it, it could be death to enter certain districts without good reason.

On his right hand was the city. On his left an elegant parkland that stretched away for several kilometers before the forest took over. There were no other cities on Seltique, though there once had been many rich metropolises. Now there was only Loger, and all the rest of the planet was ruin, jungle, forest, desert, ocean, and bare mountain. As his roadbelt swept him back into Red Dog toward his transient's accommodation, the setting rays of the sun lit the high buildings, and he knew that though Loger was the last city of Seltique, it was not the least.

His way took him past a place that looked like it might

serve food, so he stepped off the molecular belt, onto a green lawn in front of the building, where small tables were scattered, seemingly at random, among flower beds and low bushes. He went to one that was unoccupied and sat in a chair that he would have sworn had been carved from ivory. And only a block away was the spaceport. Amazing.

A living waiter came over to his table. McCade took the hand-written menu and, though the script was elaborately lettered, was able to read it. He ordered something that he guessed would be like a slice of roast with potatoes and a salad, and asked the waiter to select a wine. Then he sat back. The waiter returned almost at once with a question about credit, and McCade referred him to the Morphy Chessica. This time the waiter stayed away.

After a moment a cart appeared, the covered top of which folded back to reveal his meal, which was more like lobster with some kind of hot red vegetable. But the salad was salad, and the wine was quite good. He let the cart serve him and ate with pleasure. It was getting late in the day, and he had not eaten since breakfast, but he was used to irregular meals. His habits did not allow any kind of steady schedule.

He finished the meal and sat sipping the last of his wine, watching the sky change colors, when two young dandies came up and stopped a few feet from his table. He noticed them, but did not pay them any attention. Nor did he react when, in voices sufficiently loud for him to hear, they began commenting to each other about his looks. This, too, had happened to him before, and he had learned not to mind it. If their opinion mattered, he could change it easily enough.

Tiring at last at his lack of response, the two came up to his table and sat down, uninvited, draping themselves with practiced insolence across the chairs.

"Whacha up to, Dopey?" one of them cracked. They both laughed. McCade just looked the speaker in the eye, a small smile touching his mouth, and did not answer.

"Think he's as dumb as he looks?" the other one chortled.

"Naw," said the first. "Nobody could be that dumb."

McCade just sipped his wine. A hand shot out and smashed the glass from his fingers. He looked into the smouldering eyes of the first youth, as he leaned across the table.

"You're rude," the youth said. McCade started, slowly, to rise but just then the waiter came hurrying up.

"Leo," the waiter said anxiously, "Farn, stop, he's an unclassed."

The two young men looked at the waiter in surprise, then back at McCade.

"You sure?" the second asked.

"Absolutely. I checked his accommodation."

"Crap!" the first one said, and they hurried away. The waiter bustled up.

"I'm sorry," he said, "they just didn't know. Will there be anything else?"

"No, thank you," McCade said, getting to his feet. He glanced in the direction the two dandies had gone, but they were nowhere in sight. Then he grinned at the waiter, went back to the belt, and returned to the Morphy Chessica.

ZETESIS

ZETESIS

Larson McCade, attaché case in hand, stepped on to the transport belt in front of the Morphy Chessica. The day was bright and clear, with only a few pearly clouds in the robin's-egg-blue sky. A slight breeze ruffled his curly brown hair, and he felt himself smiling. Other people on the belt saw him and smiled too, infected by his obvious good humor. As he slid easily along he felt the music softly playing in his head. It had a rhythm that made his muscles want to move, to dance, to step along the moving belt in a way he knew would attract too much attention. He did not yield, but smiled only the more broadly, and nodded at the people going the other way. They could not hear his music, would never know what made him feel so good today, but he didn't care. His business was not such that he wanted to share it anyway.

There were very few private vehicles in Loger. On his tour a couple of days before he had seen fewer than a dozen. But then, there was very little need for them in this ancient city, where leisure was the rule, not the exception. Only members of the highest class and rank needed, or wanted, any such thing as a car. And the lower strata of this highly caste-oriented society were not allowed to have them.

He crossed the river into Aragon, a district of much higher status than Red Dog, the bottom of the heap, and turned west. There were more people here, but by no means as many as a city the size of Loger would seem to warrant. Judging by the size, McCade estimated the city should be able to hold over ten million people comfortably. But an examination of the directory indicated that fewer than one million people lived here. Though he had understood that to be the case, it still surprised him somewhat to find that it was actually so.

A few blocks farther on he left the belt and ascended a gentle ramp to a glass dome above the ubiquitous strip-park that bordered all the streets of Loger. For a moment the music in his head grew louder, and he skipped a step as he crossed the threshold of the dome.

Inside he spent a few minutes walking around the perimeter of the dome, looking out over the city from all angles. Such a strange world, with no apparent resources and only one remaining city after thousands of years of decline, and yet the lowest-caste people of Red Dog were as wealthy as the best middle classes of any other world.

At last he turned to the center of the dome, and the columns that rose from the floor to the great transparent tube that crossed the dome eight meters higher still. He stepped up to one of the columns, a door slid back silently, and he stepped inside. A moment later the door opened again, and he crossed the threshold into a tiny room furnished with a double-width reclining chair, in front of which was a low bar. The walls of the room were completely transparent, and curved over him without corner or seam. Even the door, which had closed, was invisible. He sat back on the comfortable chair, and the chamber turned and entered the tube.

"Kimberly University," he said softly, and the car shot out over the city and away to the southeast. His view of the city was completely unobstructed, and he now had a perspective much different from that offered by the belts. There were few other cars in the tube, going either direction, and the car went quickly, without the need to slow for traffic. The whole trip took only ten minutes, and McCade envied the people of Loger their maneuverability. A similar trip in a comparable city on any other world would have taken at least an hour. But then, that was how he had been told it would be.

Kimberly was a large, sprawling district in the foothills of the southern mountains, heavily wooded, sparsely populated, one of the ninth-ranked districts. His car stopped at a dome halfway between the first and second slopes, and he left the tubeways to return to the belts below.

Here there was a definite nip in the air. McCade knew that the climate of Loger was strictly controlled, but to step from the early summer of the rest of the city to the earliest autumn of this district was still somewhat unsettling. He'd never experienced anything like it before, and didn't know if he liked it. The weather was beautiful enough, and the tall trees, evergreens and deciduous, scenting the air with their crisp fragrances, made his blood tingle. It would be beautiful to live here. It was the controlled change that bothered him, robbing him for a moment of the pure pleasure of the day.

On the belts again, he went east at a leisurely pace, allowing himself the time to enjoy the scenery. Houses were set back far from the road, their privacy protected by the trees and by rugged, dense bushes. He occasionally saw an individual or small group outdoors, doing something or other in the cool air, but met almost no one on the belt. Once he passed a commercial area, but so well blended into the landscaping that it was out of sight before he realized what it was.

At last the widely spaced towers of the university appeared above and among the trees, and the beltway came to an end at a transverse road. He stepped off and onto the motionless polished-stone walkway of the campus. He shifted his attaché case to his left hand and entered.

Buildings mossy with age nestled among ancient trees and dense shrubbery. Vines and creepers climbed occasional walls and framed windows. And the people here were all young, except for a faculty member now and then. Their dress was at once less status-oriented and more extravagant than that of the rest of the people of the city. But that was natural. Most of these students would not be able to make use of any inherited or acquired class or rank for some years yet. They were learning how to fit into their society, as well as the subjects of their courses.

Almost at random, McCade ambled around the campus, taking his time, locating buildings he had memorized from the directory and atlas the day before. He knew what he was looking for and where it was, but he was in no hurry. It was important to him to get the feel of a place, to know where he was more than just by map coordinates. He was too used to being a stranger, knew too well the ways a stranger stuck out in the biggest crowd. By spending an hour, walking around, entering an occasional building, he should be able to knock off the sharpest corners of his strangeness. That he was not a student was only too obvious, and he could do nothing about that. But that he was a stranger to Loger and Seltique he did want to conceal, if he could.

He approached the building from the north, from the other end of a two-kilometer-long quad. He walked down the center, across the grass, his pace steady, his eyes neither wandering nor fixed. The music in his head was of a different beat and rhythm now, and it made his pace steady, his back straight. His grin was all but erased and his senses all alert, yet he managed to appear calm and relaxed.

He stepped from the lawn to the paved court in front of the building. Across the court, broad shallow steps climbed up to a pillared portico, the lintel of which bore the legend "Enoch Varney Sambrelli Library." He climbed the steps, passed between the pillars through the door marked "In Only" into a marbled lobby. At a desk at his left, by the "Out" door, a student was checking to make sure that books leaving the library were properly checked out. Ahead of him another student at a desk marked "Information" looked up expectantly. Without pause or hesitation McCade smiled at the girl and turned left into a large room filled with the library's catalogs.

It took only a moment to find the section he wanted. He sat down at a desk, turned on the catcom, and watched the titles of the library's holdings drift by. The book he wanted—it wasn't here.

He punched a button and tried again, this time under author. The man was there, with three entries, but not the one book McCade wanted. He knew the book was here—or at least had been here a century ago. He tried yet a third time, under subject. But the whole subject area was blank. There were no entries at all, only a few cross references to unrelated subjects.

The book had been purged. The inside of his head felt strangely hollow and silent. To have come all this way, and then meet with absolute failure on his first step. Where did he go now?

Maybe the book, and all the others dealing with the same subject, had not been destroyed. Maybe it had been only put away somewhere, withdrawn from the stacks and put in storage. This idea gave his new hope, and a soft melody once again played to him from some depth of his unconscious. He tried to think.

There was another book, one his great-grandfather had often spoken of, what was it? He checked the catalog again, and that volume, too, was not listed. But that was not surprising. The book was only a novel, written two and a half centuries ago, and would be a prime candidate for a cleanup. He stood from the catcom, picked up his attaché case, went back to the lobby and crossed to the other side into another large room where librarians worked at the circulation desk. He walked up to the high counter, laid his case on it, rested his elbows on that, and looked expectantly from one man to another. One of them noticed him, did a little take, smiled, and came up to the counter.

"Can I help you, sir?" the man asked.

"I sure hope so," McCade said, smiling sheepishly. "I'm looking for a book and I can't seem to find it in your catalog."

"What were the title and author?"

"*Pennyfargo*, by Artur Mespelioski. It's an old novel, and I checked it out of here several years ago and, well, I wanted to read it again."

The man fiddled with buttons on his side of the counter.

"You're right," he said, "it's not listed in the catalog. Are you sure you got it from this library and not some other?"

"Oh, absolutely. This is the only library I've ever been to. It was several years ago, as I said, maybe six or seven."

"I see. Well, if it was a really old book we could have removed it from the circulating stacks and put it downstairs. Do you know where the storage catalog is?"

"No, I'm afraid I don't."

"Just go through that door on your right. Across the hall, and to the other side of the room . . ."

There he turned right, between shelves of films and tapes and various viewing and listening equipment, until he came to a stair that opened off the corridor. He went down, around two turns, past a landing, round two more turns, and stepped off the stair into a low-ceilinged room with several doors. He opened the one marked "Storage" and stepped through.

The lights were dim and at first he didn't recognize the objects in front of him. Then, as he reached out to touch, he realized that they were card storage drawers. He pulled open the drawer marked "CLA-COT." Inside were about six thousand cards, bearing pertinent catalog information. He was in the subject section.

Marveling that, in this day of automated information retrieval, even the withdrawn books should be recorded in so archaic a fashion, he flipped through the cards, looking for the missing subject. It was not here either.

He shoved the drawer back in its place and moved farther into the room. Beyond the card catalog were stacks and stacks of books. There must have been almost half a million titles down here alone, he thought, peering down passageway after passageway, all lined with shelves. If the book he wanted was here, but not listed in the catalog, it would be beyond his experience to find it.

He walked as far as he could go in one direction, then turned left and followed the wall. He came to a corner, turned, and followed the wall farther. So far there were only books, but when he turned the second corner the wall continued behind the room, self-contained, which held the stairway. Where the other doors in that room led to, he did not know or care to guess. But back here, behind the stairs and the card catalog, were books that had not been touched in years, just piled at random in towers that reached up over his head. Idly he began to scan the titles, but gave it up quickly. There were too many books, even here.

Then he came to the door. He stopped, looked around, listened. At least two other people were not too far away, doing who knew what in these stacks, but nobody was near enough to see him. He touched the knob of the door, and it swung open. It was black inside. He groped along the wall until he found a switch. He turned it off as soon as it went on. A mop closet.

Farther down the wall was another door—a men's room. Then a ladies' room. Then a door with a frosted-glass upper panel, lit from the other side. He eased it open gently and beyond saw a short corridor. He stepped into it and closed the door behind him. Doors opened off the corridor, three on each side. He went to each one in turn, listened, opened, and found that the first three were a storage room, a closet, and a small untidy office. The fourth door was locked.

He checked the last two doors first. Behind one he could hear voices, and behind the other was only a small kitchenette. Then he went back to the fourth door, put down his attaché case, and took out his wallet.

His senses became super sharp. Certain courses of childhood training took over now, and he listened to each and every sound that came to him, identifying, evaluating. His body became calm, and his fingers were quick but sure as they took a thin strip of metal from the wallet and stuck it in the lock. Gently, now, he twisted, pushed, rocked, and then there was a click. He turned the knob, pushed the door open a crack, and took out the bit of metal. With his toe against the door to keep it from swinging shut, he returned his lock pick to his wallet, picked up his attaché case, and stepped through. Just as he closed the door behind him he heard the door to the fifth room open and two people come out into the corridor.

He stood stock still, listening. The voices of the two people passed up the corridor and out the door into the storage stacks. Then he turned. He was at the head of a flight of stairs, leading down into darkness. There was a switch on the wall. He touched it, and a light came on below. He went down.

There were more books down here, older books, untouched for years, if the accumulation of dust was any evidence. It was not a large room, and contained no more than ten thousand volumes, he estimated, but that was still too many for a quick search. He went round the room once, and back in a corner under the stairs he found the tiny twenty-drawer catalog.

He had to force himself to be calm. He pulled out the "C" drawer and flipped through the cards. And there it was.

Heavy rhythm flooded his brain. He memorized the number, and quickly found the shelf. And yes, there was the book. He took it down, dry, dusty, the pages yellowed, the spine broken. He flipped through it gently. Yes, this was the one.

He opened his attaché case, slipped the book inside, and went back to the stairs. In his head, the music was loud, and he could feel his face stretch into a broad grin. At the top of the stairs he turned off the light, listened carefully for a long moment at the door, then stepped out into the corridor. No one saw him re-enter the storage stacks, and the other person at the card catalog glanced at him only briefly. He looked up *Pennyfargo*, by Artur Mespelioski, found it, went to the appropriate shelf, took it down, tucked it under his arm, and went back up to the main floor of the librar, and the circulation desk. The librarian who'd helped him before smiled when he saw him, and took the book from him.

"It is an oldie," the man said. "I'm surprised anyone would want to read anything like that any more."

"Well, it's not all that good, I suppose," McCade said, "but there are memories associated with it and, well, you know . . ."

"Yes, I do," the man said. He made out a special card allowing McCade to check the book out, and didn't even raise an eyebrow when McCade gave him the Morphy Chessica address as reference.

"Hope you enjoy it as much the second time," the librarian said.

"Oh, I'm sure I will," McCade answered, putting the book into his case. He snapped it shut and left the counter.

And at the door the student there stopped him and asked to look in his case. McCade set it down on the desk and opened it. There was *Pennyfargo.* The student checked the card, smiled his thanks, and closed the case again. And with the music making his feet light, McCade left the library, skipped down the steps to the court, and walked briskly up the long quad.

He enjoyed the autumn crispness now, as he went past dorms and class buildings. The feel of the air intoxicated him, and he toyed with the idea of getting a lunch somewhere and making a picnic out on the grass. But the music in his mind was too demanding. He left the campus, got on a belt, and went to the nearest tube station. Here he boarded another tiny car, asked for Red Dog, and settled back for the short ride across the city.

He got off the tube at a point nearer his accommodation than the one at which he'd gotten on, and went immediately home. Back in his room he put the case down on the table, opened it, and took out *Pennyfargo*. He flipped through it quickly, noted the due date, and tossed it aside. Then he reached into his case again, undid a flap at the bottom, and took out the other book. This, after all, was the purpose for the whole morning's expedition. He settled himself down in a chair and began to read.

"When Seltique was founded nearly six thousand years ago . . . cultural center . . . interstellar jealousies . . . the concentrated lore of all the planets . . ."

Yes, this was it. All the things he'd heard as a child were verified here. The stories hadn't changed much with the generations, no matter how much they differed from what was publicly believed.

"The general public of the Orion Limb, at that time . . ."—about twenty-seven hundred years ago. It was a long time for a world to be in social decline. Scholars on other worlds could not explain how Seltique had been able to continue as it had. Even McCade's grandfather had no explanation for that.

"And thus the paranoid reaction put an effective embargo on all . . . the group which later became known as the Core . . . and not all its past advances were lost in spite of its cultural degeneracy."

McCade hadn't yet seen enough of Loger to make any judgement on that, but if the affair of the two youths at the restaurant was any example, the author was probably right. His own knowledge was too biased and too limited.

"Then followed a counter reaction on the part of the Seltiques . . . another three centuries . . . records destroyed, but duplicates . . . completely underground, though actual members frequently held positions of importance and had high status."

He could feel himself trembling. There was so much yet

to be done, and this was just the first step. But it was also the key. The stories he'd been told meant nothing without hard data to relate it to the real world, not as Seltique had been three thousand yeas ago, or even a hundred years ago, but as it was today.

"Underground, a certain clique or club remained . . . the true position of Seltique was eventually forgotten . . . the people themselves no longer knew . . . continued isolation relieved only by reception of regular broadcasts . . . now a secret cult . . ."

Here and there the book gave him little bits of information that turned the story he knew from an impressive if chaotic collection of reminiscences and prejudices into a complete picture. And, in turn, what he knew turned what the book said from a dry assortment of facts into a living drama with meaning. He could hardly sit still. His hands were wet and trembling, and as his excitement grew the music in his head became louder, more melodic, more emotional.

"Their existence suspected, the remnants of the Core now . . . certain hiding places . . . dispersed the objects and remaining records . . . fanatical isolationists insisted . . . resulting in a pogrom. None of the Core members were known to have survived, though many bodies were unidentifiable and certain persons not accounted for. After this time the isolation of Seltique was complete, and even today, ten years later, mention of the Core can produce the most violent response on the part of certain individuals."

No wonder the book was repressed. Only a few copies had ever gotten off Seltique, and they were now all lost or destroyed, but his great-grandfather had read the book and had acclaimed it highly.

He finished the book quickly, then had room service bring him a late lunch. He needed time to assimilate all he had learned. He needed time to think.

The island of Lestrange was the oldest part of Loger, in the mouth of the bay around which the city had grown. It showed no signs of antiquity in its architecture, however, other than what had been deliberately preserved. During the five thousand years of its existence, its streets had more than once changed their positions, and parks now grew where once buildings had stood.

Only one bridge connected the island with the peninsula of low-status Pier, and that was a beltway. Lestrange was the most isolated of all the districts of Loger, and as a general rule, liked it that way. Because there was no air traffic of any kind in the city, the island could cut itself off from the rest of the world whenever it wanted to, which, thankfully, was not today. For today, McCade had business in Lestrange, at the local offices of the Brotherhood of Administrators. In this ninth-ranked district, the Compassionate Brothers of the Capital were very powerful, and maintained, along with its own records, the records of the whole city, back to its founding.

McCade crossed the bridge to the island, surreptitiously watching the guards seated in their glass boxes at the end. He was an eminently memorable person, he knew, and there was no way for him to travel inconspicuously, but he did nothing to arouse any more attention than his bright clothes and unusual face would have done anyway.

The Capital building was in the center of the island, on one side of a broad square where flowering trees grew, brilliant all year long. There was more weather here than elsewhere in Loger, due to the ocean to the north, and the bay to the south, but as elsewhere, it was always mild and well controlled. Still, there was a salt tang in the air, and a sense of freshness that differed from other parts of the city.

McCade entered the imposing Capital building, façaded with pink and gray marble, stepped with dark gray granite worn to a high polish over the centuries. Inside the lobby, the stone walls and floor were more contrasting, dark gray and russet, and the people moving purposefully across the broad floor made the place echo with their footfalls. There was a reception desk to one side, an information desk at the other, elevators and stairs against the far wall, and an index of offices on a display in the middle. McCade stopped here and ran his eyes over the listing. He stopped at "Elex Norther, Director of Archives, 771."

The elevator took him quickly up, and he stepped out into a large vestibule. There were only three offices here, and he went to the first one. A secretary took his name and a moment later told him to go in. As he entered the inner office a man of about his own age, but taller and with strong, handsome features, stood up from behind his desk and came around to greet him.

"Ah, Mr. McCade," the man said, oddly hesitant, "I'm Elex Norther. Uh—what can I do for you?"

"Quite a bit, I hope," McCade said. "I'm sorry, but something seems to be upsetting you."

"Well, it's just that I see you're not wearing any badges of rank or class. And I'm at a loss as to how to address you."

"However you please," McCade said, laughing. "I may as well admit that I'm from off world, and therefore don't have any rank or class. As a matter of fact, I'm not really sure I understand the system."

"Oh, I see," Norther said, much relieved. "Please, sit down. So you're a visitor, a real visitor. You may know that we don't get very many of those. As a matter of fact, I believe you're the first one I've ever met. Would you like a drink?" He pushed a button when McCade nodded. "What brings you to Seltique, may I ask, and is there anything I can do to help?"

"It's a long story," McCade said, and took a glass from a cart that had just presented itself to him, "but I'll keep it short. I'm doing a monograph on the history of the Samosar Cluster here in the Orion Limb, concentrating on the period of about two to three thousand years ago. During all my early researches, I kept coming across references to Seltique, and I now find that I will be unable to finish my work without incorporating Seltique's influence on the rest of the Cluster during that period. I'm afraid that our texts on your planet out in the rest of the Limb are ambiguous, contradictory, and incomplete, and so I've come here looking for primary sources."

"Well, this is the place for it," Norther said, taking a sip at his own drink. "We have all the remaining documents from the first period, and almost all the documents from about twenty-seven hundred years ago on up to the present day. But I'm sure you don't want to see all of them. You could spend a lifetime just skimming, and only touch the surface."

"You're quite right," McCade said. "But I do have an area of particular interest. During the period which I am researching, Seltique played a very central role, for almost three hundred years, the culmination of a long period of ever increasing importance. Then, just twenty-seven hundred years ago, in fact, that role began to lose significance, until Seltique became just a name on a star atlas to most people. It is my thesis that, if Seltique had not dropped out of the greater society of the Samosar Cluster and the Orion Limb, the whole history of our galaxy from that time on would have been so different as to be unrecognizable. So you see, I am primarily concerned with those documents bearing on the reasons why Seltique—uh—dropped out."

"Hmm. I see." Norther was no longer quite so cheerful. "You touch us at one of our sore spots," he said. "We ourselves have not been able to fully evaluate the reasons for our 'dropping out,' as you put it, probably due to first-hand bias. But even two and a half millenia have not been enough to make us change our minds or wish it had never happened."

"I understand," McCade said, "that the fault lay primarily with the outside Cluster, and that your complete withdrawal was only a reaction to an externally imposed embargo."

"That's the way the theory usually runs. Do you think it's true?"

"I don't know for sure, but it's certainly plausible. Tell me, is there any way I can get to look at certain specific documents of that period?"

"Oh, yes, of course, but as I say, even that area is so broad—a thousand years of unsifted history—it would take you forever to find what you wanted."

"Perhaps not. Remember, this kind of work is my specialty. I am, in fact, a first-class 'sifter'—oh, beg your pardon, I mean an accredited expert."

"That's all right," Norther said, trying to recompose his features. "When you said 'first class' I naturally thought you meant in the context of our world and city."

"Naturally. I'll try to watch myself. But let me reassure you, I do know what I'm doing, and I don't intend to spend any more time than I have to in plowing through old newspapers, videocasts, and books. If I can get access to the materials I want, I should be able to locate answers to my specific questions quite easily and quickly."

"For your sake I certainly hope so," Norther said. "Some classification, of course, has been done, though not nearly so much as we would like. The data input is so voluminous, even these days, that we have a hard time trying to keep up with it."

"I can understand that," McCade said, finishing his drink. The cart came over to retrieve the empty glass.

"What then, in particular, are you looking for?" Norther asked.

"Documents relating to the group or organization known or referred to as the Core, specifically, what role they had to play in—"

"The Core? My God, man, do you know what you're talking about?" Norther was on his feet, surprised, frightened, and a little angry.

"As I understand it," McCade said calmly, "the Core resisted first the efforts of the outside Cluster to shut Seltique off from the rest of society, then resisted Seltique when the rest of the world wanted to retreat into isolation."

"That's just about it," Norther said, still hot, "and whatever that group may have been, they were not popular. Are you aware that the last remnants of the Core existed as recently as a century ago? And that public feeling against them was so high that they were slaughtered to a man? Even the children!"

McCade let his mouth open softly and his face go white. He collected a little saliva in the back of his throat so that when he spoke again, he choked.

"No," he said, "I wasn't aware of that. I assumed that—"

"Well, your assumption was in error," Norther snapped. "Look, man, I don't associate *you* with the Core, or with the things they did, but you *are* an outsider, and if it became known that you were interested in the Core, even your classless status wouldn't save you. The Core is a bugbear that fathers frighten their young sons with."

"I see," McCade said, and made himself flush. He clenched his teeth and drew his mouth into a tight line. "I see," he repeated, "and I appreciate your warning. But let me explain that I have already invested four years in this work, and have prepublished certain parts of it. My publishers want the book finished, and so do I. If I fail to produce, I stand to lose a fortune, and if I write the book without adequate reference to Seltique and the Core, I'll lose my reputation. It's a matter which is worth almost my life to me. I'm sorry, but you just don't appreciate the academic pressure out there, even these days when the government seems to be falling apart."

"No, I don't," Norther said. "Maybe I'm just as glad. But I had to make sure you understood just how dangerous such queries are here. I have seen enough and read enough to be able to suspend judgement in most cases, and I disagree with the anti-Core attitude on general principles. But if it's worth that much to you—"

"It is."

"Then I think I can show you the documents—at least, the area of the documents—you're interested in. But I warn you, be discreet. If my Vice Director had been here today instead of me, he'd have kicked you out and dropped a few words in a few places, and your life would have been in real danger. You were just lucky, that's all."

It was as bad as he had been told. Though he wasn't actually afraid, McCade let his face go white again and made sweat pop out on his forehead. Macrocutaneous control had been part of his early biotraining, and he had always appreciated the ability to make himself appear to be experiencing any emotion—or lack of emotion—that he desired. He swallowed noisily, then let himself return to normal so as to not overdo the effect. If Norther weren't so disturbed himself, it would already have been too much.

"I guess I am," he said. "Lucky, that is. And thank you very much for your concern. It's not all that common these days. But, as I said, it is worth practically my life to obtain this information, and if you will, I'd like to see those documents."

"As you wish," Norther said, and came around the desk again. "I admire your courage." He smiled. "Come now, I won't tell anybody if you won't. This way."

He led McCade out of the office and into the elevator. They went up and got out somewhere near the top of the building, McCade guessed.

There were no people in the little foyer, but a robotic comcon kept watch. Norther flashed a card, and the only other door in the foyer opened.

"These are the main files," Norther explained as they went past banks and banks of computer core. They came to a floating stair and climbed to another level.

"The period you want," Norther said, "is over on this side. It gets older as you go up. You'll have to start about twenty-five hundred years back. After that, the index keys to Core documents were removed, but you should be able to work forward if you have a need to. Are you familiar with Lepsecon Data Retrieval?"

McCade nodded.

"Fine," Norther went on. "Then I'll just leave you here. Try to be out by six, and stop by my office when you go, will you?"

"Certainly. I appreciate this, Mr. Norther."

"Quite all right, but listen, call me Elex. If you must be formal, it's 'Fifth Norther,' not 'mister.' Anyway, I hope you're as sharp at researching as you claim. If you need to come back, just let me know."

"I shall. Thank you again."

Norther nodded, then turned and left.

For a long moment, McCade just stood there, singing softly to himself. It had been too easy so far, and he had been too lucky. Still, the past had no effect on any future luck. Every moment was the start of a new game.

Then he went to the console Norther had pointed out, and punched out the index. There *were* references to the Core, but they were few. He did not read out any of them, but instead took careful note of the index numbers, then shut off that machine, went to the next one, and punched them in.

Here were more titles, but the index reference was slightly shifted. He made notes and went to the next computer. Again he found documents pertinent to the Core, but again the index was shifted slightly. Three more checks and a pattern to the shift began to emerge.

It took him all the rest of the morning and most of the afternoon to work up to the recordings, on the floor below, of just a century ago. The index had continued its shift, and he was now punching out numbers far from what the original subject had been, but that in itself didn't bother him. He was closing in on what he wanted, and that was all that mattered.

Then he ran the file on the year of the pogrom. There was plenty of material submitted both before, during, and after that slaughter of all people found to be involved with the Core in any way, but the references stopped two months after the event, and the Core was not mentioned again. But this was it. This was what he wanted.

He checked his watch. It was a quarter to five, and he had no time to read all those documents now. Carefully he made an experimental print-out of an innocuous document relating to belt maintenance. No alarms lit up. And the print-out was on microfine paper. Quickly, then, he set up a search program to find and print out at high speed all the documents under the index codes that were now assigned to the Core. Forty-five minutes later he had a stack of paper two meters high and weighing almost a hundred kilograms.

Time was running out. He set his attaché case down on the floor, opened it, and lifted up the false bottom flap. Inside, he touched a stud, and the true bottom of the case seemed to drop down out of sight.

Then, grabbing the print-out in big bunches, yet being careful not to break up any whole document, he stuffed the whole pile into the case. The little device he'd picked up on Farside Dexter allowing a four-dimensional internal expansion of the case was just what he needed. Then he touched another knob which had the effect of neutralizing the added inertia, closed the case, picked it up, and left the records room. The robocom at the door paid him no attention. He went down to Norther's office and was told to go right in.

"Well, did you have any luck?" Norther asked as McCade seated himself.

"Yes and no. I found all the references to the Core that I could possibly desire, but I'm afraid, from the few that I read, that they, at that time at least, were not instrumental in developing Seltique's isolation."

"That's very interesting," Norther said. "It was certainly the Core that generated the strong feelings one, two, three hundred years ago that made our separatism final."

"That may be, but it's way beyond my area of interest. It's surprising, though, that the group managed to survive so long, and that they continue to be so strongly hated."

"Isn't it, though? Some of that is due, no doubt, to the Pro-Galaxy Group, which has always claimed that Seltique should maintain some form of contact with the Cluster and the Orion Limb. They are the ones responsible for the fact that all during this tme we have continued to receive broadcasting from other worlds. But they, too, are beginning to go a bit rancid, I'm afraid, and if they continue their fanatic activities, there may be another strong overreaction, and we'll find ourselves cut off completely. And that would be disastrous."

"I agree. Well, Elex, I want to thank you again. I think I have found out what I needed—though not what I wanted—to know on the subject of the Core, and my researches will have to turn elsewhere."

"I'm sorry to hear that, but I must confess that at the same time I'm relieved. But wait—I have an idea. It may not help your book much, but perhaps it will give you some perspective on what kind of people we are now, if not about our ancestors of three millenia ago. And you might be able to meet some people who could help you on those other lines of research."

"I don't understand," McCade said.

"Oh, I'm sorry; a party is what I'm talking about. Nothing very special, just the usual sort of gathering. But then you're new to all this, of course. Then you must come. Day after tomorrow. Here's the address." He scribbled on a piece of paper.

"Oh, no, really," McCade protested. "I'm really not sure I should. I don't know anybody and I am, as you said, an outsider, and I won't know what's expected of me."

"You'll do just fine," Norther said, putting the paper in McCade's hand. "And as for not knowing anybody, all the more reason to come. Don't worry about what's expected; as an outsider you could hardly do anything wrong—except mention the Core, of course."

"Of course. But really, I have a considerable amount of work to do and—"

"Nonsense. You'll come. I'll let First Saranof know so you won't get lost the minute you get there."

"Well, if you insist . . . all right, I'll come."

"Excellent. I'll see you then, the day after tomorrow, at about eight."

"Thank you very much," McCade said. Then, suddenly very tired of humility, he made his goodbyes and left.

All the way back to the Morphy Chessica his mind swung between the upcoming party and the contents of his attaché case. The one intrigued him as much as the other. He'd heard enough stories and had always wondered if the inhabitants of Seltique were as decadent as the stories claimed. So far he hadn't had the opportunity to find out. This might just be the chance he needed. After all, with what was at stake . . .

That brought him back to the volumes of material in his case. There was an awful lot of stuff to go through, and he started as soon as he got back to his suite. Fortunately, he knew exactly what he was looking for, and was able to throw out whole masses of material after only a cursory glance. By noon the next day, he still had a meter-high stack of paper left, and what he wanted could have been anywhere in it.

He began a more methodical search, now that the dross had been eliminated, and by midnight he had what he wanted. Names. Names of every single person known or suspected to be a member of the Core. A few of them were familiar; most were totally strange to him. He made up a list, and after each name recorded what pertinent data he could find, which wasn't much. When he finished at five in the morning, he had four hundred names, only twenty-seven addresses, and very little else. Still, it was a start. The book from the university had told him that the thing he suspected of being on Seltique might actually be here, and the list of names included one—which one he did not yet know—of a person who might have had that thing at one time. So he had a start.

He had something else. Several times he had run across mention of certain data not related to his own searches, but which seemed to have to do with the existence, at one time, of an office of Planet Master. It was held not necessarily by the person with the highest caste, though the person who held the office naturally acquired tremendous status and real power. And from what he could tell, that office had terminated with the pogrom of the Core. It intrigued him, especially since the references indicated that the office was still valid, just unfilled. The idea crossed his mind, as he dropped off to sleep, to check on *that* point as well.

The address of the party was at the top of Celadrin, the seventh-ranked district, in the southeast corner of the city in the mountains above Kimberly. It was one of the first-order districts, a place where people of lower than first or second class did not come unless by invitation. As McCade understood it, unwanted visitors to any of the seven first-ranked districts just didn't come out again. It went against all he knew of the outside galaxy, and his own beliefs in personal freedom. McCade valued his freedom highly. He had always gone where he wanted to, when he wanted to, in company he chose, to do anything he wished. Though the restrictions of Seltique had not yet made themselves strongly felt to him, he was already beginning to chafe with the knowledge that here, in Loger, there were places, public places, where he would be casually shot by whomever happened to be handy with a gun. He'd been told of this, but he hadn't really believed it.

He was going to Arvin Saranof 's party, long black cloak covering his party clothes, and now he had to face the truth of the situation. The tubeway took him all the way to the edge of town, where he got off, before running across the parklands to the wilderness beyond. He was surprised to discover that though the distant destinations of the tubeways had long been vacant and were crumbling into ruins, the tubeways themselves still functioned—though nobody used them, of course.

From the tube station he had several blocks to go by belt to get to Saranof 's residence, and it was then that he discovered the truth of the stories he'd heard as a youth. A man lounging on his lawn spotted him and, leaving the cover of magnificent trees which framed the mansion beyond, came up to the belt, a smirk on his face, drawing a strangely designed pistol as casually as if he were just going to plunk tin cans. Before the belt could take McCade past the man, it stopped. Just stopped dead.

"I never cease to be amazed," the man said, "at the temerity of you lower classes," and took a bead on McCade's forehead.

"I have no class," McCade said softly but distinctly. The man stopped, then looked at McCade again.

"You've just removed them," he said, and started to aim again, casual, unhurried.

"I came on the *Dovetail* a week ago, from Phenolk P'talion," McCade said further.

The man lowered his gun a moment, a slight frown on his face.

"What of it? This is still a restricted district."

"I'm expected at First Saranof's."

"Bullshit."

McCade just shrugged. But while he worked to maintain a calm, relaxed exterior, inside he was triggering certain neuromuscular systems. If this man actually shot, he would be in for a surprise.

"Beat it," the man snapped suddenly and, turning, shot a low branch off a nearby tree, then stalked away toward his house. The belt started again, and McCade slid on toward his destination.

But before he got there he met two women on the belt going the opposite way. They saw him a hundred meters off and, giving each other significant glances, assumed easy postures of unarmed attack.

The distance between McCade and the two women was closing rapidly. He had no time for arguments or explanations. Quickly he triggered again his body's internal preparedness, and when the two women came at him—fast, graceful, deadly, from two sides—he kicked into overdrive, accelerated to five times normal speed, and ducked between them and ran as stiff fingers and sharp boot-toes came at his throat and groin.

He hated to flee. But he hated even more the thought of what might happen if he had actually killed these two women. After two hundred meters he dropped back to normal and looked behind him. The two women were just recovering from their missed blows and staring after him in utter surprise. He waved cheerily, turned, and went on his way.

A few moments later the belt turned a corner, and he stepped off. A walkway of tiny stones set in a solid matrix of some dark color led through beautifully trimmed hedges and around exotic flower beds carefully tended to look natural. Ahead of him the wings of the mansion rose up in the evening dusk, and between them a blaze of lights around a broad porch at the entrance. From inside, as he neared, McCade could hear the sounds of voices mingled with a strange and muted music that touched something in his own mind. Adding counterpoint and syncopation in his head, he approached the house and stepped from the dark walkway into the brilliance of the porch. He climbed the stairs, and loosed the cloak fastened at his throat as he did so. The music swelled, in his ears and in his brain, and he felt himself grinning as he flipped the cloak off to reveal himself dressed in crimson and gold, brilliant but superbly cut. It was eight-thirty.

An elegantly dressed woman came to the door, a slight question in her smiling face.

"McCade," he said and, handing her the cloak, strode past into a vestibule and beyond to a huge room where at least fifty people sat or stood or lay, drinking and munching, talking animatedly, laughing, while bar men and women, dressed uniformly in dark, tight clothes, moved among them with trays of glasses and foods. McCade turned to the elegant woman, now standing behind him, still holding his cloak, a wry expression replacing the question.

"Forgive me," McCade said, and took the cloak from

her. "I have been on Seltique for only a week, and I'm afraid I'm prone to gaffes such as this. I am terribly ignorant of your life here."

The woman smiled.

"You are forgiven," she said. "I am Arvin Saranof."

McCade's jaw dropped, then he laughed.

"Milady," he said, "I should have known." He handed the cloak to a servant, and took Saranof 's arm. "Do me the kindness please," he said, taking her in among her guests, "to set someone over me to keep me out of trouble."

She took a glass from a passing tray and handed it to him.

"Are you sure it would do any good?" she asked, smiling. "You seem to have a will all your own. I doubt you'd bow easily to our customs."

"Very true, milady, but I am here to learn, and you must teach me."

"Very well, then. I shall endeavor to give you your first lesson myself. But after that you must fend for yourself."

"I am most grateful," McCade said, bowing slightly while still holding her arm, and smiling as broadly as he knew how.

"First," she said, "as a classless person, I suppose you might get away with certain familiarities not otherwise allowed." She gently disengaged her arm from his. "On the other hand," she went on, "as a classless person you might be expected to show deference to everyone present." She looked at McCade with curiosity. "However, Elex Norther tells me that what is expected is not what we must expect from you. So my one bit of advice for the evening is," and she became serious, "walk carefully." Then she smiled brightly, turned, and disappeared into the crowd.

Mentally, McCade kicked himself. He'd played it very badly and only extraordinary good luck had saved him from a debacle. He sipped his drink and, maintaining his external composure, moved slowly among the people. First he noticed that the style of his dress was quite severe by comparison with everyone else, although its color was the most brilliant.

As usual, he stuck out.

Slowly, he circled the room, looking closely at each person, trying to evaluate them, discover what kind of a crowd he was in. Occasionally, someone would look up from their conversation and notice him, but by the time he'd gone around the room once, everyone was aware of him. He paid no attention to this, but continued to move, took another drink, smiled whenever he caught someone's eye, and said nothing.

"McCade," someone called, and he stopped and turned to see Elex Norther coming through the press of people.

"Larson," Norther said, taking his hand. "Arvin told me about your entrance. I don't know where you get the gall."

"Where I come from," McCade said, smiling softly, "it's not so unusual. But then, where I come from, we're not so status-conscious."

"Of course, of course, but you're in Loger now, not out in the heathen galaxy. You'll have to conform, at least a little bit, or find yourself in deep trouble, or dead."

"So I discovered," McCade said, and told him about the two incidents on the beltway.

"Some people are too touchy," Norther said. "Theoretically the beltways are neutral, if you're just going through, but some of the higher-ups, especially if they're not of the first or second class, tend to be overly particular. Do you carry a gun?"

"No, I don't."

"You should. If someone assaults you on a belt or tube, or in any building or area that is strictly public, you have a right to defend yourself."

"Thanks for the warning, but I've seldom found a need for weapons."

"As you wish. Well, what do you think?" He gestured vaguely at the room and the now nearly seventy people in it.

"Too early to make judgements," McCade said. "But it looks like quite a mixed group to me."

"Oh, it is. People here from almost all classes and ranks. Most of them personal friends of Arvin's. She makes it her business to move among all levels and give help to those who need it."

"Very impressive. I hope I haven't destroyed *my* chances for help."

"Not likely. She's had experience with offworlders before, which is why I suggested you make your first social contacts here. That pilot or captain or whatever, Ben Toledo, has been here before."

"I see. Very interesting. By the way, I've been wondering—he wouldn't tell me anything on the trip out from Phenolk P'talion—just what does he transport back and forth?"

"I haven't the slightest idea."

"Excuse me," said a man, tall, elegant, fiftyish. "But I understand that, uh, you have *no class*, sir."

"That is correct," McCade said. "I'm from off world."

"So I understand," the man went on, "but still, how can one exist without class? Or rank?"

"I'm afraid I don't understand the distinction."

"Between class and rank? Why, class is one's status, and rank is one's level within a class."

McCade shook his head.

"Class," Norther said, coming to his rescue, "is a more or less permanent level of status, what one is born with, so to speak, and barring degradation or promotion, it does not change throughout one's life and requires no maintenance. Rank, on the other hand, fluctuates. A person of a given class can gain rank by performance in certain fields, by joining a Brotherhood, by elimination of opponents, and so on. In a certain way, rank cuts across class. A first class of the second rank is in some ways inferior to a second, or even a third or fourth, class of the first rank."

"Still not very clear," McCade said, "but I'm beginning to get the picture."

"So you see, sir," the tall man said, "we just don't know what to do with you."

"Why, nothing," McCade said, and his voice became just a bit acid. "It's what *I* do with *you* that you have to worry about."

The man was taken aback, and mumbling something about outsiders, went off.

Arvin Saranof returned to fill the vacuum, with several people in tow.

"Larson McCade," she said, "I'd like you to meet Eleventh Derk Renseleau, Master Artist of the first rank. Ninth Valyn Dixon, student-patron. And Sixth Mort Skopoloth, a member of the Inner Circle of the Understanding Brothers of the Institute of Science."

"I'm very happy to meet you all," McCade said, looking from the short round youth, to the attractive girl, to the elderly gentleman. Renseleau snickered.

"I beg your pardon," McCade said.

"Nothing," the artist said, trying to straighten his face. "But do all offworlders have such unique physiognomy as yours?"

"Really, Derk," Skopoloth said. "I apologize for his manners, ah, Mr. McCade. He has just recently been promoted to eleventh class and his rise has gone to his head."

"That's perfectly all right," McCade said. "I'm used to comments on my face."

"Why, what's wrong with it?" Dixon asked. McCade looked at her sharply. She was more than just attractive.

"Some people think it funny, Ninth Dixon," he answered with a gentle smile.

"I think it's cute," she answered seriously.

"Really, Valyn," Skopoloth said. "Sir, the young lady pretends to be learning to become a patron, but she has yet to learn proper behavior."

"My great-grandfather once told me," McCade said, "that behavior was proper when it achieved the effect one desired."

"Indeed, and who was your great-grandfather?"

For a moment, McCade's mind went blank, but he recovered himself quickly.

"A refugee," he answered, "with no name when he came to Lamborge. He took the name Dugal McCade there."

"I see. Then you are a person of no background."

"On the contrary, I have considerable background. Take any young man here, of about thirty say, rip him from his world, his class, his rank, and set him down on another world that had not yet been completely civilized. What do you suppose would happen to him?"

"Why," Skopoloth said, taken aback, "I assume he would die."

"Indeed. My great-grandfather, in very similar circumstances, owned half of Lamborge when he died ten years ago. My grandfather built an interplanetary transport company while his father was carving an empire out of the wilderness. My father united these two enterprises, and developed several research institutes, each worth a city. I have considerable background."

"And what about you?" Renseleau asked.

McCade grinned. "I'm striking out on my own," he said.

"I think that's marvelous," Dixon said, and McCade now saw that, whenever her face grew animated, she was absolutely lovely. He looked at her for a long moment, becoming aware of the shape of her body under her clothes.

"Thank you," he said. "I prefer to stand on my own feet and be beholden to none. My great-grandfather approved."

"Well," Skopoloth said, a bit ill at ease, "I see that, even though the essentials of society are not recognized on other worlds, you are in fact a person of some status. Why don't you go to the Academy and see if you can get it regularized."

"No thank you," McCade said. "I'll establish myself as I am. And for the moment, I prefer my . . . anomalous position."

"Indeed," Renseleau smirked, "that could be quite interesting, if it didn't involve certain disadvantages."

"Nonsense, Derk," Skopoloth snapped. "If he were truly classless, like the Planet Masters used to be, he would have every advantage."

"You mean," McCade said, suddenly paying sharp attention, "that there actually have been classless men on Seltique?"

"Oh, yes, indeed, but not for a century or more. You can't just become classless at will, you know. Outsiders like yourself don't count. Bottom-rung people don't stand a chance. Only first-class, first-rank individuals stand to become classless, and unfortunately, the secret of the technique has been lost. When the last Planet Master died, he left no records as to how he had achieved this truly anomalous state, and so no one has been able to succeed him, though several people have tried to discover the secret."

Now the conversation was beginning to get interesting, but before McCade could pursue the subject any further two other people came over to join in, primarily to satisfy their curiosity about him. After an hour or so he discovered that he was the center of attention, with people asking him all kinds of questions about what life was like on other worlds. From their questions and from their reactions to his answers, he learned more about them than they did about him, and though he didn't show it, he didn't like everything he heard.

Then he felt a tugging at his arm, and turned to see Valyn Dixon.

"Come on," she said, "you've supplied enough entertainment for a while. There are plenty of other things going on in other parts of the house. Let's explore."

He let himself be pulled away. They passed from room to room, staying in each place just long enough to satisfy McCade's curiosity. In one room, lit with ultraviolet, people were dancing to musicless rhythms, performed by four men on a variety of drums. The beat was hypnotic, restless, and intricate, moving from four-four to seven-four to nine-three to five-two, then playing three on four or six on eleven, with first one player, now another, taking over the lead, and the others improvising around him.

In another room games of chance were being played. As money was not used in Loger, the stakes were honor points, which obligated the loser to perform a service for the winner, the specific service being strictly defined by a scaling system and depending on the number of points lost.

In another room four men and four women were involved in an elaborate sexual structure. McCade backed out as soon as he saw what was going on, though Dixon seemed in no way embarrassed.

"Call me Valyn," she insisted at one point. "One can carry formality too far."

The hours passed and eventually they returned to some of the rooms they had visited before. In the gambling room McCade was fascinated by a game played with a hundred-sixteen-card deck, but when he heard what some of the losing penalties were, he declined to play.

He especially noted one thing during the course of the evening. Valyn Dixon seemed to have acquired an attachment to him. He dared not encourage it. Despite all the things he'd learned at home and here, he knew too little about male-female relationships in Loger to risk allowing himself to get involved. And besides, he did not want to find himself obligated to any person in any way. He still had many things to do in Loger, and to do them he needed absolute freedom, a quality he prized highly in any event.

So he tried, several times, as gently as he could, to disengage himself from Valyn, but never with any success. If she was aware of his discomfort and intention to leave her, intensified by the attraction he felt toward her, she didn't show it, but stayed by his side, patiently answering his questions, commenting on things that caught his interest, sharing her evening with him in a way that struck him as almost too natural.

About two in the morning, when the party was at its peak, they returned to the front living room where they had started out, and found an argument in progress. There were only twenty people present, all silently watching the two people in the center of the room, as they exchanged words that grew ever warmer as the moments passed.

"You really don't deserve your rank," the younger of

the two, a woman, said. "I know your connection with Baldair. You satisfy her sexually and that's your reward."

"You can leave her out of this," the man said. "How a person of your status got into this party is beyond me."

"Arvin invites *all* sorts of people," the woman sneered. "At least my rank was fairly won."

"Fair, yes, if you call tricking people into duels they can't win fair. You won't get to me that way, Twelfth Dorkis."

"Come now, Twelfth Rean, why should I want to? I just don't like it when you parade your phoney status around in front of honest people."

"Are you calling me a liar?"

"Of course not. You wouldn't know how to lie."

"I know a hell of a lot more than you give me credit for," Rean shouted. "I know who you were before you became anybody."

"Everybody knows that," Dorkis laughed. "What you don't know is how to keep your mouth shut."

Reflexively, Rean lashed out and hit Dorkis across the face. She staggered back, but there was a light of triumph in her eyes, and Rean's face went white.

"You also don't know," Dorkis went on quietly, "how to control your temper. Can't you take a little criticism? If you didn't like it, you could always have gone away."

"And have you following me, hounding me all over the house? No, let's get this over with. Maybe you're not as hot as everybody seems to think."

"Maybe I'm not," Dorkis said, but it was obvious that she knew better. One of the servants brought in a wide, shallow box, and opened it. Inside were two pistols. Dorkis took one, Rean the other. Rean examined his carefully, but Dorkis just stood, relaxed, the pistol in her hand by her hip.

"Point blank," she said, and Rean looked up, startled.

"Wha—what?"

"Point blank. On three, Now."

"Now wait a minute, Twelfth Dorkis," the man said, "that's suicide. How could you hope to win a fight like that? If it's suicide you want—"

"One."

"Now wait a minute." He was sweating, and his face was chalky. "What about all these people here? You wouldn't want any of them to—"

"Two."

"From a draw, Dorkis?" He was desperate. His own hand hung limply at his side. As Dorkis started to say three, he started to bring his hand up, but Dorkis never raised her gun. It just pointed up at Rean's chin, and "Three" and the shot came together. The top of Rean's head came off, the gun fell from his fingers, and the body slowly slumped to the floor. One or two people applauded.

"That takes you over the top and into the next class," one of the bystanders remarked. McCade just moved away.

"I think I'll go home now," he said grimly. "This party seems to lose its appeal for me."

"Is death so shocking to you?" Valyn asked.

"Not death. I've killed a few myself. It's the manner of death and its reasons. I'm not criticizing. It's just not my way."

He went to one of the servants and asked for his cloak.

"Let me come with you," Valyn asked.

"I didn't think anyone would work as a servant here," McCade said, avoiding her suggestion.

"Surely, why not? It's a part of the Brotherhood of Service. These are all members of the Temple. They have a limited membership, and many applicants are turned away."

"Does it confer status?" he asked as his cloak was brought. "To work as a servant?"

"To provide good service always brings status," Valyn answered, putting on her own cloak. "There is a four-year training period before the members can go out and work."

"Very strange," McCade said, and went to the door. Valyn hurried after him.

"You don't have to go home so early," she said as they stepped out into the cool night air.

"No, I don't have to, but I want to. I have other things to do."

"Like what? You don't belong to a Brotherhood, so you can't work."

"I'm self-employed," he said as they got on the belt. He chose a different route back to the tube.

"What is self-employed?" Valyn asked. "Everybody is self-employed, to do what he thinks best with his life."

"It's a long story," he said, "and I don't think I'll tell it to you. Ask Norther some time for one version, if you wish."

"What's the matter, Larson? Did the duel upset you so much?"

"I guess it did. There was no reason for that man's death."

"Yes there was. Dorkis needed a kill of her class or higher in order to advance to the next class."

"Is status seeking so important to you, then, that you'd kill for it?"

"I never have, but it's common enough."

"My grandfather was right," McCade sighed as they entered the tube dome.

"About what?" Valyn asked.

"He said I shouldn't come to Seltique."

"What does *he* know?"

"Nohing firsthand, I'll admit. But more is known about you out in the Cluster than you're aware of."

"Come home with me," Valyn said. They seated themselves in the tube car.

"What for?"

"Just because I want you to. Wouldn't you like to?"

"Yes, I would, but not tonight. Red Dog," he said to the car, and they started off.

"It would do you good," Valyn insisted.

"Perhaps, but I'm tired, and I have things to think about."

"Like what?"

"Like this Planet Master business."

"*You'll* never be Planet Master. Only a native-born can become one."

"And what else?"

"I don't know. Nobody does any more."

"That guy, Sixth Skopoloth, said some people were trying to find out. Who, for instance?"

"Well, First Njaird, Second Korothom, Second Kelso, Third Rotique, Fourth Esmert. And some others. Why?"

"Just curious."

"Is this the business you have to do?"

"No, this is something else."

"And you won't tell me what it is that's so important to you."

"Not tonight."

"And you won't come home with me and make love."

"Not tonight. I'm sorry, Valyn, I don't understand your ways, but neither do you understand mine. I can't explain."

The car stopped at Red Dog and McCade got out. He looked back as it started up again, carrying Valyn Dixon away, but she wasn't looking at him.

McCade sat near the rear of the church. The service was almost over, and he was just as glad. None of it made any sense to him, based as it was on the social situation peculiar to Seltique. As far as he had been able to understand, the religion of Loger revolved around a philosophical rationalization and justification of that system, and today's sermon had sought to explain the significance of certain portions of that system. To McCade, it all seemed too artificial, too cut to order, though his researches had uncovered the fact that the Church of Loger had its origin long before the intense social stratification began back when the Cluster, jealous of Seltique's influential position in the Orion Limb, had put up the embargo on the planet and begun the process of closing it off from the rest of the galaxy.

Instead of trying to make sense of the introverted nonsense of the service, he considered again the justification for his own proposed course of action. The print-out from Norther's files had contained names, and one of those with addresses had been of a man who had been prelate of this Esterhazy branch of the Church of Loger. And the book he'd stolen from the library of the Kimberly University had mentioned that at one time the Esterhazy branch of the Core had been responsible for the inventory of the artifacts and documents held and guarded by the Core from the days when Seltique's reaction to being denied the galaxy was to deny the galaxy in turn. Further researches had hinted at the fact that the prelate, before the pogrom, had compiled a list of all inventory hiding places, and that from the first day of the pogrom until he was killed by a mob toward the end, he had not left this building, the church.

In querying the Loving Brotherhood of Service, McCade had learned further caution, but also that all the churches were built to the same plan, and on one pretext or other, he had learned that plan, over a period of weeks, by visiting other churches. From all that he was able to discover, he could eliminate every part of the church as a possible hiding place for the list of inventory hiding places. Every room and corridor, every vault and cellar, was cleaned and purified at one time or another, and the architecture of the places was such that there could be no secret rooms or cabinets. There was only one place that was never open to inspection or ritual cleaning, and that was the cabinet under and behind the altar, the holy of holies.

The service came to an end. He rose with the rest of the congregation, but did not leave his pew. He waited while the people—almost all of the eighth class, but a few higher, a few lower—filed out, leaving the church empty. Finally the last worshiper was gone and the clergy absent from the altar area. Only then did he leave his pew and in an attitude of hesitant respect walk slowly toward the altar.

He stood at the step, waiting, listening, his senses hypersharp. He heard no sound, no noise of approach. So, maintaining his attitude of reverence and awe, he mounted the steps to the altar and, carefully keeping his hands clenched behind him, examined the tiny silver sphere, the gold bell, the copper dagger, the embroidery in the white altar cloth. And still he listened.

There were voices, somewhere. He went down the steps, across the nave to a side door, and out into a corridor, where the congregation sometimes gathered before services to gossip. Seated on a bench against the far wall was an old priest, silently contemplating a scrollwork in the ceiling. Behind him, the voices passed beyond a closed door and went away.

"How can I help you, my son?" the priest asked, kindly enough.

"Forgive me for intruding," McCade said, "but I found myself overcome in there and when I realized where I was everybody had gone."

"That's quite all right," the priest said, rising to his feet. "I take it you do not come to church regularly."

"I'm afraid you're right, father," McCade said and mentally kicked himself.

"You should, you know," the priest went on. "How can we hope to know ourselves better, make our world a better place in which to live, and insure our continued existence if we don't take instruction?"

"I'm sure I don't know, father. But something moved me to come today, and I'm still wondering at it."

"The Spirit of Life is always to be wondered at, my son. Perhaps this is the beginning of a new life for you. Tell me, are you affiliated with any church at all?"

"No, father. Red Dog, somehow . . ."

"I understand. You set your sights high, to come all the way from there, but perhaps there is a reason."

"I don't know, father. I feel that I am just beginning something. I need time yet to find out what, and how to best approach it."

"Of course you do, my son, of course you do."

"And my father keeps pressing me so," McCade complained.

"That is a shame. Truly. When a man is called by the Spirit, he should allow no other to divert him from his course."

"That's what I feel, father."

"Very good. Well, I must apologize, but we must move on to our afternoon prayers now. But let me reassure you," he said, walking McCade to the outer door, "that any time you wish to come back and talk with me, I'll be glad to see you."

"I'm grateful, father," McCade said, standing in the open door. As he went out he brushed against the latchplate. The door closed, and cursing himself, he stopped and listened carefully as the old priest's footsteps receded down the hall. He stood there waiting a full ten minutes before putting his hand on the door and gently pushing it open.

The corridor was empty. He pulled the piece of magnetic film from the latch hole, put it in his pocket, and on feet that were as silent as any cat's went back to the nave of the church.

The lights had been dimmed, but altar flames burned at the back. He climbed the steps, moved behind the altar, and without touching anything, examined the altar carefully. The cloth hung down only halfway in back, and he could see that there was a small door set into the wood.

And then again the sound of voices approaching from somewhere off on the side. He backed into the shadows at the rear of the altar, and the side door opened. Two men and a woman entered, talking about what they were planning to do that afternoon. One of them said something about races. McCade pressed back farther into the shadows.

Behind him was a tapestry, and behind that a wall. He stepped to the corner nearest the three speakers, cutting them from sight by the projecting wall of the altar enclosure. But they kept coming.

He felt behind him, at the same time stepping up his neuromuscular system. There was a knob. Carefully, so as not to make the tapestry sway, he pulled the cloth aside and opened the door behind it. As he slipped through and let the tapestry back into place he saw the three people beginning to mount the steps to the altar. He closed the door and looked around.

He was in a vestry, dark but for a small light high up on one wall. There was another door on the other side of the room. He went to it and passed through just as the door behind the tapestry began to open.

He was in another hall and from his previous research knew that this was a part of the building forbidden to all but members of the Brotherhood. If he were caught here, he would be put to death on sight—no questions asked. Across the hall was another door, and from beyond it came other voices. He was trapped.

Up one way the hall ended abruptly in a blank wall, at the right side a stair spiralling up to the dormitories. In the other direction the hall stretched for perhaps twenty meters with other doors opening off it. Here were offices, the refectory, and private chapels. One door was partly open. He went to it, looked inside. A library. The door opened outward into the hall, and swung away from the dead end of the hall. In the library, he could see a monk, facing away from the door with a book in his hand. Behind him the door to the vestry started to open.

He flattened himself against the wall of the hall and pulled the door all the way around against him. Through the crack he could see the three people emerging from the vestry. One of them went to the door across the hall and knocked. After a pause it opened and two women came out. The group spoke a word or two and started up the hall toward the library and the refectory. At the library door they stopped and one of the women poked her head in. She was only inches from McCade, and if she had turned she could have seen him through the crack between the door and the jamb.

"Come on, Kim," she called. McCade could not distinguish the answer. "You can look it up later," the woman went on. "If you want to get to the races before they start, you'll have to eat with us now." Another muffled answer, the sound of footsteps, and the monk who had been reading joined the five in the hall.

"I'll put odds on Black Prince," the monk said.

"You're on," another man answered. "Black Prince is getting fat and doesn't stand a chance."

"Nonsense," said the woman who had called Kim to the hall. "In his last race he nearly broke the record for the five hundred meters." They moved off down the hall toward the refectory.

They passed the door, moving slowly. If one of them turned around now, McCade would be in plain sight. But they didn't.

When they had all entered the refectory, McCade let out the breath he had been holding and stepped out from behind the door. But he did not relax his neuromuscular systems. Tense, tight, all senses humming, he went back to the vestry and through it to the altar place and the altar. He bent down, lifted up the altar cloth, and looked at the little door. It was fastened with a mechanical latch, a trick device as ancient as the church, which required the use of eight fingers, all pressing the proper lever at the proper time to the proper degree to open. Gently, he placed his fingers on the levers of the latch, and concentrated all his attention.

The church faded away. His body did not exist. There were just the eight levers, of which he was a part, and the only sound was the faintest of scratches as the levers slowly moved. He did not feel the latch; he *was* the latch. After moving each lever separately once and all together once, he knew the trick, and the levers slid home.

He came to himself. The little door swung open. Inside were a few ancient objects, and four sheets of paper. All the papers were old, but one was much younger than the rest. He slipped it out from under a crystal goblet, and saw that it was a simple list. Each item was an abbreviated address followed by two key words. One was a specific locator, the other was a sign as to what was located there. He folded the paper, tucked it in his shirt, closed the altar, and stood—to see the old priest on the other side, looking disapprovingly at him.

"This is sacrilege, my son," the priest said gently.

"Yes, father, I know," McCade answered evenly.

"I think you were deceiving me," the priest said, "when we were talking before." There was an unmistakable trace of sadness in his voice.

"I was," McCade admitted.

"I had hoped . . ." the priest said. "But I can see now that such a hope was foolish. I will have to inform the elders, you understand."

"Please don't," McCade said softly. "I'll go away and not come back again." He came around the altar and stood facing the priest.

"I'm afraid that won't do," the priest insisted. "The altar will have to be opened, and its contents checked. You did take something from it, didn't you?"

"No, father."

"I don't know how you have learned the secret of the latch. There will have to be an investigation." He started to turn away toward the side door. McCade put out a hand to stop him.

"Don't you touch me," the old man cried angrily. "You deceived me, and you have tampered with the holy of holies. What kind of a man are you, anyway?"

"A desperate one," McCade answered. "Please, I beg you, let me go."

"No. You have sinned, and you must be punished." Again he started for the door, and again McCade grabbed his arm.

"Let go of me," the priest hissed.

"No, father," McCade said. "I'm sorry, but I can't let you call for help."

"Help? What help? I don't need any help with you, you young monkey." The priest flew foward with his fingers stiff, jabbing at McCade's throat.

In high gear, McCade ducked aside and his own hand came up and over the priest's, and into the bridge of the man's nose. There was a soft snap, and the man fell.

McCade shook himself, took a deep breath, and bent to inspect the body. Splinters of bone had been driven deep into the old priest's brain, and he was dead. McCade sighed. He hadn't wanted to do that. A wave of pity crossed his mind, but he brushed it away. He couldn't just leave the man here. Suspicion would fall on the altar immediately, and too many people had seen him during the morning service and would remember him.

At the back, on the side of the nave opposite the corridor, was another door. Quickly he went to it, opened it, stepped through into a small antechamber, to another door which opened onto a small enclosed courtyard. He hurried back to the priest, lifted him, and carried him out through the antechamber to the court. There he laid the body down gently behind some bushes. He went back to close the doors, then went to the far wall of the yard, jumped up, caught the top with the tips of his fingers, and pulled himself up. On the other side was a wooded yard, and beyond a beltway. He clambered over, let himself down, and ran to the edge of the wood. He looked out from the trees to the beltway, watched the people move by, and wished for an alley. But there was no way to avoid being seen.

He paused a moment, composed himself, then strolled out from the trees, casually crossed the strip of lawn to the belt, smiled at the people on it, stepped on, and rode away.

Foxes was one of the strangest districts of Loger. Long, serpentine, it twisted past several other districts of higher and lower status, and was almost a law unto itself. Eleventh class, first of the third order, its architecture was bizarre, its streets garish, its inhabitants unorthodox by any standards. McCade had been through a section of Foxes before, on his first day in Loger almost a month ago, and it had intrigued him. He was taking a holiday now from his researches and studies of public records and news files, to satisfy a curiosity that had been with him since the first day.

The tube that ended at the spaceport in Red Dog was the same one that serviced Foxes across the city; it snaked around all over Loger, sometimes looping on itself. He rode it the full route, all the way to its other end at the beach at New Port, then back again into the heart of Foxes. From there he had taken to the belts and had gone first one way, then another, trying to see as much of this eccentric district as he could.

Just as he was passing some very tall buildings with huge display windows, he got the first sensation of someone following. He stayed on the belt and did not alter his course, but as he went past the brilliant displays of elaborate furnishings and decorator items, he kept on the lookout for a pane of glass angled just so. But a mirror in one of the windows served his purpose just as well. He saw himself approach in it, and scanned the figures as they came into view behind him. Though the crowd was not too heavy and he could see each person clearly, none of them stuck out as the obvious tail. He went on.

A few blocks later he got his chance. A cross-belt going into Emeraud was empty, and he got on it. He did not look back. He did not change course again until he had rejoined the traffic. And then he left the belt and walked across soft green grass to a park. He slowed as he neared a fountain, which he circled. Now he was facing back the way he had come.

There were several people in the park, sitting on benches or on the grass or standing talking under the elegant trees, but four of them he had seen before, in the mirror in the store window in Foxes.

Three young men, and a girl who seemed to be barely out of her teens. Quite casually he walked up to them, and laughed inwardly as they tried to pretend they didn't notice him.

"It was the mirror," he said, and they looked up startled. "In Gorgoran's," he added. "I saw you then."

"Why don't you buzz off, mister," one of the young men snapped. He was a wiry individual with reddish-brown hair and seemed to be the leader.

"Button your lip, punk," McCade snapped back. "You think you're fooling anybody?"

"I don't know what you're talking about," the youth said hotly.

"Easy, Kyle," the girl said, "he's got no class."

"*I* know that," Kyle said. "You got the wrong bunch, bub," he said to McCade.

"Sure I do. So have you. Don't let's act more stupid than we are, shall we? You're picked, man, and you can blubber there all you want but that isn't going to change anything. Any time you want to know where I'm going, why don't you just call up ahead of time and ask."

"Listen, mister," Kyle began, but his friends interrupted.

"Easy, boy," one of the other young men said. "Don't make a fool of yourself."

"Shut up, Lupus. Let's get out of here."

"Hold on," McCade said, putting just the tip of one finger on Kyle's shoulder. With a hiss the young man spun and smashed the hand off. In return, McCade gently tapped him on the jaw and Kyle went sprawling.

"Why, you—"

"Easy," McCade said, "I believe you struck first."

"He's right, Kyle," the other youth said.

"Shut up, Billy," Kyle said, and got to his feet warily. He hadn't expected this odd-looking character to actually be able to defend himself.

"I just want to know what the idea is," McCade said, standing easily.

"No business of yours," Kyle said.

"No business of mine? Indeed, I do not understand. It seems to me that if you go following me all around the city it's very much my business."

"Nothing to do with you," Kyle insisted.

"Just picking me out at random, hmm? Pick up a few points by knocking the dummy off, hmm?"

"You're too smart, mister," the girl said.

"Or maybe it's something else? Well, how 'bout it? You gonna let me in on it?"

"Listen, buddy," Lupus said, stepping between Kyle and McCade, "we made a mistake, okay? Sorry we got you all ruffled," and he insolently flipped the tips of his fingers across McCade's jacket, then jumped back clutching his hand.

"Mustn't touch," McCade said. "I break fingers next time," he went on.

Cursing, Lupus and the others retreated a few paces, then turned and walked quickly away. McCade stood staring after them.

He was sure they were after something more than just a quick rumble. The girl was no good at acting, and if the others hadn't been so frightened, he might have learned something from them. As it was, he was completely in the dark. And now he had something new to worry about. Who wanted him followed, and why? He didn't give Kyle and his friends the credit to be the brains behind the action. They were just toughs with no minds of their own.

So whom had he made an enemy? So far, he could think of none, except those two kids he'd met the first day, but they were just products of their culture, and there had been nothing mysterious about them. Had the Brotherhood of Service figured out that he was responsible for their priest's death? But if it was the Church, they certainly wouldn't take their justice this way. Who else did he know? Elex Norther, but that made no sense. Arvin Saranof ? No reason for her to be nasty that he knew of. Valyn Dixon? Perhaps, though he gave her more credit than that. Certainly he had disappointed her, and he supposed that she might actually be unsophisticated enough to want to get back at him, but surely not this way.

Had he, perhaps, stirred up something in his prying

about? That was the possibility that seemed most likely, and which afforded the least chance of confirmation. It was also the possibility that worried him the most. If someone didn't like the research he was doing, that person had a good idea what McCade was looking for. And that could mean big trouble.

In his reverie he lost track of where he was going and was surprised to find himself staring in the window of "Emeraud's Largest Sporting Goods Store," as the sign in the corner put it. He was staring at a boxed set of dueling pistols.

He didn't believe in carrying firearms. He had never found them necessary. His biotraining as a child and youth had turned his whole body into a potential weapon if he needed it. That had been his great-grandfather's idea. After the old man's experience in fleeing from his home world, he had decided that none of his children would ever be as helpless as he had been. McCade was the third generation to receive such training, and it had stood them all in good stead at one time or another.

Nevertheless, he went in. Out in the Cluster or the rest of the Orion Limb, if a man had to defend himself, he did, and as long as the laws were satisfied, everything turned out okay. But here there were entirely different customs, with which he was still exceedingly unfamiliar. If he violated a custom, he could die, no matter how right he was. The laying on of hands was evidently a severe social crime, while shooting apparently was not.

It was a large store. He wandered around for a while, looking at the displays of more innocent equipment—clothes, balls, fishing gear, handsome board games and such—and gradually worked his way over to the firearms section.

There was plenty to choose from. Pistols of all types, rifles, even automatic weapons. And over on one side was a collection of foils, épées, rapiers, light axes, daggers, and knives. Apparently, dueling was a serious business in Loger.

"Excuse me," he said to a woman standing behind the counter, "but how does one go about purchasing a gun?"

"Why, in the normal way, of course," the clerk answered, surprised.

"I'm sure," McCade said dryly, "but I'm afraid I don't know the regular way."

"Why, where have you been?" the clerk asked, peeved at being distracted from whatever else she had been doing.

"Out in the Cluster for the last thirty-five years," McCade said. "I'm afraid I've gotten behind the times a bit."

"Good heavens! Are you an offworlder?"

"Yes, ma'am, I'm afraid I am."

"Well, sir, I'm afraid I just don't know exactly what to say to you."

"How about telling me what the normal procedure is for the procurement of a firearm. Do I need to acquire a license first?"

"No, of course not. Really, sir, if you are not a native of Seltique, I cannot see why you would want a firearm."

"I couldn't myself until a half-hour ago, but now I feel I have reason to fear for my life. What do I do, just pick one out?"

"Of course. I assume you do know one firearm from another. And if your life is in danger, perhaps you should leave Seltique."

"My problem at the moment is getting to the spaceport. They're outside waiting for me."

"Really, sir!"

"Really. How much is this one?" he asked, indicating a small caliber pocket pistol.

"Two hundred credits. But sir, if you're an offworlder, how can you pay?"

"Money won't buy it, I suppose?"

"What is money? Never mind. Sir, I really don't think we can help you."

"Well, you haven't so far. Tell me, once I buy one, must I register it?"

"Well, of all the—of course you must. What do you think we are?"

"I'm only beginning to find out," he said, but his game

was interrupted by a presence at his elbow. He turned to see a conservatively dressed man, ostensibly examining the pistols. McCade had not yet learned all the subtleties of caste markings, but he could see this man's low-caste badges distinctly. Apparently the man was twenty-seventh, next to the lowest class. And yet there was something in his behavior that belied the marks.

After being stared at for a long moment, the man looked up and smiled.

"Hello," he said. "I'm Jon Dorn."

"Pleased to meet you," McCade said, curious. The clerk moved off.

"You're Larson McCade," Dorn said. "I recognize you. It isn't hard. There's only one offworlder on Seltique—and you're it.

"Yes, that's who I am," McCade admitted. "What can I do for you?"

"It's the other way around, I think," Dorn said. "Our friendly clerk here seemed most reluctant to tell you what you wanted to know."

"She certainly was. Perhaps you can fill me in."

"I shall try. First, anyone over the age of eighteen is allowed to carry a weapon, provided that weapon has been duly registered at the Academy. Registration is done by the store. You don't have to do anything yourself. This ensures that all weapons will be on record with the Academy, since careful inventory is taken frequently, and if a store has any weapons unaccounted for, it stands to lose its license. It's easy."

"So it would seem. Tell me, if you had to choose, which of these guns would you pick?"

"You are unaccustomed to firearms? No, of course not. We do have types here which you would not find anywhere else. To tell the truth, I prefer a heavy knife. But if I were to choose a gun, I think it would be that one." He pointed to a longish, slender automatic type. "Ten caliber, fully automatic, soft nosed, high velocity, thirty rounds to the clip."

"Quite a beasty," McCade said. "But, uh, why do you prefer a knife?"

"A knife has traditionally been a low-class weapon," Dorn said, smiling broadly and leaning one elbow on the counter.

"But you are not really class twenty-seven," McCade said. "You wear your badges too flamboyantly. I'd guess you're at least third order."

"You are right," Dorn said, smiling even more broadly. "At least, I was born a thirteen. But I don't believe in all that crap. It's all artificial, promoted by the eight Brotherhoods. Ever since I turned eighteen and was able to fend for myself I've lived as a twenty-seven. I've never claimed any rank for any kills. I always keep my status low. After all, even the lowest in this world have all they want. Who could want more?"

"Indeed, who could? But you're on the wrong world, Dorn. You should catch the *Dovetail* on its next stop here, and head for any of the worlds of the Cluster."

"Out of the question," Dorn said. "How could I do Seltique any good that way? This world is decadent. It's sick and dying, and it will take strong medicine to put it back on its feet again."

"I see," McCade said, beginning to sense that not all was right inside Jon Dorn. "And what kind of medicine do you propose?" he asked.

"I haven't figured that out yet."

"I see. Well, listen, I thank you very much, but I wasn't kidding when I told that clerk that they were outside waiting for me. And if I don't get moving, they're likely to come in after me."

"Then move, by all means," Dorn said, his face suddenly serious. And McCade did, taking a side exit.

He looked up and down the belt, saw no one suspicious, told the belt to take him to any other gun store and was whisked away. He wished he knew the secret of verbal commands for public transportation. It certainly saved a lot of bother and could be worth a large fortune out in the rest of the Galaxy. With the lack of any political control of trade in the Cluster these days, a person could do pretty much as he wished.

He spun down out of Emeraud, across a neck of Foxes, and into Blackstone. The belt took him into the central business area, then out the other side and into the suburbs, to a squat, plain building set far back from the road and concealed by trees and flowering shrubs. There it stopped.

He crossed the lawn up to the small paved court and now he could see the tiny gold letters above the door. "Christie Armory," they read. He opened the door and walked inside.

He was in an airy room, with a few widely spaced display cabinets and a coffee table in the center, around which were several comfortable chairs. A well-dressed—even for Loger—man, who was seated at the table reading a magazine, looked up when McCade entered and rose to greet him by extending a hand.

"How do you do," the man said as McCade accepted the hand. "I'm Fourth Zepo Martins. May we be of service to you in any way, sir?"

"I think so," McCade said, taken somewhat aback. "I must explain that I am an offworlder and may be unfamiliar with the proper formalities." Martins did not respond at all, except to indicate that his full attention was at McCade's disposal.

"I have discovered," McCade said after a pause, "that I may have reason to fear for my life, though I do not participate in the normal social competitions of Loger, and for that reason, desire a gun."

"Of course. May I inform you that, for purposes of dueling, automatic weapons of any kind are forbidden. For matters of decency and discretion, large weapons should be discouraged. But for simple self-defense, in a non-competitive situation, may I suggest this item." He walked over to one of the counters, lifted the glass top, and took out a short, snub pistol, heavy and ugly. "Twenty-five caliber magnum, ten-round clip, accurate up to a hundred meters, low kick-back, will stop anything on this world or most others. Can be fired auto or single. Reasonably heavy for good balance."

"How much?" McCade asked.

"Four hundred."

"I think my account at the Morphy Chessica is good for it."

"If not, we do accept currency. One of the few establishments that do, I might add."

"I'm surprised, Fourth Martins. Do you get much off-world trade?"

"Captain Toledo has stopped in here on occasion."

"I understand." He took out a packet of credit vouchers, black with gold scrolling and figures, and pulled one off.

"I shall register your credit balance with your hotel, Mr. McCade," Martins said and pressed a button at the side of the display case.

"Does everybody know me?" McCade asked wryly.

"Not everybody, sir, but you are an offworlder, and the Academy has taken note. And, too, you were at Arvin Saranof's a while back, I believe. I was there, too, though we did not meet."

"I see." Another man came from the back carrying an elegantly wrapped parcel which he handed to McCade.

"Registration has been taken care of," Martins said. "Thank you very much for doing business with us. And may I add, sir, that I hope you will find your purchase superfluous."

"Thank you, very much," McCade said, and left, feeling just a little light-headed.

It was a beautiful day, and though he was a long way from his hotel he decided to take the belts rather than the tube. But he had not travelled for more than a half-hour before he once again sensed that he was being followed. He sharpened his hearing, listened for anything behind him that might give a clue about his followers. But whoever they were, they were saying nothing.

Being as open and casual about it as possible, he simply turned around so that he was sliding along backwards. A hundred meters behind him he saw the smirking faces of Kyle and Lupus and Billy and their girl friend. He waved. They did not wave back. He turned back facing the proper way and decided to ignore them completely. He had taken the belts so that he could see some more of the city, and four tails or no, he was going to see it. He went on a random route, letting his fancy choose his way, and gave no thought to the four people behind him, except to turn around once an hour or so to make sure they were still there. They were, and each time he waved. They did not seem too happy.

Eventually he began to tire and want his supper, and so he directed the belt to take him back to the Morphy Chessica. As he stepped off onto the lawn by the building's entrance he turned once again and watched as Kyle and his friends slid past. They laughed, slapped each other on the shoulders, and pointed derisively at him, but he just grinned back, and went in to supper.

He skipped a little dance step as he brought his pot of coffee from the kitchen to his study. The music he was hearing with internal ears was happy and melodic. Today he felt very good indeed.

He set the pot down on the desk and sat. In front of him were notes extracted from the book he'd taken from the library, the last few sheets of the print-out he'd gotten from Norther, and the list from the church. Near at hand were other notes from his other, less strenuous researches. He had classified everything last night and this morning was prepared to spend the day correlating all he had gathered and learned so far, meager though that was.

For one thing, the book verified and was more specific about many of the stories McCade had heard concerning the cultural leadership Seltique had enjoyed until its embargo twenty-seven hundred years ago. It also held information unavailable to his earlier sources. He wondered, now, what had happened to the author of that book, who had dared to publish so soon after the pogrom of a century ago.

Then, the print-out with its list of names of all who had been involved with the Core. There were significant names there, especially in light of newer information. It was through comparing those names with certain entries in the book that McCade was able to determine who the true leaders of the Core had been—and who had been responsible for the safekeeping of certain documents and artifacts held by the Core since the embargo. The stories he'd heard of old had marvelous things to say about what some of those artifacts and documents were, and the book verified that they were real and gave an explanation as to how they had come to Seltique.

As acknowledged cultural center of the Limb three thousand years ago, Seltique had been a haven for scholars, artists, scientists, social leaders of all sorts. As Seltique had developed, its subtle but profound influence on and leadership of the Cluster, the Limb, and the Galaxy as a whole had become ever stronger until certain other worlds had become jealous of Seltique's influence, had convinced the rest that Seltique was out for galactic dominion, and shortly after, had caused the embargo.

Before then, the scholars, scientists, artists, philosophers, all had brought something to Seltique. Sometimes just the contents of their minds. Sometimes a stuffed notebook. Sometimes a shipload of crates. The intellectual wealth of the galaxy had accumulated on one world. No wonder the others were jealous. And no wonder the rest had progressed only fitfully since the embargo.

Among certain less well documented legends was that of a thing or process or bit of knowledge known as the Book of Aradka. There was no clear idea of what it was or what it was good for, but the hints were too many, too consistent even in their brevity. And through a lifetime of wandering, McCade had picked up little bits and hints here and there and had acquired as much knowledge of the fabulous Book of Aradka as was to be had. He was sure that, whatever it was, it was here on Seltique, in Loger, and had at one time been in the possession of certain members of the Core.

He took out the list from the church. Just a list of addresses, each followed by two key words, such as "blueshelf" and "semimunitions." Some of the code words were easy to understand, others were more obscure. The first of the two, it was obvious, referred to some specific place at each address. The second was a clue to the nature of what had been hidden there. But that was too easy. For security's sake, the compiler of the list had abbreviated the addresses. That seemed obvious, at least to McCade's eye. But what places they actually represented was another question. And there were one hundred fifteen of them.

He took the print-out he'd gotten from Norther. Only twenty-seven of the four hundred some odd names had addresses. These he copied out, then began the long, tedious process of comparing each of these twenty-seven addresses with each of the one hundred fifteen names from the church list. The odds were against him. There was good reason to assume that the material wealth of the Core, represented by artifacts and documents, had been hidden away in the homes of its members. There was no reason to assume that any of the computer's twenty-seven addresses were among those on the church list.

But one was. Out of all the possible combinations, one matched. Now he knew how to read the addresses on the church list. "1-429-16037" meant simply: first-class district —of which there was only one; four hundred twenty-ninth street—easily determined by examining public works plans of the area; house number sixteen thousand thirty-seven—to be found in the directory.

The comcon buzzed. He switched on, and the face of a woman appeared, dignified and severe. She was somewhat over sixty he guessed.

"Larson McCade?" the woman asked. "I am Senna

Reddy, Director of the Academy. Am I interrupting you?"

"No, of course not," McCade said, noting her first-class status badges. The Academy. The Police. Military, the Guard.

"Good. Mr. McCade, I was informed, as a matter of course, of your arrival on Seltique a month or so ago, and I was also informed when you did not depart with Captain Toledo. Naturally, I've been keeping an eye on you. It is seldom that an outsider comes to Seltique, even more seldom that he or she stays any longer than a few days. Most rare of all is for an outsider to purchase weapons on Seltique."

"I believe I understand so far, First Reddy," McCade said. "I can assure you that my purpose here is perfectly legitimate, and I can explain my purchase."

"I'm sure you can, Mr. McCade. Please do so."

"As to the first, I believe I've explained to one or two others that I am in the process of writing a monograph on—"

"Yes, I know that. I have made inquiries. You are discreet, Mr. McCade, but so am I. About the gun."

McCade took a deep breath and told the Director about Kyle and his friends.

"I see," Reddy said. "I know Twelfth Kyle, and his behavior, as you describe it, is consistent with his character. May I assume that you have no idea as to his motives?"

"You may."

"But you see our situation, I hope," Reddy went on. "I understand the position you find yourself in—alone on a strange world, confronted by customs you don't understand, finding yourself threatened by people you don't know. It is only reasonable that you should want to defend yourself. But you are a man without status, Mr. McCade. No matter what you may think of us and our society, we do have very precise rules and laws, strictly enforced. And you, Mr. McCade, are an anomaly. You do not fit in. Nothing in our laws covers you, a man with no status."

"I'm afraid I don't understand," McCade said. "If someone kills or injures someone else, isn't that considered in the laws?"

"Certainly, but only when both parties to the incident are members of a class and hold rank. And as you can see, Mr. McCade, that covers *all* such incidents as they are likely to occur on Seltique. There is absolutely no one in Loger without registered status—except you. In all cases, the evaluation of any act of violence is guided by the regulations of attack and defense as defined by the code of status adjustment. There have been no cases in the last two thousand years in which a statusless person was involved. If someone were to kill you, Mr. McCade, what would we do with him or her? How could the act be classified? As a statusless person, technically you do not exist. And yet no one could deny that a man had been killed. How would that affect the killer's status? Should he be promoted or degraded, or tried for murder? There are no answers to these questions in our laws as they are formulated today.

"And suppose, Mr. McCade, that you should kill someone else. No question of motive or reason need be brought up at this point. That's trivial. But what would become of the status of the deceased, and his non-inherited property? What would your status be after the fact? Your status, whatever it may be before a kill, *must* be affected by that kill, one way or another.

"You see, Mr. McCade, our problem?"

"Yes, Director, I think I do, though I must admit I don't sympathize."

"I don't expect sympathy, Mr. McCade, just appreciation."

"Yes, Ma'am. Well, what can I do? I couldn't leave Seltique now, even if I wanted to, which I don't."

"You could register for status. Every child born on Seltique is automatically registered to inherit status when he or she comes of age at eighteen. It would not be difficult to register you as newborn on the day of your arrival, your coming of age to occur at the time you apply for registration. As a man of status, Mr. McCade, almost all my problems concerning you would be solved."

"But what problems could be left?"

"Just who you are, and why you're here."

"But I've already told you. I can show you my papers."

"I'm sure you can, Mr. McCade, I'm sure you can, but now is not the time to go into that. Will you come down to King's Lake and register?"

"I really would prefer not to, Director Reddy."

"I'm aware of that, Mr. McCade, but perhaps I can offer you arguments that might change your mind. For example, a statusless person has no rights in Loger. As an outsider on a visit, you are protected by certain common laws. But once that outsider becomes a resident, he loses his visitor status—a very real status, by the way, though outside the scope of the normal system—and unless that visitor acquires new status, he becomes a nonentity, legally speaking, though I must admit a very troublesome one. For example, should you find yourself in a duel and not be killed but only injured, there would be no way you could obtain medical treatment."

"I have plenty of credit," McCade said, "and can obtain more if I need it."

"Medical treatment is not a matter of credit, Mr. McCade, but of status."

He sat silent for a long moment. "I see," he said at last. "And there are, I assume, other similar situations where credit is nothing and status is all?"

"Precisely. For example, if someone should make a claim against your person or property. Should someone accuse you of improper behavior or a crime. There are many other such situations. I know a little about the outside universe, Mr. McCade, and I can assure you that however the situation may appear to you and however it might be out there, on Seltique the status system works quite well."

"How long do I have?" McCade asked.

"For what?"

"Before my visitor status goes out of effect."

"Forty days from date of arrival."

"That's the day after tomorrow."

"That's correct."

"I begin to appreciate the problem," McCade said. "However, I would prefer not to act on your suggestion until I see that I have no other recourse. I will think about this in hope of coming up with another course of action that will both satisfy you and allow me to keep my non-status. If I do come up with such a solution, I will inform you. If I fail to think of one, I shall come in and register no later than five P.M. the day after tomorrow."

"As you wish, Mr. McCade. But please be careful. Even as a visitor, you can get into trouble that you would find it hard to get out of."

"I'll be very careful, Director," McCade said, and switched off. He leaned back in his chair and stared at the blank screen. How much trouble was he really getting into? He hadn't counted on the Academy's surveillance being so thorough.

He reached for the directory and flipped it open to the section on group affiliations. Under "Pro-Galaxy Group" he looked for the secretary, found the name and address, then stood. He hesitated a moment, thought about using the comcon again, decided against it, opened a drawer in his desk, took out the gun, made sure it was loaded, and dropped it in his pocket. He left his suite and the hotel. On the belt he thought about taking the tube but decided against that too. He still had much to learn about the physical layout of the city, so he stayed on the belts with all the people going places in the late afternoon and headed north through Aragon and Rocky Point into Starkey. Near the west side of the district, in a quiet area of private homes, he found his address, left the belt, and walked up to the door. He announced himself and waited for a moment. The door opened and he entered.

A rather harried-looking woman met him in the hall.

"Ah, Mr. McCade?" she said, using the neutral honorific uncertainly. "I'm afraid we haven't had the pleasure of meeting."

"No, we have not, Eleventh Regulus."

"Call me Van, please," she said and smiled.

"Van, then." He smiled back. "And I'm Larson."

"Very glad to know you, Larson. Won't you come in?" She led him into a large and very comfortably furnished living room and fixed him a drink without asking.

"Now, Larson," she said when they were seated, "what can I do for you?"

"I come to you," McCade said, "in your capacity as secretary of the Pro-Galaxy Group."

"Oh, dear, I'm sorry. I mean, you're not from the Academy, are you?"

"No, Van, I'm not. I am a visitor from Phenolk P'talion, doing research on the withdrawal of Seltique from the society of the Samosar Cluster."

"Oh, my goodness. Well, really Larson, I'm sorry, but I'm not much of a historian."

"It's not as a historian that I come to you, Van, but as a person who through your affiliation with the Pro-Galaxy Group, is interested in seeing Seltique once again becoming a functioning member of the Orion Limb."

"But Mr. McCade, I mean Larson, I don't understand."

"I shall try to explain, and I think with you, Van, I can be very frank. The research I am doing is for a society on Skopalos which has ideas very sympathetic to your own."

"You mean they want to rejoin the Galaxy, too?"

"No, Van. They want Seltique to rejoin the Galaxy. Though you may not be aware of it, the Pro-Galaxy Group has friends all over the Cluster and the Limb, people who have forgotten that there ever was a reason, however specious, for the infamous embargo, and who feel that Seltique has much to offer the rest of the galaxy—and much to gain."

"Goodness gracious. I think I begin to understand."

"I think you do, Van," McCade said, as straight and as sincere as he could make himself. "We, on Skopalos, have done considerable work on the Seltique Problem, as we call it, and are almost ready to present our data to the Cultural Tribunal. We think we can win them over."

"Why, that's marvelous."

"Indeed it is, thank you very much. It has been the work of several generations. But after all is said and done, we find that there is still a major stumbling block before our goal."

"Seltique itself," Regulus said, bitterly. "Yes, Larson, I do understand. The Pro-Galaxy Group is a duly registered political body, but I'm afraid we're not very popular. It's all we can do to maintain our registration, let alone convince people that our present policy of all but absolute isolationism is wrong. Most people don't even think about all those other worlds out there, and those who do are either afraid or think that if we open up we'll lose our culture and way of life."

"How silly," McCade exclaimed. "The Cluster is not what it was three thousand years ago. Each world is autonomous. Only things which affect the Cluster as a whole are decided by the Cultural Tribunal. Each world is allowed to be whatever it wants to be."

"That's what we keep on saying," Regulus said, "but nobody believes us."

"Why I come," McCade said after a pause, "is because we of the Society believe that we know a way to convince the people of Seltique that rejoining the greater society is the proper thing to do. Now, before you get your hopes up, we may be wrong. We think we have the answer, but we lack certain information. If we can acquire that information, we will be able to make a better evaluation. Then, if our theory is correct, we can put it into practice. If, on the other hand, our theory proves to be invalid, it's best that we know it as soon as possible so that we can get off the dead end quickly and try a new approach."

"That's just wonderful, Larson. Can you tell me the theory?"

"I'm afraid I cannot, because I don't understand it myself. I am not a psychosociologist, and their terms mean nothing to me. I am just a supporter, who is doing his bit for the cause by acting as an agent."

"I see," she said doubtfully, her enthusiasm somewhat dampened. "But what can I do to help?"

"We have learned," McCade said, "that an old group, known as the Core, at one time held certain information which, properly used, would have brought about the desired end, but that, due to lack of personnel and political suppression, they were unable to bring that information to bear. And I believe that, even in *your* hands, you would be unable to make proper use of that which the Core once held."

"You are in dangerous waters, *Mister* McCade."

"So I have learned, Van, much to my sorrow. But you see, I feel very strongly about this and am prepared to take the risk."

"You are a brave man, and I hate to disappoint you, but when the Core was destroyed a century ago all their papers were lost. At least none of them were ever found in the searches."

"So we understand. But tell me, have not you—a group which has always shared at least one ideal with the Core, that Seltique should give up its isolationism—have you not kept certain records on the Core, even back to the days before it was destroyed?"

"Yes, we have."

"It is as we have hoped. Van, I'll be as frank as I know how. We are looking for a book, written long ago, that was at one time in the possession of the Core. We want to find that book. We know that all the possessions of the Core were hidden shortly before the pogrom. We know who the members of the Core were at that time, and we have a document supposedly indicating the hiding places of many of their secrets. But so far we have not been able to correlate our data. I have sought out public records, but the information I seek has been removed. I hope you can help me."

"What is this book, Larson?"

"As we understand it, it is a precise account of the origins of the status system, how it was developed, and how it was planned to make the system compatible with the rest of the Cluster and the Orion Limb without destroying or significantly altering that system."

"I see. I can't pretend to understand all that, Larson.

I'm not a what you said either—sociopsychologist or whatever. But I do believe I can be of assistance. If you will excuse me for a moment."

She got up from her chair and left the room to return a moment later with a minirecorder, which she set down on the coffee table in front of McCade.

"This," she explained, "contains our copies of all the files on the Core compiled by the Separatists just prior to the pogrom."

"That's amazing," McCade said, feeling a feather of music tickle the back of his head. "Those are the very documents which have been removed from the public files."

"I know."

"May I look?"

"Certainly."

He turned on the recorder, keyed the index, ran through it quickly, and found the entry he wanted. He punched the selection and watched as several pages of a directory of a century ago scanned across the screen with little marks by certain names.

"May I make a copy of this?" he asked.

"Certainly," she answered again.

He ran the recording back to the beginning, took a small recorder from his pocket, connected it to the auxiliary line, and ran through the entry again.

"Thank you very much," he said, disconnecting his recorder from hers.

"You're very welcome. Do you think you can find the book?"

"I hope so. And I hope it will prove to be what we think it is. But there's no telling now what may happen next."

"I understand, Larson, but may I offer you some advice? Be discreet. The Separatists still exist, and though they find little cause for action, they are still very strong."

"I'm surprised. Are they so paranoid, then?"

"That, and power-seeking, especially their president, a man named Kelso. He's dangerous, Larson, and if he heard any word that you were trying to break Seltique's isolation, he would crush you. And us."

"I shall be most careful, Van," McCade reassured her. "I've heard of this Kelso before, though I've never met him. Can you tell me anything about him?"

"Not very much. He has very high status, of course, and is very prominent in the University, though socially he is almost completely inactive."

"I see. Well, I can promise you that he shall hear nothing about this"—he patted his recorder—"from me."

"Nor from me. Good luck, Larson McCade."

"Thank you, Van Regulus, to you and the Group."

She showed him out, and as he stepped on the belt he noticed that the young man whom Kyle had called Billy was waiting across the street. The young tough got on the belt when McCade did and followed him openly. After a block or two, Billy came up and rode beside him, smirking at him in a manner designed to be provoking.

"You carry a gun now, I understand," Billy said.

"Yes, Billy, I do," McCade answered quietly.

"Thirteenth Sereg," Billy snarled, "my name's Thirteenth Sereg. Only my friends call me Billy."

"I apologize."

"The hell you do. What do you think you are, some kind of a hot shot?"

McCade just smiled softly.

"So now the Visitor has a gun," Billy Sereg went on. "Isn't that interesting. Could he be planning murder? Or is he afraid of somebody?" He laughed uproariously, and the other people on the belt, who had been watching with some concern, began to move away.

Again, McCade said nothing, but instead of heading straight for home, angled southeast.

"You're going to fight me, McCade," Billy Sereg said.

"I have no status," McCade answered.

"That don't matter, *punk*. You'll still fight me. You're so full of it I can hardl wait to drill it out of you."

"Senna Reddy wouldn't like that," McCade said.

"What the hell does she have to do with it, buddy?"

"She's the Director of the Academy."

"So what? It's none of her affair."

"She called me this afternoon," McCade explained. "She seemed to think that anyone who killed me, without my having any status, would automatically be tried for murder."

"Bullshit."

"Ask her yourself," McCade said. "We're going to her office now."

"Hah! Hiding behind the law, punk? You can't do that forever. There are four of us. We have all the time in the world. You're a stranger here. You don't know the rules. All you have to do is make one mistake, and you've had it."

They were just entering the district of King's Lake, and McCade asked for the Academy. The belt whisked them along, McCade standing easily as Billy Sereg moved around him, pawing at him but not touching, mocking him, calling out to other belt passengers to look at the funny-looking coward. They reached the Academy building.

Like a nasty dog that nips at a pedestrian's heels, Billy Sereg followed McCade into the building, up to the Registration Office, and over to the counter where a comcon clerk took his name and told him to wait. After a moment, Senna Reddy came out.

"Well, Mr. McCade," she said. "Have you found an alternate solution?"

"No, Director Reddy, I haven't," McCade answered.

"He couldn't find his nose with his finger already in it," Sereg sneered.

"I see," Reddy said. "Then may I assume you have come to register?"

"You may," McCade said.

"Oh, my," Sereg chirped, "aren't we polite today?"

"I have the forms already made out," Reddy said and touched a button on the comcon. A sheaf of papers came out. "All you have to do is sign them."

McCade flipped through the form, grasping its total import with just a few quick glances. Then he took a pen from his pocket and put his name on it. Reddy took the papers from him, and McCade turned to go—and turned right into Sereg, who had been breathing over his shoulder. The young man staggered back. "You struck me," he cried. "You low-class scum." He started to reach under his arm.

McCade hesitated just a fraction of a second, punched his body into high gear, reached out with one hand, grabbed Sereg by the neck, and squeezed. His fingers met through the flesh, and the bones of the neck crumpled. Sereg flopped once in his grip, then went limp. McCade let go, and the body fell heavily to the floor.

There was silence in the office. McCade turned to Reddy, who was staring openmouthed at the body bleeding on the floor.

"Properly done, I hope?" McCade asked.

"If you mean according to rule, yes."

"That's good. I'd hate to break a rule my first day as a citizen. There are some questions about this form I'd like to ask."

"Certainly, McCade." She pressed a button on the comcon. "Please come into my office." She led him into an inner room just as the sanitation robots arrived to dispose of the body.

"You're a cool one, McCade," she said as she sat down behind her desk.

"I have to be to stay alive," he answered.

"So I see. Please sit down. Now, what were those questions?"

"I notice that you have me registered as nineteenth class. How did you arrive at that level?"

"By an analysis of your apparent status relative to your ostensible position off Seltique. But that status won't hold any longer. You've moved up a point to eighteen, by killing in self-defense. Sereg's tactics would not have passed the Academy statutes. He did not provoke an assault on his person, though that was what he wanted. His actions were too ambiguous, and as he was the provoking agent, the assault would have been considered his. He should have known better.

"And another point. Billy Sereg has no heirs. Therefore, you inherit his property by default. That marks you up to seventeenth class. Sereg was thirteenth, but that's no problem."

"What do you mean, I inherit? I don't want anything of his."

"That's not the point. We do our best to ensure that property does not stand ownerless. You inherit by law, as much for the sake of the property as for yourself."

"How about the state?"

"I don't understand," she said.

"In my experience, if a person dies intestate and with no heirs, the state inherits the property."

"I still don't understand. What state? Property has to be owned by a person."

"Never mind, Director, I guess it doesn't apply here." He paused a moment, trying to sort things out. "What happens next?" he asked at last.

"I'd suggest that you move out of that accomodation and into Sereg's home in Sands. Its former occupant will not reflect on you. Then I suggest you contact a member of the University's Cultural Education Department and learn a few things about life in Loger—Citizen."

"Yes, Ma'am," he said.

McCade had to admit, once he had moved in, that his new home in Sands was much more comfortable than the Morphy Chessica had been. He had more rooms than he knew what to do with, and accordingly had instructed the housekeeping mechanisms to close off all but a living room, parlor, kitchen, study, library, two baths, and two bedrooms, all toward the front. The rest he had no use for at present.

He spent two days getting settled and then took up Reddy's suggestion about calling the University, at least to the extent of finding out how to handle his credit, of which he now had plenty without using his own funds, and the precise rules and regulations concerning duels and other means of killing people for status or self-defense. He was rather appalled to learn that ritual murder in one form or another was exceedingly common, and that there were even seasons during the year when some or all of the rules regulating homicide were suspended. This killing off of people was, he learned, Loger's prime method of population control.

After he was settled, he made a print-out of the recording obtained from Van Regulus and set to work correlating it with his other data. It took him another two days to decipher all the addresses in the church list, but he still was stumped by the specific location and content codes. It would be impossible for him to go to each of these one hundred fifteen places, search them from top to bottom, especially since most of them were homes or offices whose residents might object to his intrusion. Somewhere, somehow, he had to find a key to those two codes, so that he not only knew what to look for, but exactly where to look.

He learned something else in his researches, another piece to the riddle of the Planet Master. It wasn't much, but it helped. From certain references in the Norther file, along with certain entries in the Regulus directory, he learned that the Planet Master had always, before his elevation to that non-status, been referred to as the Number One of Loger, a person of the first class and the first rank who by performing some feat or service or ritual or something, had taken just one more step and transcended the whole status system of Seltique.

Second Kelso was one of those interested in becoming Planet Master. Kelso was president of the Separatists, who a century ago had precipitated and led the pogrom against the Core. And Kelso was undoubtedly aware of McCade, even as Reddy and so many other people in Loger were. He wouldn't be surprised if Kelso was the one behind Kyle and his bunch. Well, there was one fewer of *them* to worry about.

He was interrupted in his reverie by the door announcing a visitor. He directed the door to admit the caller, and a moment later Valyn Dixon came into the study.

"Welcome, Valyn," he said, getting to his feet as she entered. "How are you?"

"Pretty well, Larson," she answered. "I see you've at last achieved status."

"Not as much as yours, I'm afraid, and not in a manner to my liking. But I had no choice in the matter, as Director Reddy will tell you."

"I've heard the story," Valyn said, taking a chair. "I went to the Morphy Chessica, and they told me where you'd moved. I was curious, so I called Arvin, and she told me all about it."

"Where did *she* hear it?"

"From Reddy herself. They're close friends."

"Now she tells me. Well, that's the way it goes. But tell me, what brings you here?"

"I just wanted to see you again. I know you're an outsider, Larson, even if you do have status now, and your ways are different, but surely they aren't so different that men and women don't find each other attractive."

"No," McCade said, smiling softly, "that happens all over the galaxy."

"I do find you attractive, Larson."

"I figured that out. Listen, Valyn, you're a nice kid and all, and on your world you're a high-class person who's going to be higher some day, and important. But I'm not of your world. I'm not of any world, really. I've spent most of my life traveling from planet to planet. I've been on my own since I was fifteen, in spite of close family ties. I've been places you can't even imagine, done things that are unheard of on Seltique."

"That's part of your charm," Valyn said. Her smile was

broad and happy, and she seemed to be quite comfortable. "Don't you think," she went on, "that sometimes, some of us here in Loger realize just how small and restricted our world is? Sometimes I wish I could just go away somewhere, but I don't know where, or how, or what I would do when I got there, without my class and rank to fall back on."

McCade stared down at the floor in front of Valyn's feet. He could sense the thing that was developing in this room, and he didn't want it. Not that exactly, rather, he couldn't allow it.

"You're a beautiful woman," he said, "when you smile." Her warmth radiated throughout the room. "And I'd be a liar," he went on, "if I said I didn't like you, didn't want you. But Valyn, I'm here with a purpose, and not just to revel in the luxury your world has to offer."

"I know that, Larson," she said softly, still smiling. "Already you've acquired enemies."

"Indeed I have. I've met a little opposition so far, but there's more. I have to move fast, without waiting for questions or at the necessity of other obligations. Do you understand?"

"I think so. But how can that prevent us from making love if we want to? I want to, and I think you do too."

"Dammit," he said, getting to his feet, and turning away from her, "I do. And you're not making it easy. But Valyn," he turned back to her, "I have to be careful. My life is balanced on a slenderer edge than you realize. I believe certain people are beginning to move against me. I have status now, and they can get at me. If I let down my guard for a minute, it could be my last minute. If I get involved in one other thing than my quest, that involvement could entangle me to my death. Do you understand *that*?"

"I guess I don't, not really." She was very subdued. Either she's a good actor, he thought, or she's more naive than I'd imagined.

"Valyn," he said, "what do I do? I have this mission, self-imposed I admit, but I have it nonetheless. I'm here. I've spent a lot of money, invested a lot of time, and taken considerable risk. I can't jeopardize all that, let alone the future."

"I don't want you to," she said. "But maybe *you* don't understand certain things. I know very little about what life is like on other worlds, in spite of the broadcasts we get from a dozen planets or more. Here, Larson, a sexual relationship does not necessarily involve social, financial, or family responsibilities. I think perhaps it's a good system in that respect. I am not obligated to any other person unless I choose. People in your broadcasts make such a big thing of love. So do we, but in a different way. It's not the be-all and end-all of a man-woman relationship. It is a phase, an aspect, a function of something that may be, but doesn't have to be bigger. If I want to make love with you, that does not mean I want to bear your children, or even live in your house. It just means I want to love you. Can you understand *that*?"

"Not very well, but I've got the idea. That's how I've survived so long. Do you want to bear my children?"

"Yes."

"I was afraid you did. Which is why I've been trying so hard to discourage you."

"You've been very gentle about it."

"I'm not all rocks and iron, you know. So what do we do, Valyn? You know my position. I can only guess at yours."

"Just do what I've been suggesting all along. Maybe it will wear off after a while. Maybe one of us will change our mind. Maybe you'll get what you want and won't have to be so careful any more. But how can we tell until we try?"

He looked at her and realized that he was defeated. "All right," he said, grinning and taking her hand, "let's try."

"Why are you really here?" she asked as they lay together in the dimness.

"I told you," he said sleepily.

"I know, but that isn't all. Or it isn't true. What could you be doing that would make you such powerful enemies?"

"What kind of enemies, Valyn?"

"The Separatist League."

"Hmm. Yes, that's a bad bunch, from all I know."

"Worse. They know about you, Larson, and they don't like you. I don't think they know what you're after any better than I do, but they're suspicious."

"How do you know about all this?"

"My father knows several of the officers."

"I see. Puts you into rather a delicate position, doesn't it?"

"I guess it does. I'm worried, Larson. You're meddling in things that are too big for one person."

"Like what?"

"I don't know. Something to do with the Pro-Galaxy Group, I think. You're an outsider, Larson, and they're afraid of you. You don't throw parties; you don't participate in sports; you don't have a job; you travel around the city, visiting people the League doesn't like; and you spend a lot of time alone. They're afraid of you, afraid you're going to try to open up Seltique to the rest of the galaxy, and they don't want to do that. Is that why you're here—to break us out of our isolation?"

"That's part of it," he admitted, "but that's only incidental. My real purpose is just as I told you, to find a certain thing."

"What thing, Larson?"

"A book, I think."

"A book?"

"It's called the Book of Aradka. I don't really know what it is, but I do know it was a thing brought to Seltique long ago, very long ago, and that when the Cluster began to impose its embargo, it fell into the hands of the people who later became known as the Core. And I know that it never left their possession before the pogrom and was not found afterward. Therefore, it was hidden by them, somewhere, and is still there."

"It sounds all very romantic, but I can't see that a book

or anything else could be so important that you'd come here and risk your life for it. There must be more."

"There is, but I can't tell you. I can't trust you that much, Valyn. You're just a beautiful stranger in my bed, and that's all I know. All I can say is that this quest of mine has been on my mind for twenty years. It's something I've directed my whole life toward. Whatever results it may have on the rest of the Cluster and the Limb, my commitment to myself is to continue my search at all costs. I've worked for so long, I can't endanger it now."

"After it's all over . . ."

"That will be a different story."

"I don't like it. It's so obsessive. Just like Second Kelso and his Planet Master business."

"Ah, yes, that's another matter." He swung his legs over the edge of the bed, sat up, and turned on a light. "I keep digging up clues about that, too."

"Surely you aren't trying to become Planet Master, too?" she cried.

"God no! Such an odious responsibility is the furthest thing from my mind. I want no part of that business. I'll just get this Book of Aradka, if I can, and go away, a free man. Seltique will be opened up in the process, but that has to be done anyway. The Orion Limb is stagnating. It has no leadership. Each world does all right for itself, but there just aren't any people capable of governing the whole system. Only here, on Seltique, is there the culture, the background, and the talent for that sort of thing. The embargo put a stop to a unified Cluster and Limb twenty-seven hundred years ago, and the galaxy has been hurting ever since. But that's all beyond my interest.

"No, what I meant about the Planet Master was that, in the same matrix, so to speak, as my own quest, I find references to this Planet Master business, and I think some clues as to how a Planet Master is made. It's an interesting side track, that's all."

"Oh. Well, I'm glad for that, at least," she said, sitting up beside him. "There are other people interested in that besides Kelso and the League, and you've got all the enemies you need right now."

"More than enough, Valyn. You seem to be pretty well informed on the subject, by the way."

"Not really. I mean, I'm learning to be a patron—art and society and all that—and in order to be a good patron, one must have lots of contacts. And with lots of contacts, one hears lots of things."

"Yes, I suppose one would." He thought for a moment, and then started to get dressed. "Maybe you could help me," he said idly.

"In what way?"

"There is still a lot I have to know about the Core. For example, how they managed to keep secret for so long, and how they were finally discovered."

"That's all beyond me," she said, standing up and stretching. He patted her belly.

"One thing I've run across several times," he said, "is mention of a place called Khethespi. I can't find it anywhere. It's not a district, or a street, or a park, or a person. Do you know what it is?"

"Of course, it's another city."

"Another city? But I thought Loger was the only one."

"It is, silly, now, but before, there used to be lots of cities. At least that's what the history books say."

"Another city. Is it inhabited?"

"I surely don't think so. Why?"

"Just curious." He left the bedroom and went into the study. There he switched on the comcon, and asked for an atlas of the planet. The comcon was a long time in responding, and when it did, all it printed out was a thin booklet of some twenty pages. He felt something soft pressing against his back.

"What are you looking for?" Valyn asked. She was still naked.

"Khethespi," McCade answered. "One of the pieces to this puzzle is there."

"Well, if it's in Khethespi, it's out of your reach."

"Why? Are the tubes wrecked?"

"No, of course not, but Khethespi is a ruin, and besides, it's on the other side of the world."

"So I'll go to the other side of the world, or at least as far as the tubes will take me."

"But you can't."

"Why not?"

"Leave the city? But that's unthinkable. No one ever leaves the city."

"I was born on another world, remember? Leaving one city for another is trivial."

"But it's a ruin. How will you live? No food, no water, nowhere to sleep."

"I've done worse," he said. "Here it is." His finger pointed at a spot that was not truly on the other side of the world, but only halfway there.

"Yes," she said, "that's it. Larson, don't go, it's too dangerous. The rest of the world is a wilderness. It's full of animals and who knows what."

"I'm going, Valyn," he said, "and right now. It's like I said before. I have this thing to do, and I can't let anything deter me."

"I won't let you."

"You can't stop me. I'm sorry, but I tried to explain."

"I know, but I don't care." She followed him into the bedroom, where he changed into more rugged clothing.

"If you won't stay for my sake," she pleaded, "how about your own?"

"It's for my sake I'm going," he said and went back to the study. Still naked, she padded after him. He took his gun from his desk, made sure it was loaded, and stuck it in a pocket. He took a box of extra cartridges from the drawer and put them in another pocket. Something hit him in the back of the head and he staggered forward, clutching at the desk. He turned painfully, just barely managing to keep on his feet, and saw Valyn holding a statuette by the head, her hand to her mouth in shock and surprise at what she'd done.

He shook his head to clear it and straightened up. He concentrated for a moment on the area of his skull where the pain was. Nothing was broken. He adjusted his blood and lymph flow to the spot to speed up healing, and made the nerves stop sending pain signals. "I'm sorry," he said, looking at Valyn, then made his body accelerate to five times its normal speed and moved on her.

She seemed to be in slow motion as he reached up, brushed past the rising statuette, and touched her at the base of the neck. He decelerated, and she slumped to the floor. Gently picking her up, he took her into the bedroom, laid her down, and covered her with a sheet. Back in his study he replaced the statuette, then left the house. He took the belt to the nearest tube dome, got into a car, and said, "Khethespi." The car shuddered a moment, then started off.

There were few other cars in the tube as he sped east, and when he neared the eastern edge of the Rand district, he was all alone. Without hesitation his little glass bubble shot down the tube out of the city and over the parkland that bordered it. Below him he could see acres of grass, tended bushes, groves of trees, and the mobile robots that took care of it all. A few moments later the tube leapt over the edge of the forest and he was in the wilderness.

There were no signs of age or wear in the tube. He guessed that the system was a unit, maintained as a whole in spite of what might have happened to the cities it had once serviced. At least he hoped so. If this transport stopped before he reached Khethespi, he would be stuck. There were no roads, so even if he had a car he couldn't use it. And never once had he seen any signs of any kind of air vehicle. But the Core had gotten to Khethespi somehow, and so he should be able to, too. He sat back and watched the trees go by.

The sun was setting, and the pillars of the tubeway now ran closer to the ground. It was unnerving to see the trees rushing up at several hundred kilometers per hour, but they could not touch him. They had grown up around the crystal walls of the tube, and his car rushed on.

Just as the sun dipped below the horizon he came out of the forest and saw the tubeway stretching in great arcs over a flat prairie land. Herds of some kind of grazing animal browsed here and there, taking no notice of his passage. The sun set, and he rushed along in the darkness. Overhead the stars came out, and a moon rose swiftly ahead of him. A few more hours, and suddenly the sky was blotted out. He had entered another forest. He dozed.

He woke with the first light of morning and saw that now the tubeway was plunging through a wet and steamy jungle. There were animals on the ground and in the trees, but those near enough to see went by too quickly for him to make out any details. At midmorning the car began to slow and he was afraid he had come to the end of the line. He was a long way from Khethespi yet and didn't know if it was possible for him to make it on foot, assuming he could find his way.

But the tubeway was intact. Ahead the jungle cleared a bit, and he saw the ruins. How long this now nameless city had lain rotting here he could not tell. Except for the slightly twisted tube still held by its dome stations, there was little left of the place other than walls covered with vines and mosses. The car had slowed simply because of the distortions in the tube caused by several sunken stanchions.

There wasn't much to see, and what he did see wasn't encouraging. After a moment the ruins were past and the car sped up again. The ground began to rise now, and in the thinning clearings of the jungle he could see mountains rising ahead. The car reached them by noon.

The tube zigzagged and climbed steeply, occasionally cutting through short tunnels, but in the main keeping to the open air. Once he slowed almost to a walk as the car inched along a section where there had been a landslide and the tubeway had slumped all the way to the rocky ground.

Still the way was intact, and once past the sag the car picked up speed again.

In a high pass he passed through another ruined city without slowing. It was much better preserved than the one in the jungle had been, and McCade estimated it to be about half the size of Loger.

On the car went, over the pass and down the other side of the range, picking its tortuous trail. It ran into another jungle as it reached the foothills, and just before dusk left the dense foliage, shot over a short expanse of desert and slowed to a stop at the edge of yet another city. Khethespi.

It was Khethespi, all right. It was right where it was supposed to be, according to the atlas. He directed the car to take him to the center of the city, where he got out and, leaving instructions that the car was to wait for him, made his way down from the dome to the street below.

There were no strip parks here, though the road was a molecular belt as in Loger. It was not functioning, however. He had no map of the city and had no idea where he was, but that would have to come later. Now he was very hungry, and dusk was deepening. He would need supper and a place to sleep for the night.

He walked up the deserted roadway, keeping to the center and examining briefly each gray and moss-covered building he passed. After two blocks he came to a park which he entered cautiously. He set his senses on full, kicked up his neuromuscular system, and listened. Ahead and to his left he heard the sound of something relatively large moving through the bushes. Moving more quietly than the wind, he rounded the overgrown shrubbery to a point upwind and ahead of the sound. He sharpened his eyes, and peered through the gloom that now was not so gloomy. He caught a hint of movement.

He took out his gun and crept closer to the source of the movement. The animal moved again, and stepped out onto the grass. It looked something like a cross between a deer and a dog, with a bit of giraffe thrown in for laughs, as big as a sheep and very plump. He aimed and shot it through the eye.

Moving quickly now, he took a knife from his pocket, opened it, and sliced a haunch off the animal, then left the park and went back into the streets. He looked for and found a recessed doorway, which was locked. There, with bits of wood he gathered from one of the overgrown side streets, he built a fire, cooked his meat, and ate as much of it as he could. He made himself as comfortable as possible in the doorway and settled down to sleep. His only precaution was to leave his hearing at super keenness.

It was the sound that woke him. The sky was light, and dawn was only moments away. He had slept long because every time he made use of his biotraining to increase his body's performance, he used up energy at a greatly increased rate, and his body needed a longer time than usual to recuperate.

But it was the sound that woke him, not the light. He cracked his eyes open the merest bit and looked out from the doorway into the street. There were three men, not very clean, wearing rough clothes of skins. They were squatting on their heels just twenty meters from him, watching him warily.

Slowly, without moving, he opened his eyes. They saw he was awake. They mumbled softly to each other, and he thought that perhaps, if he tried hard, he could understand them. It had not been so many centuries since civilization had retreated from Khethespi, leaving the ancestors of these pitiful remnants behind, and though their language had changed in that time, it was still somewhat intelligible.

Cautiously, he moved just a little bit. The three neosavages sprang to their feet, brandishing lengths of iron pipe. McCade froze. He felt sorry for them. They had retrogressed so far. Going back to nature was one thing, but there was no need to return to the club as a weapon and give up all other means of securing one's survival in the wilderness.

"Hello," he said softly, and the three men jumped again.

"Can you help me?" he asked slowly and clearly. They jabbered among themselves again, but more loudly this time, and now he could understand them.

He sat up, picked up what was left of his meat, brushed off ashes and dirt, and began to eat it. Slowly, the three men crept closer. When they were only ten meters off, he held out the bone to them, still with plenty of meat on it.

"A gift," he said. "It isn't much. Will you share?" One of the others left his companions and came timidly forward. The man reached out gingerly, touched the bone, and took it slowly from McCade's fingers. He backed up until he was with his friends again. They all squatted. The first one took just one bite, handed the bone to his neighbor, who did the same, and passed it to the third man, who took one bite. He then brought it back to McCade. Just to make sure, McCade took one more mouthful himself, then put the bone down.

"I come from Loger," he said, and the three men's eyes went wide.

"Not to stay," he went on, "just to visit. Can you help me?"

"Whayawan?" the first man asked, doubtfully.

"I want to find a certain place, a building." He indicated the one against which he was sitting. "It's a place where the Core once was."

"Core? Oynowit."

"Will you take me there? I have nothing to give you."

"Sokay. Howlongya stayin?"

"Just long enough to see if there is a thing there I am looking for."

"Whazit?"

"A book."

"Lossabooks."

"This is a particular one. It may not be here, but I might find something else."

"Sokay. Lesgo."

The three men got to their feet and McCade followed suit. They started off up the street, while McCade kept his distance behind them. They seemed to prefer it that way.

They traveled several miles over ruined roads, some of them dense with undergrowth, others filled with rubble. Several times they went through buildings which had been emptied of all furnishings. Never once did McCade see any more of these people.

At last the trio ahead stopped in front of a building in the middle of the block, undistinguishable from any others.

"Scorbildin," the spokesman said. "Sokay?"

"Just fine," McCade said. "I thank you very much."

The three men nodded once, then turned and walked away. When McCade looked again, they were gone. He shrugged his shoulders and entered the building. It was dim inside, and he had to turn up his eyesight to be able to see. He would have a headache later, but there was no choice.

He was in a foyer, empty of all furniture. Toward the back, stairs went up to the upper floors, and there was a vacant space where the elevators had once been. He went across the gritty floor, found a corridor that led to the back, and followed it. Near the end another set of stairs led down. He descended, and now he was in pitch darkness. He reached into a pocket and took out a tiny flash. It didn't make much light, but with his hyped-up vision, it was enough.

There were more pieces of furniture here, and signs still hung on the doors. He went from one to another until he came to one marked "Officers Only." Disregarding the warning, he put his shoulder to the rotting panels and pushed the door open.

Beyond was what appeared to be a security vault, filled with safety deposit boxes, most of which had been forced open. In the far wall was set the circular steel door of a safe. McCade went up to it and touched the knobs. They still spun. He put out the light, leaned his head against the door, placed his hands on the knobs, and let his senses flow into the locking mechanism. He was not aware of the darkness, the room, or his body. He knew nothing but the subtle vibrations of the turning cogs inside the door. He lost all sense of the passage of time. He was just a tiny motion, a bit of friction, a slither of metal on metal. One way would bring life and light. All other ways were death. He felt, he was. And then a click.

He opened his eyes and returned to himself. The door was open. He turned on his little light again, swung the door wide, and stepped through.

He was in a chamber of wonders. The walls were lined with shelves, each of which held objects of light and fire. He went from one to another: a jeweled skull, something that looked like a miniature comcon, an ancient volume actually made of paper and cloth. Here was a hoard, a veritable wealth of ancient treasures culled from all over the galaxy, each representative of a peak of art, culture, science, or philosophy. If he could have taken the contents of this vault back out into the Cluster, he would be a man rich as no other before him had ever been.

Here were inventions long lost, art long forgotten, truths unremembered by even the most active cults. Yet all this was the residue, just the dregs of what had come to Seltique over the ages. All that was the best, the Core had taken, and kept with themselves in Loger. Here was an empty shelf, a vacant case, the marks where something had once lain. Not too many, but a few.

And here was something new, something put to rest just a short century ago. A notebook. McCade picked it up and opened it. Yes, this was what he had come here for. An inventory. A listing of all the treasures that had been taken away from this vault and from hundreds of others around the globe. He closed the notebook, left the safe carrying it with him, and closed and locked the heavy door behind him. He left the vault, the cellar, the building, and walked up the street in the sun toward the tubeway, his head singing, his feet dancing. He felt as light as a bird. He didn't have all the pieces yet, but he was so close, so close. He danced on his way, whistling a wild melody, hardly mindful of the ruins around him.

As he capered along he became aware of a bird, flying in gay swoops over his head, going the same way he was. It was a large bird, black with yellow and white feathers in the wings and tail. It seemed to be keeping time to McCade's music.

"Hello, bird," McCade called.

"Hello, man," the bird called back in a husky soprano voice.

McCade stopped. "You can talk!" he exclaimed.

"Of course I can," the bird said, settling down to land on the ground two meters in front of him.

"But I mean, you're not trained, you can really talk."

"Yes, man, I can. Forgive me, I thought you were a native of Loger."

"No, I'm not. I'm an offworlder. How did you know?"

"Your surprise. My people are not unknown in the city. I have been there myself. Have you come out here to live or just to look around?"

"Just a visit," McCade said. "Forgive me, but I can't get used to this. Are you really a person inside all those feathers?"

The bird squawked. McCade guessed it was a laugh. "Of course I am," it said. "Am I really such a marvel, then?"

"You are indeed," McCade said. "What do you call yourself?"

"I don't call myself anything, but others call me Klooshkai. And who are you?"

"Larson McCade, at your service." He bowed deeply.

"Much obliged, Larson McCade," the bird said. "Aha, I see you've been taking notes."

"Indeed," McCade said, aware again of the notebook in his hand, "and literally too, from the safe in the basement of the Core Building."

"That old business," the bird mocked. "When will it ever end? It's all for nothing, you know."

"No, I don't know it, and I'd argue the point with you except that I want to get back to the tube before dark."

"What, leaving so soon?"

"Yes. This is what I came for and now that I have it I must go home."

"Where is home? May I accompany you?"

"You may," he said, starting on his way again. "Home for me," he went on, "is a world called Lamborge. At least, that's where my parents live."

"Lamborge," Klooshkai the bird said, fluttering up to perch on McCade's shoulder. "Never heard of it. But then I'm not one for astronomy. Will you go back there?"

"Eventually, I hope so."

"You won't if you don't take care at the tube dome," Klooshkai warned. "If that's where you're going, you'll find a surprise."

"What kind? The tube hasn't collapsed, has it?"

"No, but there are three little cars there in the station, and four big men hiding in the station."

"When did you see this?"

"An hour or so ago. I was just flying over and got curious. I didn't know you were here then. I thought they were waiting for somebody else to come through, but if you say you've been looking for Core stuff, then I guess it's you they're after."

"Thank you for the warning, Klooshkai. Maybe, now, I'll have a little surprise for them instead."

The bird stayed on his shoulder all the way back to the tube station, which McCade approached as if in total ignorance. But instead of taking the regular way up, he mounted to the dome by the back service stairs, and came at the ambushers from behind.

They were all four in plain view from where he stood at the upper service door, though if he had come up the public way they would have been well enough hidden. He pulled out his gun and with no compunction fired four times. There was no thrashing, no outcry, just four heavy thumps.

"You're a damn good shot," Klooshkai said.

"Yes, I bet my life on it," McCade answered. He inspected the bodies one by one, but though all were armed, none bore any identifying marks. They were as anonymous as the furniture they had been hiding behind.

McCade left the bodies and climbed into one of the tube cars. The bird fluttered in after him.

"Hey," McCade protested, "you can't go along."

"Why not? It's my world, too. If you kick me out, I'll just fly to Loger. It's been a while since I've been there, and I have the sneaking suspicion things might just be getting pretty exciting there soon."

"For my sake I hope they're not," McCade muttered. "Okay, come along if you wish." He closed the door and the car started for Loger.

He read the notebook while they traveled. The bird just slept. Besides the inventory, there was a note, scrawled hastily on the last page.

"Merenthar is dead," it read. "Only Sterpreen has the key now." Merenthar had been the last Planet Master. Then who was Sterpreen?

Twenty-four hours later the car neared Loger. McCade was very hungry and anxious to find a good restaurant. Klooshkai wasn't too cheerful. As they passed the first station in the city, the car slowed for traffic, and McCade saw a man standing in the terminal, watching him approach. There was no mistaking it, the man was expecting a car from outside the city. But when the man saw McCade, his face went grim, and he turned and quickly walked away.

"Another friend, I see," Klooshkai croaked.

McCade left the tube a few stops further on, and Klooshkai, with a simple farewell, flapped off on his own. Not really sure what to make of the bird, McCade watched it go, then got on a belt and asked for a restaurant.

The men in ambush had bothered him. Whoever his enemies were, they must have decided to stop playing. And off in Khethespi, without the rigid rules of Loger to follow, the opportunity had been perfect, except that the bird had blown their cover. In a way, McCade was safer now that he was closer to his enemies. They would have to follow the rules.

The belt stopped him by a low sprawling building surmounted by a broad, squat dome. He walked up a gravel path to the door, entered, and found himself in a dimly lit room, simply but elegantly furnished in leather and rich ruddy wood. A floating sphere greeted him and took him to a table already laid out, the translucent porcelain resting on a rich brocaded cloth, the utensils of silver and gold. There was no menu. McCade just told the floating sphere what he wanted, was served with a huge tray of mixed hors d'oeuvres and a glass of liqueur. He nibbled and sipped, and after a remarkably short time for a restaurant, the food was brought to the table on a floating hemispheric cart. The waiter-sphere sprouted arms and served him. Then McCade noticed that each table had its own waiter. As he ate, the waiter-sphere continued to serve him. The food was superb, and he filled himself to repletion. When he had had enough, the table was cleared, a wine was brought, and finally coffee and cigars were offered. McCade left the cigars and wine but sat back comfortably in the easy chair and sipped the coffee, the best he'd ever tasted.

As he started on his second cup the sphere returned once more, with two people behind it. Lupus and the girl, Kyle's friends.

"Hello, Seventeenth McCade," Lupus said, not flippant now but softly surly. "Remember me?"

"I do, Fifteenth Lupus," McCade said, "though I haven't had the pleasure of a proper introduction."

"You know my name, I know yours—that's enough."

"What about her?"

"I'm Thirteenth Finewalls," the girl said, subdued but seething underneath. McCade wondered for a moment if these people were always angry or if it was just his presence.

They sat down at his table without being asked.

"You'll treat us, won't you?" Lupus said.

"No," McCade answered shortly. "I was having a pleasant time until just now."

"Well ain't that too bad," Finewalls hissed. "Billy Sereg isn't having *any* kind of a time, now."

"So whose fault was that?" McCade asked. "I didn't ask for it."

"You killed him."

"And if I pulled a gun on you, what would you do to me?"

"Wipe your ass all over the wall," Lupus said. "He was a friend of ours. Kyle isn't very happy." Logic got nowhere with them.

"If Kyle isn't happy," McCade said, "he should maybe take up a hobby."

"Listen, McCade," Lupus snarled, leaning across the table, "I don't like it either, and I just want you to know you're going to have to watch your step."

Somewhere in the back of McCade's head a rocking melody began to take form, like a saxophone playing in the distance. "It would appear," he said, a lazy smile beginning to grow on his face, "that that bit of advice would do better going to you, don't you think?"

"Not really, McCade," Lupus said, grinning nastily. "Once you leave here—" But he was interrupted by Finewalls grabbing his arm. She was looking past McCade, over his shoulder. Lupus looked at her, then followed her gaze. His face went white.

"All right, McCade," he said through clenched teeth. "You get off this time. Just remember, there are three of us." Then the two hoods got up and, with another glance behind McCade, left his table and faded into the distance. When they had gone, McCade turned around to see what had upset them so. But all he saw were other people, singly, in couples, and in small groups, eating and enjoying themselves. He turned back and finished his coffee.

Though it was well into the night when he left the restaurant, his notebook tight under his arm, he decided to see what he could find out about Planet Masters. He directed the belt to take him to the Capitol Building of the Amaranth district, where Merenthar, the last Planet Master, had had his offices. He didn't know what he would find there, but he hoped something that would enable him to deal with whoever had sent the ambushers to Khethespi. He suspected Kelso, and if he had the secret of the Planet Master he might be able to buy Kelso off.

The Capitol Building of Amaranth, one of the ninth-class districts, was an imposing structure. Two blocks wide, forty stories tall, its façade was designed to present an image of power and strength, a unified design in black and olive stone that dominated the broad avenue on which it stood and made the neighboring buildings, even the taller ones, seem insignificant by comparison. Broad white marble steps led up to ten wide glass doors, above which crystal windows glinted with light from inside. McCade strode up the deep steps and into the main foyer, half as wide as the building itself and three stories high, floored with an intricate mosaic of intertwined geometric shapes. There were no desks, no clerks present, no index of occupants. There were sleek couches, coffee tables, comfortable chairs, pots of exotic plants, and statues, but no sign of any way to get to other parts of the building. He stopped in the center of the huge room and watched the thirty or so other people who sat or moved around as if they knew where they were going. He saw one man walk up to a blank wall, in which a recess suddenly appeared. The man stepped inside, and the recess closed again. Nothing to do but try the same thing.

But which part of the wall should he try? He'd feel silly if he went up to the blank brown-and-beige marble surface and nothing happened. Oh, well, he'd just have to risk it.

He picked a spot and walked toward it. As he drew nearer the wall he could see fine cracks in the surface. He changed his course slightly and when he stopped, a recess appeared, just as it had for the other man. He stepped inside. The panel closed.

"Planet Master," he said, and the panel opened. He stepped out onto a deep plush carpet, in a small, tastefully furnished office. A human secretary sat behind a desk of lustrous wood. McCade walked up to the man.

"How do you do," he said. "I'm Larson McCade." No sense in trying to disguise himself. "I've been doing research on the lives of the last three Planet Masters, and I was wondering if you could help me."

"That would depend, sir," the secretary said, "on what kind of help you required. Most of this office's history is well represented in the various university libraries, and much of the rest is not open to public inspection. There is very little here that cannot be found elsewhere."

"So I understand," McCade said, "but the other sources are highly disorganized, I find, and broadly scattered. I was hoping to be able to accomplish in one stop here what would take me several days of library-hopping elsewhere."

"I see. Well, in that case, perhaps we can be of some service to you after all. May I ask the nature of the information you seek?"

"Certainly. Merenthar, the last Planet Master, died without passing the keys of the office on to his successor, as you know, and I have been trying to find documentation that might indicate just why he failed to do this."

"I see. I thought you said you were researching the last *three* Planet Masters."

"I am, but as I'm sure you're aware, Merenthar's predecessors left no enigma such as his. They have been no problem to me so far."

"I see. Well, Seventeenth McCade, I don't really think we can help you. Others before *you,* as I'm sure *you* are aware, have sought the solution to that particular mystery, as well as to the nature of the key of the office, and none has so far succeeded."

"Indeed I know that, sir," McCade said stiffly. "However I have been fortunate in uncovering some evidence which I have found in none of the other studies on the subject.

With this new evidence I feel sure that I can at last get at the truth of the matter. Provided I have access to certain other information."

"Such as?"

"Such as the names of Merenthar's close friends and associates. None of his biographers are precise in this matter, and they are inconsistent with each other."

"I see. I'm afraid, Seventeenth McCade, that you are entering areas closed to public inspection."

"I was afraid of that. All I can say is that the information I seek is vital to my study, which, if successfully completed, might mean that Seltique once again will have a Planet Master. And I can also assure you that Seltique will need a Planet Master in the not too distant future."

"I'm sorry, Seventeenth McCade, but I cannot let you have the information you want."

"Is there, then, something to fear in knowing precisely who Merenthar's close friends and associates were?"

"Yes, there is. This office, too, has gone into the problem you say you are researching, and while I cannot tell you the results of our investigation, I can tell you that they frightened us, badly."

"I see," McCade said, mockingly. "And may I assume that some one among those close friends of Merenthar's was the cause for your fright?"

The secretary said nothing, but McCade could read the man's face, and the answer was clearly affirmative.

"May I add," McCade went on, "that the additional evidence I spoke of also relates to some one of Merenthar's close friends or associates?"

The secretary still said nothing, but his face began to go white around the corners of his jaw and eyes.

"Unfortunately," McCade said, "what I found was not enough. Perhaps, however, if I also had what you have, the answer might be seen."

"I'll have to ask you to leave, sir," the secretary said.

Casually, without overt threat, McCade took his gun

from his pocket and placed it on the edge of the desk. He did not point it at the man or leave his hand on it. Technically, he was just relieving himself of a cumbersome object. But the secretary's eyes went wide at the sight of the gun and stayed fixed on it as it lay there.

"A friend of mine," McCade said very softly, "just recently shot himself in the ankle. It was a soft slug that expanded rapidly and took away most of the bone. He says that his new artificial foot is nowhere near as good as the natural one was."

The secretary's eyes snapped up to McCade's face.

"Are you threatening me, sir?" he croaked.

"It doesn't look like it," McCade said, crossing his arms. "Nor does it sound like it, I believe. As I was saying, between us, I'm sure we can put an end to this mystery, and open the way for a new Planet Master. Which, I can assure you, will not be either you or me."

The secretary swallowed hard, explored McCade's face with his eyes, and his fear began to abate.

"Really, sir," he said, "I think you had better leave. You can get into a lot of trouble displaying weapons in this building."

McCade's face, without any significant change, went hard, and his voice when he spoke was flat and almost inhuman.

"I do not intend," he said, "to obey any of the rules or principles of this city of yours. I intend to have that information I spoke of. If you do not comply with my request immediately, I shall commence to remove parts of your body with my little toy until such time as you either do comply or are dead. But I must warn you that once I start on you, I shall make sure that you will never be able to inculpate me in the matter. There are ways of doing that without killing, such as removing the tongue and eyes, breaking the eardrums, and permanently crippling the fingers—provided, of course, you have any fingers left by that time."

The secretary went white, then red, then gray. His voice

was only a gasp; tears appeared in his shocked eyes and slid down his mottled and twisted cheeks. "My God," he squeaked over and over, "my God, what kind of a monster are you?" And he sobbed, his protruding eyes glued to McCade's face.

"Not a very nice one," McCade said gently, and let himself soften completely. "I'm sorry, I didn't mean to frighten you quite that badly."

The secretary gasped and panted, wiped his face, and still wide-eyed, struggled desperately though futilely to make some recovery of his composure.

"But," McCade said, just as gently, "I meant what I said."

The secretary choked, climbed to his feet, and gripping the desk and then the wall, staggered over to a door and into another room. There, the poor man opened a cabinet, took out a bottle and a glass, poured himself a huge drink, and gulped it down. Then he spun on McCade and, his face white with anger and fear, hissed, "All right, dammit. All right, you monster, I'll give you your damned information, though they'll kill me for it. At least it will be clean!"

"No one will kill you," McCade said gently, "because no one will know. All you have to do is make me a copy of what I want and give that to me. The originals you can return to their places."

The secretary gasped and panted and began to recover himself somewhat. He dabbed at his face with his handkerchief. The immediacy of the threat of mutilation and total incapacitation was gone, and the gun was not in sight. McCade was not a bad-looking guy, and he was being very gentle and had offered means of covering himself. All in all things could be worse. All this McCade read in the man's still smeary and distorted face.

"All right," the man said again, but this time more calmly. "All right. Come with me, please." He led McCade through several back rooms and offices into a file room. The walls were filled with cabinets, all labeled cryptically.

"Just what do you want," the man asked sullenly.

"Just a list of close friends and associates and information identifying them, especially anything concerning any person or associate with whom he had frequent but unexplained meetings or conferences, particularly if that person is unnamed or goes by a code name."

The secretary's head snapped around. "Then you know?" he whispered hoarsely.

"Not yet," McCade answered, "but I will."

The man continued to stare at him a moment longer, then went to one of the files, opened it, and took out a folder.

"It's all here," he said.

"Copy it."

The man took the folder to a machine in the corner, fed the contents to the machine one page at a time, put the originals back in the folder, and handed the copies to McCade.

"Thank you," McCade said. "I can find my own way out." He turned and left the room, stopped at the front desk to retrieve his gun, entered the elevator, and returned to the street. As he stepped onto the belt, he noticed another man, half a block away, getting on at the same time. He rode aimlessly for a block or two, changing directions frequently, until he was sure. The man was a tail.

But it was not Kyle or Lupus or Finewalls. There was nothing distinctive about the man other than his constant presence. McCade rode on a bit farther, then got off the belt and strolled casually into a park. He rounded a clump of high bushes, accelerated, sped around to the other side, and slowed down just behind his follower, who had started to run when McCade had gone out of his sight. He touched the man on his shoulder, and the other spun, startled.

"You'd do better to stay closer," McCade said.

"God dammit," the man gasped, "how'd you do that?"

"Trade secret," McCade said. "How about we talk a bit?"

"Listen, buddy, I'm not looking for trouble."

"Too bad, you've found it."

"Hey, look, man, take it easy," the man said, holding up his hands defensively and stepping back, "all I'm supposed to do is follow you and report back where you've been."

"That's very nice," McCade said, "but I don't happen to like the idea. Maybe you've heard how much I don't like it."

"Yes, I've heard, but I've got my orders."

"That's also very interesting," McCade said. "I thought that in this wonderful world of yours every man was his own boss. Speaking of which, I don't believe I know yours."

"You're not supposed to," the man blurted.

"Too bad again. I like to think I know more than is good for me. For example, that the man who's been bugging and tailing me lately is named Kelso. Is that right?"

The man nodded.

"Okay, then," McCade went on, "you go on back home now, and give Kelso a message for me. You tell him to keep off my back, and that any time, *any* time he feels he *really* has to know what I'm up to, he should come to me and ask me politely. Got that?"

The man nodded again.

"That's good. Now git."

The man got.

The door announced a caller. McCade shut off the news program from Phenolk P'talion and signalled admittance. Elex Norther entered, and McCade stood up to greet him.

"How are you doing?" Norther asked, shaking his hand. "It's been quite a while."

"I've been busy," McCade apologized. "How's yourself?"

"Doing pretty well. I'm glad to see you've decided to stay with us, but what about that monograph you were writing?"

"Still working on it," McCade said. "Care for a drink? I'm afraid I've got a long way to go yet, which is why I decided to take up residence. My publishers keep complaining, but all I can do is tell them to wait."

"How do you keep in touch with them?"

"Messages at the spaceport. It's not easy to get one out, but it can be done."

"I didn't know that. Thank you." He took the tall chilled glass and sipped. "Very good," he said. "What is it?"

"Scotch. Very popular out toward the edge of the Limb. Had a hell of a time trying to find it here, though. Well, what brings you around?"

"Today's the first day of the Sagger Month Opens. I thought you might like to go and watch a few matches."

"Very kind of you, but I'm afraid I don't know what Sagger Month is."

"One of the four months during which the regular rules of dueling are relaxed. Helps keep the population down. During Sagger Month, any person may challenge any other person of the same rank but lower class. There are also a series of formal duels, held in the Whitefriar arena. That's where I'm going. The arena itself is off bounds for free-lance challenges, as is a person's home or office. I don't participate myself, not since I was twenty-three at any rate, but I like to see a good fight. Like to come?"

"Hmm. I'm not sure. Ritual murder was never my style. Only for money." He laughed to show it was a joke. "But I guess I might as well. I still have a lot to learn about this place."

"Good. Take your gun if you have one. We'll be fair game on the way there."

At his suggestion, McCade took his gun from its desk drawer, checked it, and also took a handful of extra cartridges.

"Actually," he said, "I never go out without it any more."

"Yes, I've heard Kelso is steamed at you. How did you manage to get *his* back up?" He finished his drink.

"I'm not sure, but I believe he thinks that because I'm from outside, I want to open up Seltique to foreign exploitation, or something like that."

"That's right in character, all right," Norther said. "Well, shall we go?"

They rode the belts to Whitefriar, the number two district of Loger, and much to McCade's relief they received no challenges. He knew he could defend himself if he had to, but he didn't want it to be known just how well. They reached the arena—actually an interlocked cluster of buildings, many of them roofless—and went to the central plaza, where the events scheduled for the day were listed.

"Don't care much for pistol matches," Norther said, looking over the illustrated display. "Anyone can shoot a gun. But it takes skill and training to handle a sword or knife, or to master one of the forms of unarmed combat. How about this one?" He pointed to a panel which depicted two men with crossed rapiers.

"You know this thing better than I do," McCade said. "You be the judge."

"Okay, then this one it is. Matches every quarter-hour. I know some of the contestants. Should be good for a couple of rounds anyway."

They went through a maze of patios and corridors, past the entrances to other arenas and theaters and innumerable stands where refreshments of all kinds could be obtained. That much, at least, wasn't any different from anywhere else in the galaxy.

At last they came to the proper auditorium, a rectangular room with steep rows of seats on two sides and a long strip of bare floor down the center. They entered, found places near the middle halfway up one side, and waited as an attendant with a vacuum-mop cleaned up some blood on the strip.

Then two men came out onto the floor, one from either end, and approached each other. They wore only tight-fitting shorts and soft, snug shoes, and each carried a long, thin-bladed rapier. They neared each other at the center of the strip, saluted each other, backed off a step, fell into a crouch, and when a bell sounded, commenced to fight.

It was brief and bloody. Both men were very good, and both received several superficial wounds. The bout was won when one of the men ran the other through the thick part of his thigh. They did not fight to the death.

They stayed for two more bouts, and McCade grew more impressed with the swordsmanship with each one, but at last Norther tired of it and suggested they leave. The next place they went to offered something very akin to karate.

Here, too, they watched three rounds before going on.

"These aren't just regular citizens, are they?" McCade asked as they stopped at one of the little counters for sandwiches and beer.

"By no means," Norther said. "The contestants are all members of the athletic branch of the Academy. This is their profession."

"I thought they were awfully good. I know a little about such things, and aside from my older brother, I've never seen fencers as good as those."

"I didn't know you had any family."

"Oh, yes, a brother, two sisters, and a heap of cousins. My great-grandfather had three children, ten grandchildren, and thirty-seven great-grandchildren. And several of my generation are beginning to start another set. We're a growing family."

"Where did your great-grandfather come from originally?" Norther asked.

"A place I've never been," was all McCade would say. "He was very bitter about it."

They wandered up and down the intersecting concourses for a while, watching the people. Then three young women came up in a group and greeted Norther.

"I thought you gave up on all this," one of them said.

"Just as much as you have," Norther returned. "Larson, I'd like you to meet some friends of mine: Alice, Dalyr, and Merthy, with a lisp."

McCade smiled and nodded to each of them, and they smiled and nodded back.

"I think I'd like to see some more fencing," he said when the greetings were over.

"Not for me, thanks," Norther said. "Can you manage alone?"

"Certainly. Tell you what. I'll meet you at the central court at seven, and we'll all go over to my place and have a little. If you can find *me* a friend, that is."

"Sounds fine," Norther said, laughing, "and don't worry about friends."

"We'll see you later, then," Alice added, and he left them.

He stopped in at a few more theaters, just to see what was going on, but didn't stay at any one place longer than one bout. He was surprised at the variation in combat styles, and decided that his own education along those lines had been decidedly lacking.

He was just leaving a competition where a girl smaller than Valyn Dixon had drubbed a giant of a man at quarter-staves when he saw Arvin Saranof in the crowd. He went up to her and said hello.

"Larson McCade," she exclaimed, "things have certainly changed for you since the party. I had intended to offer you my services, but I begin to doubt you'll ever need them."

"Thank you for the thought anyway, First Saranof," McCade said. "But I'm still a stranger here. Can you explain to me just what a Patron is and does?"

"Why certainly. Not everybody, you must understand, who wants to improve his or her status knows very well how to go about doing it. A Patron is sort of like a graduate tutor in Cultural Education in that respect. What we try to do is to teach an aspiring person how to better himself, how to discover which of many possible options and courses of action are best for him or her, and guide the person in the upward climb. We only work, of course, with people of lower status than ourselves. We'd be of no use to anyone higher, and after one reaches the seventh class, the first order, he or she is completely on their own."

"I see. That's very interesting. You may be able to help me yet, though I don't have any aspirations at the moment."

"If I've judged you correctly, Larson," she said dryly, "any assistance I give you would be purely nominal."

He smiled his best boyish smile. "That's very kind of you," he said.

"Not at all. But I was hoping you'd become a little more social than you have been. You're quite a character, you know. You make a big impression on people."

"Bigger than I sometimes like," McCade said.

"Like Kelso, you mean? Yes, he's not one of your friends, I'm afraid. But I don't think you're afraid of him, are you?"

"Not in the least."

"I didn't think so. Maybe that's foolish of you. I don't know what you've done to upset him so, but he's very displeased. And he's a dangerous man when he's angry. I don't like him much. He bends the law to suit his own purposes, and uses people in ways that are hardly proper. Still, he is a man of considerable importance and influence, and his status is much higher than mine. Still, there have been times when I've thought of calling him out just to teach him a lesson, if I thought I could get away with it. The only trouble is people who become his enemy seldom get a chance to confront him personally."

"You'd call him out?" McCade asked. "What's your weapon?"

"Axe."

"Oh. Well, remind me never to pick a fight with you. That's one weapon I've never used."

"It's not very common," she admitted, "but very effective. I've defended myself several times with it and though I don't duel much I keep in training. Who knows, someday he may call *me* out."

They were interrupted by a squawk from overhead and a flutter of feathers. McCade looked up to see a large black bird with yellow and white wing and tail feathers soaring down to land on his shoulder.

"Hot blood, it's a roaring good fight today," the bird squawked.

"Now where did you come from," Saranof exclaimed. "Off with you, shoo." She waved her hands at the bird, who flapped its wings but kept its perch on McCade's shoulder.

"Not so rough not so rough," the bird squawked.

"What is it?" McCade asked, appearing nervous and curious at the same time.

"Just a corvis. They're harmless but can be a nuisance at times. Like now. This one seems to have picked you for a roost. Well, I must be going. I only came for a little break. I have a couple of protégés who are going to try to improve themselves during the Sagger Month, and unlike yourself, sir, they need all the help they can get."

"I'm sure they'll do well," McCade said and watched the woman walk away.

"Keeping in trouble, I see," the bird said in its throaty soprano.

"Is that you, Klooshkai?"

"It's certainly not Senna Reddy," the bird retorted. "I've been scouting around. That little incident at the tube dome in Khethespi got my curiosity up. Purely personal, you understand."

"Oh, of course."

"Anyway, I met somebody here I think you'd do well to get to know—for ten minutes or so, anyway."

"Anything you say. I'm certainly open to suggestions."

"Like hell you are. You'd be surprised how much a bird like me can find out by listening at open windows. Haw, haw, haw!"

"I have doubts about your sanity," McCade said, chuckling.

"You'd not be alone," the bird answered. "Anyway, are you interested?"

"I don't know. You haven't told me who this person is."

"Words cannot describe. Come with me, that way." It pointed with its beak. McCade went where he was directed, up one concourse, down an alley, across a court, and through a door into what was obviously a dressing room There was only one man present, who looked up with surprise when the mismatched pair entered.

"Who are you?," the man asked.

"Larson McCade. My friend here," he poked the bird, "suggested I come and visit you."

"Indeed." The man looked skeptically at Klooshkai. "You picked a poor time. I'm due to go into the arena in ten minutes."

"Then, not denigrating your abiity, I'd say we came just in time," McCade said, "though I still don't know why," he added to the bird.

"Larson," Klooshkai said melodiously, "meet Reverend Eighth Pedar Subriente."

"Reverend?" McCade exclaimed. "But I thought all the contestants were members of the Academy."

"This is a blood match," Subriente said, buckling on heavy wrist-straps. He wore the tight shorts and snug, soft shoes of the professional fighters.

"Someone call you out?"

"Yes. But he's in for a surprise, I think."

"I hope so, for your sake at least. Klooshkai, why are we here?"

"The Reverend has knowledge of the Core," the bird said sweetly.

"Damn that bird," Subriente muttered.

"Is that true?" McCade asked.

"Yes, it is." He opened a locker and took out a small, long-handled, broad-bladed axe, spiked opposite the blade. "My grandfather was almost caught in the pogrom. At the last minute the Separatists found out he was innocent and let him off. That was their mistake. He had been innocent, before then, but sympathized with the Core afterward. It was too late by then, of course."

"I'd like to talk to you about it, if I may."

"That's nice, but I'm afraid someone is ahead of you." The Reverend walked to an inner door and opened it. "Ninth Notokris has first dibs," he said over his shoulder and walked through. McCade followed, the bird still clinging to his shoulder.

They were on the floor of an arena. Subriente was walking toward the center to meet a slightly larger and much younger man. The two saluted, stepped back, then the bell rang.

Instantly, the younger man sprang at Subriente, swinging his axe in short, vicious arcs. The Reverend just backed up, keeping his own blade held out stiffly in front of him, parrying clumsily. And yet McCade could see that the parries were all effective, and that the older man was making the minimum effort, while the younger, though fast and seemingly sure of himself, would quickly wear himself out.

Subriente retreated, letting his opponent press him back, but he curved his retreat, so that they circled the floor. The straight-on attack obviously wasn't working, so the younger man changed tactics. He made short, deadly lunges, first to one side, then to the other, but every time Subriente managed to interpose his own axe between himself and the other blade, and soon the young man was dripping with sweat. His back was to McCade now, so he never saw clearly just what happened next. The younger man seemed to hesitate for just a moment, his blade in seventh position, out to the side and down a bit, and Subriente's axe suddenly whistled through the air at the level of his face. The Reverend stepped back then, while his opponent just stood there, then all of a piece fell forward. The crowd screamed. Subriente chucked his axe into the floor, and without a glance at the cheering mob walked steadily back to the dressing room, a grim expression on his face.

"I'm sorry," McCade said as the man brushed by him.

Subriente stopped. "You understand," he said.

"Yes, I think I do. I've been in that situation myself."

Subriente nodded, and turned his head away.

"They never learn," he said. "Just because I left the Academy for the Temple twenty years ago, they think they can put me down." He faced McCade again, his face still grim. "There has been no other first-ranked axeman since I left," he said.

"Then perhaps they deserve their fates," McCade said softly.

"Perhaps they do. But you wanted to talk about the Core?"

"Yes, sir, if you don't mind."

"Oh, I mind, but sometimes one must do what one minds. What do you want to know?"

"Did they have anything to do with the cessation of the Planet Master?"

"No. That was the Separatists. It was an accident, but their fault just the same."

"Did any of the Core members escape the pogrom?"

"I don't know for sure, but Grandfather said that young Scott, of Scott's Woods, the son of the Number One, did escape on a merchant ship. But there was no verification of that. Of course, his body was never found, either."

"And the treasures the Core had hidden, were any ever found?"

"None."

"Have you ever heard of the Book of Aradka?"

"Yes, I have, but I don't believe in it. Just a fortune telling device, like a Tarot deck, but with one hundred sixteen cards instead of seventy-eight."

"More about the Planet Master, how did he get involved?"

"As Planet Master he was impartial, but he was visiting some of the Core people, just as a personal friend, when they were raided and he got it too."

"Have you ever heard of Sterpreen?"

"Sterpreen? Person? Place? Thing?"

"Person."

"No, I don't think so."

"That's too bad. Just one more thing. Would you support a rational movement to return Seltique to the greater galactic culture?"

Subriente was silent for a long moment, staring hard at McCade, as if he would read his mind.

"Yes," he said at last, "I would."

"Thank you," McCade said, and started to leave, but Subriente touched his arm.

"Be careful," he said. "There is a man. His name is Kelso. He'd kill you for the questions you've asked me. And me too."

"I've heard of him before," McCade said, "but we've never met."

"You're very lucky, young man."

"I would like to meet him, though," McCade said softly, "if I only knew how."

"Why don't you try the directory," Subriente answered, just as softly.

At two hours before dawn, the third-class district of St. Germain was anything but a welcome place to be. McCade stood in the bushes, watching Kelso's house, and wishing that there were some other way. He had avoided the electronic sentries that surrounded the district, walked the whole way in to Kelso's place so as not to trip the sensors on the beltways, had scouted the grounds around the mansion, and found the only safe path in. Several times on his way here he'd had to hide. As a seventeenth class in the third-class district, he was liable to be shot on sight or worse for being here after dark. Especially during the Sagger Month, when even legitimate business wouldn't excuse him. During the Sagger Month, there was no legitimate reason for a lower-class person being in any of the first-order districts after dark.

The grounds of the mansion were fitted with death traps. But then, Kelso was not really typical of the second class. He was paranoid, and surrounded himself with defenses. He had even remained in the third-class district because he couldn't trust building new defenses in the second-class district. Yet, ironically, like all first-order homes, his house had no locks. It just wasn't done.

He watched a while longer, just to make sure that he knew exactly what his approach to the house would be and that he was unobserved; then he moved, his whole body keyed to its highest pitch.

The route he took was not a straight one, but dodged here and there, seemingly at random. In actuality, it was the only way he could go in order to avoid tripping any of a dozen booby traps and alarms. But luck—and his over-extended senses—was with him, and he made it to the side of the house untouched. It was an easy matter, then, having penetrated this far, to work his way around to one of the side entrances of the main wing and just walk inside.

He had no idea of the layout of the place. He had tried to secure municipal documents, but the files had been closed to him, and this time there had been no one he could intimidate. Computers don't care about tongues and eyes and eardrums and fingers.

He passed from room to elegant room, each more voluptuously furnished than the last, until he found the library. He didn't have much hope of finding anything here, but he dared not pass it up. Quickly he scanned the titles of all the books, touched every shelf, felt all the tables and chairs. Nothing. Nothing at all. He left and continued his explorations.

Somewhere farther on, deep in the main part of the house, he came to a study that held more promise. As a preliminary he examined the walls, shelves, and furniture. He found a safe, opened it easily, found nothing inside but jewelry—why bother?—then went to the desk. The drawers were locked, but he had them open in minutes. Nothing here. Nothing there. Time was passing. But what was this? A note on a scratch pad, "Vault needs cleaning."

Vault. Now where would a vault be. Why a vault in the first place? Unless he kept things in it that would damage his status if made public.

Relocking the desk, he left the study and went on with his explorations, but more quickly this time. If there was a vault somewhere in this house, the thing he was searching for would be there.

He covered the whole main wing, from attic to cellar, without finding any sign of any vault. At one point he almost got caught when he was quietly leaving an unoccupied bedroom, and the door across the hall opened and somebody came out. Quickly, McCade made a guess and ran silently down the hall, hoping that whoever it was would go the other way, and that the person would be sleepy enough and the hall dark enough that he wouldn't be seen. His luck held all the way, and he stood at the dead end, in plain sight, as a woman in little more than her hair padded sleepily down the hall in the other direction and went into another room. A moment later, as he sped past to the stairs, he heard the sound of splashing water.

He left the main wing and ran quickly through the ground floors of the other parts of the house. Ballrooms, game rooms, another library, dining halls, studies, no vaults. He went to the cellars. Outside the sky was beginning to get light. Storage rooms, game rooms, love nests, an interrogation room, no vaults. He sped on, to the end of the house—and then just a little farther.

A covered passage had been built between the mansion proper and another, much smaller building that had once been part of a separate estate. The adjoining door was locked. He picked it and slipped through.

At the other end of the passage he found himself in the kitchen, on one hand an elegant dining room, on the other a pantry. He went there. Beyond was another pantry, then back stairs. He went down. In the basement he found not much more than dust, but in the dust was a cleared trail that ended in a blank wall. Perfectly in character. It took him just a moment to find the stud that opened the secret panel. Beyond was another stair. He went down.

There was the vault. But it worked with a key. He took out his wallet, from it took a piece of plastic, trimmed it with his knife so it fit the keyhole, and slid it in. He twisted it once in each direction, then took it out again. On the plastic were the clear marks of the wards. He whittled at the plastic, stuck it back in the lock, and twisted it again. It clicked. He grabbed the bar handle and pulled the door open.

A light was burning inside. He stepped in and quickly surveyed the whole small room. Time was running out. He went first of all to a filing cabinet, opened the top drawer, and on the flap of the first folder saw the words, "Execution follow up." Inside were reports of a totally paranoid search for survivors of the Core, begun soon after the pogrom and continued, by one person, down to the present day. And the reports from Kelso's period were both most paranoid and most thorough. Nothing had ever been found, of course, but that did not deter the Separatists. They were beyond rational behavior, as individuals and as a group.

There were other files, and McCade went through them quickly. Many were gibberish, most were useless. But one interested him highly. It spoke of searches made in an empty house in the first-class district of Scott's Woods. He took a tiny camera from his pocket and photographed the whole document, noting as he did so other references of a failure to find a certain hiding place.

Some of the documents confirmed some of his earlier researches, and others clarified certain other clues he had dug up at one time or another. But nowhere did he find anything that could help him translate the location codes on his church list or which explained in any more detail what the Book of Aradka was or who Sterpreen was and what he had to do with the Planet Master.

But the house in Scott's Woods interested him greatly. He made sure he had missed nothing, then put the room back in order, left the vault, locked it and removed his plastic key, and went up the stairs to the pantry.

It was fully daylight outside, and soon people and machines would be moving around. He had to get out now, or he would never make it at all.

He left the house. It was too dangerous to stay inside

any longer. Staying close to the wall, he worked his way back to where he'd first come to it, then, in reverse, repeated his zigzag course back to the bushes. From there it took twenty more minutes of painstaking work to get off the grounds.

Now he ran. People would be up soon. He'd have no defense if he was caught out in the open. He accelerated to five times normal speed, then seven, then eight, and moving like a human bullet, sped through St. Germain and out into Eastbridge beyond.

Music was playing. It wasn't all in his head, though it made him want to skip and dance like his own music did. But no, this was coming from somewhere else. Someone else. He rocked where he sat on the floor and let the music take him for a while. The song was so beautiful it made him want to cry.

He opened his eyes and looked around the room where he was sitting. It was large, with a high ceiling and a parquetry floor, but no furniture of any kind. On his right, sitting cross-legged, was Martins, and on his left was Jorgen. On the other side of the bonfire Ephraim and Lucias sat, also moving to the music. It was coming from Martins, who was blowing into a thing like a long, fat whistle, with lots of finger holes. How he could get so many sounds out of one instrument was beyond McCade's understanding.

It was Jorgen singing, soft words about sunshine through the summer rain where winter winds don't blow. On and on, and now McCade could see that Ephraim and Lucias were as deeply moved as he. And the bonfire, not very big really, jumped and sparkled in time to the music.

"What I remember most," Jorgen said, "was that when I was very small we used to go out in the boat all the time and fish for clams. We'd drop this line into the water, you see, with a pearl tied to the end, and the clams would reach out and grab the pearl. Then we'd pull them in. They weren't any good to eat, of course, but they sailed nicely over the back shed. One day we had nine of them sailing, all in a row. You had to take them out of their shells first, though."

"What do you think of that, Larson?" Martins asked. He had put the flute down, but the music went on, and somewhere, off in the dark edges of the room where the light of the bonfire didn't reach, a drum came in, a gentle yet driving rhythm on all five skins.

"I think it's a great story," Larson said, "but don't take him too literally. He's been known to shovel it before, you know."

"Come on, Larson," Ephraim said, "we haven't got all night. We're supposed to be having a party. Didn't Arvin teach you anything?"

"I've never taken lessons from her," Larson said. "But you can dance if you want to."

A guitar joined the drums and flute, at least the sound of one did. There were no instruments visible anywhere.

"I remember," Martins said, putting his flute away in a fancy ebony gun box, "when we used to hide in the palm trees and wait for the pirates to walk by underneath. Then we'd throw these big seeds down on them, and they'd stick in the pirates and sprout. After a while, though, we didn't have any more pirates and had to stop planting seeds."

"You're full of it," Lucias said. "You're worse than Jorgen and not as good."

"I play pretty well, though."

"Only when you aren't trying."

Jorgen brought out a handful of long, tweezer-like tongs, all silvery filigree, and handed them around, one pair to each person.

"It used to snow when I was a child," Ephraim said. "I can remember it very clearly. These big flakes would float down out of the sky and cover everything. It doesn't do that any more. They've taken all the fun out of winter."

"How did they do that?" Larson asked, snapping his tweezer-tongs. They were fully eighteen inches long and very slender, and the two legs had depressions and lumps in them up near the hinge that just fit his hand.

"I'm not too sure," Ephraim said. "I think it was when they decided that the weather should always be pleasant—whatever that means."

"I never had any childhood," Lucias said. "I was born old." His wrinkled face and hands were proof of that. He snapped his tongs at the fire once or twice. "But I do remember," he went on after a while, "the time I discovered light. Everybody else was gone, and there was a bulb missing from the lamp. It was one of those, you know, with the big bulb in the center and three little ones around it? Well anyway, one of the little ones was gone. I don't know where." Martins started to sniffle. "So anyway I climbed up on the back of the chair so I could reach the place where the light had been. I reached inside—I could get three fingers in at once—and found this little paper tube. It was the prettiest little thing." He held it up so that the rest of them could see it. "Well, I thought to myself, since there was nobody else present at the time, that there just might be another one of those little tubes in there, and so I reached in again. And that was when I discovered light."

"You weren't very bright, were you?" Larson said.

"Yes, for a moment there I was."

Larson reached into the fire with his tongs and from it plucked a small, perfect, glowing red coal, as big as his little fingernail. He looked at it a moment, waited for the music to change themes, then popped the coal into his mouth. He crunched it and began to feel warm all over. The others, too, picked out coals now, and ate them.

"I remember," he said, "but some of it wasn't much fun." He ate another coal. He began to feel a little light in the head, and a little thick, too, at the same time.

"I remember," he said again. "Great Grampa was very old. He used to tell stories a lot. That was about all he did, any more."

"What kind of stories did he tell?" Jorgen asked. Larson ate another coal. His head was beginning to get tight, and the edges of his sight indistinct.

"About when he was a boy, and a young man, before he

became a refugee," he said. "Some of the stories frightened me, especially how he just managed to escape alive. And some of them made me angry, like how they had to hide all that money and couldn't spend it, but most of Great Grampa's stories made me want to go to where he'd been born, and see the place. Except of course I couldn't."

"Why not?" Ephraim asked.

"Because I was too busy with biotraining, learning how to control my heartbeat, and my muscle cells, and my glands and stomach and nerves and skin and all those things. It wasn't hard, and I always felt good when I'd mastered a new technique, but it took a long time."

"Did you live with your Great Grampa?" Lucias asked, eating more coals.

"No," Larson said, "he lived with us." His forehead was very tight now and his body far away. The whole room had grown dark except for the fire which lit the faces of his friends and made the small, perfect coals which he kept picking out with his long tweezers and eating. "Great Grampa lived with us, because he was so old, over a hundred. He could have lived longer if he hadn't worked so hard all his life. All my family works too hard. They're very rich, but they never have any fun. They marry well, but I don't think they know anything about love. I was always different."

"No you weren't," Martins said, trying to make him feel better.

"Yes I was," Larson insisted. "I was funny looking. And I learned too fast. And I didn't want to work. My big brother—he works, and he owns factories on seven worlds. Built them all himself. Dad gave him only a million to start with. But I don't work. I took my inheritance when I was fifteen and went away."

"Where did you go?" Lucias and Jorgen asked together.

"All over. I did things for people. I ran errands. I was a spy once, for a while. I made money, but I didn't work. I wanted to travel, see the galaxy, visit strange lands, find love, enjoy my freedom. I've done most of that." He was very high now. The whole room swam, and his friends' faces were just warm orange blurs against the darkness. He tried to eat another coal, but couldn't.

He felt restless. His friends went on talking, but he didn't pay attention any more. He got to his feet, very unsteadily, and looked down at them as they sat around the fire eating coals. Faster and faster. His head was a tight fuzz, and he couldn't see very clearly. He turned away from the fire and went over to the wall where it was cooler.

A huge machine sat there. On it were lights that glowed and blinked. A lever went up and down and wheels spun. Pistons moved in and out, and from certain dark recesses, fiery noises sparked out at him.

"Where are the treasures of my yesterfather?" he asked.

From somewhere a non-voice answered, "In the recesses of the soul."

"But where do fire falls, and other breathing spaces?"

"Beneath thy brow-lines, in endless wilderness."

"Can you see me?"

"That which has no eyes can only hear."

"This isn't making much sense," he said.

"I know it isn't, dearest," the non-voice answered. "Over-exertion breaks even the strongest chords."

"If that's really true," Larson said, "then maybe I have a chance after all."

A piano joined in the chorus, and the music started all over again from Bach.

He felt a touch on his arm. He turned. It was the shy girl. She had soft brown hair and big brown eyes, and she smiled sweetly up at him.

"What are you doing here?" he asked, but she only shrugged and cast down her eyes. He put his arm around her shoulders. He felt very protective.

"This is a strange place for you," he said, and drew her closer to him. She was very shy. She buried her face in his chest.

"I don't have to touch you," he said, and started to unbutton her blouse. He could feel himself getting bigger.

She pushed away from him, gently, but seriously.

"If you don't want to," he said, "I won't," but he was very disappointed. She stood away from him a little bit, her back to him and her head bowed.

"May I touch you?" he asked, and put his hand on her shoulder. She didn't take it off, but she didn't come to him either.

He left her there and went back to the group by the fire. They were all pretty serious now.

"Where is her lover?" Larson asked. They looked up at him as if they didn't know what he was talking about.

"You know what I'm talking about," he said. "She's lonely, and I won't do. So I've come for her lover."

"The price is high," Jorgen said.

"I don't care, I'll pay it."

"He's not for sale," Ephraim said.

"Of course he is. How much?"

"I don't know," Lucius said.

"Oh, for pete's sake, what's the matter with you guys, can't you take a joke?"

Martins stood up and stepped into the fire.

"It's time," he said, "that we came to some agreement about all this." The flames roared up around his legs.

"Exactly," Jurgen said. "We've danced too long. It's time to pay Marten."

"So pay him," Larson said. "He's your piper, not mine. But I want the girl's lover, and I mean to have him."

"What's your offer?" Efraim asked.

"As much as I have."

"Let me see the color," Lucus demanded.

Larson reached into his pocket, but all he had was a half-dollar. He brought it out anyway. It was silver.

"It's a good color," Maren said.

"I don't like it," Yurgen retorted.

"It's mine anyway," Larson protested, "and I mean to keep it."

"What about your lover?" Efram asked.

"Not mine, the girl's."

"What do you care?" Lucis demanded. "You're a free man."

"And I'm going to stay that way, but her lover—"

"Okay," Eram said, "you win."

"I do?"

"Yes," Yugen answered. "He's yours."

"Let me see the contract."

"Right here," they all said together.

"How about my half-dollar?"

"You can keep it."

"What the hell's going on anyway?" he cried out, and struggled to free himself from the encroaching darkness.

"Be quiet," the non-voice said. "You've just burned yourself out. It will take a day or two."

"Okay," he said.

The light rain of the night before had made everything in the park fresh and clean, and McCade and Valyn walked through it, side by side, not touching but very close, enjoying the dewy morning smells. Blackstone, of all the districts of Loger, had the most beautiful parks.

"Thank you for helping like that," McCade said.

"What else could I do? You came staggering up like a zombie."

"Even after I slugged you and went off into the wilderness?"

"Well, I 'slugged' you first. So we're even on that score."

"But you're up on me now. I can't be in your debt, Valyn."

"I know. It's okay."

"Valyn."

"So, it isn't okay. I can't help it. I didn't want it. It just turned out that way."

"I'm sorry."

"No you're not."

"Yes I am. Truly. If things were different—well, they'd be different."

"But you have this 'quest' of yours," she said bitterly.

"Yes, I do."

"I wish you'd give it up."

"Will you go away with me?"

"What do you mean?"

"We'll go to the spaceport right now. I'll send a message to Ben Toledo. I'm sure I could get him to come to Seltique. It would only take a couple of days. Then we could leave here. Go anywhere we wanted. I'm not poor, you know."

But her face was white, and she was shaking her head vigorously.

"No, Larson," she said, "not that. I couldn't leave. Not ever."

"But you said once that you used to think about doing just that. I'm giving you your chance."

"That's just it. I could think about it then, because there was no chance. A daydream. A fantasy. But to actually leave, no, it would be impossible."

"Not even for me?"

"No, I'm sorry, Larson. Not even for you."

"But you expect me to give up something that means just as much to me as your life here does to you."

She had nothing to say. She turned away from him.

"Do you understand?" he asked.

"Yes," she said, "now I think I do. Is it really that way?"

"You saw me when I was recovering from my little expedition to Kelso's house. You nursed me. You told me about my ravings, the coals, the shy girl. Would I willingly subject myself to something like that if what I was doing didn't mean almost as much to me as life itself? "

"I suppose not."

"So you see where things stand. I have a task to do. I didn't ask for it. It just grew in me, from the first thought I can remember. I *had* to come here. I *had* to do this thing.

I have no choice. If I were to put this thing aside I would just cease to be, though the body still walked and the brain still talked. What can I do?"

"Just what you're doing, I guess. But I wish it didn't have to be. Or that you could get it over with."

"I wish that myself. Would you help me?"

"Now wait a minute. I don't think I'm ready for the kind of things you seem to take in stride. Breaking into a third-class house during Sagger Month—or any other time—is not my idea of a pleasant morning's work."

McCade laughed, and felt a delicate little melody spin softly through the back of his brain. He danced a step or two and led Valyn to a bench, where they sat down.

"My dear girl," he said, "I wouldn't ask even Pedar Subriente to do a thing like that, and he's the kind of man who would, I think. No, what I want, what I need, is a friend. I've been here over two months now, but I am still ignorant of many things. Oh, I heard lots about this place when I was a boy, and learned much more in my travels and here. But I'm an outsider, Valyn, and nothing can change that. There are many things that you take for granted so much that you never think of them, but those things could make the difference between success and death to me. I would like, if you're willing, for you to just tell me things about Seltique and about Loger. As if I were a backward child who knew nothing. For in a way, Valyn, that's what I am."

"Well," she said, "I guess I can do that." She talked about life in Loger, about the things she did, about the people and the customs and the struggles. Much he had heard before, but hers was a fresh perspective and a firsthand one, an insider's view. He learned more that morning and afternoon than in all his thirty-five previous years.

At first she was embarrassed at times, to be talking so earnestly about things that were so common, so everyday, so patently obvious. But by his questions, his own earnestness and seriousness, he eventually convinced her that every last detail was important to him, and she lost her self-consciousness and let her words pour forth in an almost unconscious stream. He absorbed the culture of her world as if she were a fountain and he the basin into which she flowed.

But at last she tired and complained of hunger.

"We've gone right through lunch," she said, "and I don't know about you, but I need to eat once in a while."

"I do too, so let's." He led her to the nearest beltway, and took her to the restaurant where he'd confronted Lupus and Finewalls. She had never been there before and was quite impressed.

"But doesn't it hurt your credit balance?" she asked.

"I don't have any other expensive hobbies," he said, "so why not this? Besides, I'm getting richer by the minute."

They ordered, and while munching hors d'oeuvres, McCade thought over what she had told him that afternoon.

"You mentioned a cult," he said. "Tell me about it."

"The Fishermen? Well, I don't really know much about them, except that they're not a part of the Temple, don't have many members, but have avoided proscription so far."

"There's something about them," McCade said. "I can't put my finger on it, but somewhere in the back of my mind there's a tickle."

"Want me to scratch?"

"Sure. Can you take me to one of their churches?"

"Whatever for?"

"I don't know. But like I said, I have this funny feeling about them. Have had, since you first mentioned them."

"Well, if you really want to, but I think they're a bunch of nuts."

"That may very well be, but I can assure you I have nothing religious in mind. I just want to scratch that tickle, okay?"

The food came, and for a long while they were too busy to talk. Replete at last, they sat a while longer and then went back to the beltways.

She led him to Newisle, twenty-seventh class, just one step above Red Dog. There, in a backwater residential section she took him to a stone building that looked more like the churches McCade was used to seeing on other worlds. They mounted the few steps to the doors, went in to the vestibule, and through that into the nave. There was an altar at the far end, a simple affair with two crossed bars mounted on the wall behind it. In one of the front pews a priest or monk was sitting praying.

Diffidently they approached him.

"I beg your pardon," McCade said, "I don't mean to disturb you but I've heard about your church, father."

"Brother," the monk corrected.

"Excuse me, brother, and I would like to learn more about it." Valyn looked at McCade in sharp surprise.

"We don't take many converts," the monk said.

"I understand that," McCade said, "but you see, I'm an outsider, from off world, and after living here for over two months I find myself spiritually starving."

"We have barely enough to feed ourselves," the monk said. Valyn was trying hard to keep a straight face and stayed out of the monk's line of sight.

"I'm so sorry to hear that," McCade said, in his most sincere voice. "I wouldn't have bothered you, but for that what little I have heard struck me as very similar to the Holy Catholic Church of Skopalos. I hope that I was not mistaken."

"I'm afraid you are," the monk said. "We are affiliated with no other church."

"But the symbol above the altar is the same," McCade said in wonder.

"Indeed, is it?"

"Yes. It is the cross, is it not, on which the Lord was hung?"

"Ye-es," the monk said, not pleased. "Please, I assure you, though there may seem to you to be resemblances between us and some other church somewhere else, there really is none. You would be better, if you are an offworlder in need of spiritual nourishment, to return to the world from which you are off, and seek it there."

McCade remained humble to the last, and with his face

expressing only disappointment and sadness, turned, took Valyn's arm, and slowly, but with dignity, walked out of the church, down the steps, across the lawn, and up the side of the belt for a half a block. At last Valyn could hold it back no longer and burst out laughing and laughed until she cried. McCade stood and supported her, chuckling himself, caught up in her mirth.

"You—did—that—so—well," she choked between guffaws.

"I've had a lot of practice," he said.

"No wonder you've made so many enemies if you can b.s. like that."

"It's a well-developed talent," he admitted, still grinning, "that I've spent considerable effort perfecting."

Suddenly she went serious. "Have you been feeding that to me too?" she asked.

"No," he said, the smile still present, but a touch sad, "though you'd never know it if I did."

"You're the perfect liar," she said.

"I am. Not all the time, but only I know when I am or not."

"Maybe I was wrong about you from the beginning."

"I tried to tell you that once, remember?"

"Yes, but—but, your delirium. You couldn't have been lying then."

"I could have been, but I doubt it. Why?"

"Just that what you've told me and what you said in your delirium match. That's all. So I think you've been square with me."

He said nothing.

"Oh, Larson," she cried. "What are you getting into?"

He just smiled ruefully.

Then her eyes widened and he spun. Behind him was a large man, wearing a holstered gun at his hip.

"I believe you're Larson McCade," the man said. "You've been running us quite a race. Second Kelso says that he has no desire to meet you whatsoever."

"Did he send you all the way out here to tell me that?" McCade asked coolly. "He could have saved himself the trouble and kept you at home."

"I'm afraid not, McCade," the man said and smiled grimly. "I'm fourteenth class, twelfth rank. You're seventeen-twelve. It's Sagger, McCade. I challenge you."

"I don't carry a gun."

"Come now, the bulge in your pocket is obvious. Draw."

McCade kicked into high gear, accelerated to five times normal speed, pulled his gun out, and fired twice while the other man was still clearing his holster. He dropped back to normal, and the challenger flopped backward, sprawling on the grass. McCade put his gun away.

"My—God," Valyn gasped. "I've never seen—"

"It's like the other day," McCade explained. "Twelve years of extensive biotraining, since I was three."

"I didn't realize—" she started.

"I know you didn't," he said. A crowd had started to gather.

"Points for you, sir," one of the bystanders said. "He challenged, he drew first. That's two. You're on your way up. Good shooting."

"Larson," Valyn said, "I don't like this."

But something was stirring in the back of his mind. That tickle was still there, but now he knew where it was coming from. One of those stories he'd heard so long ago.

"Go home, Valyn," he said. "I've got something to do."

"Go home? But what about you?"

"I'm going back to the church." He grabbed her shoulders. "Go home," he said, "and don't come looking for me. I'll come for you when I get through. Will you go now?"

"Yes," she said, then she kissed him once and hurried off. McCade pushed through the crowd in the other direction, heading back toward the church. He leaped up the stairs and strode in through the porch. The monk was still seated in his pew. McCade marched up to him and clamped his hand down on the man's shoulder.

"I'm sorry, brother," he said, "but I'm going to ask you to come with me."

The monk looked up, startled and frightened. "Y-you're not the Academy," he stammered.

"No," McCade said, "I'm worse than that. I'm the devil. Let's get going." He hauled the monk to his feet.

"Not that way," he said. "Inside. We're going down to the vaults." He tightened his grip on the man's shoulder and urged him on. The man staggered along, going where McCade directed. McCade did not know the way, but read from the monk's muscle twitches which was the right route and shoved him in that direction. They left the nave and went into a corridor, along it to the back and down the stairs to the basements, through a couple of rooms full of people who looked up with surprise, down another flight of stairs to a heavy stone door.

"Thank you," McCade said and tapped the man gently behind the ear and eased him down to the floor. Then he opened the door and stepped into a lighted chamber lined with books. An aisle ran off to right and left. It was just like the story. He turned right, passed the cross-aisle, and came to another stair, a square well down which the stairs spiralled landing after landing. He went down.

Ten landings later he came to the bottom. He went up a short, narrow hallway, past shelves of jars and pots, into another little room and lifted up a trap door set in the floor. Rungs were set into the wall below him. He lowered himself into the hole and descended.

At the bottom he stepped out of a little recess in the wall into a broad, well-lit hallway running off in two directions. He got his bearings and set off in the westerly direction.

The corridor ran straight for several kilometers with here and there equally wide, equally brightly-lit side branchings. He kept to his course until the hall forked. He took the south fork and went on several kilometers farther. Here and there he passed a door, each clearly marked but in an ancient script he could not read. He glanced at the markings idly as he passed but did not stop.

A few kilometers farther on he took another turn, and this time kept on it till he came to another recess like the one by which he'd entered these catacombs. This time, he went up.

He climbed steadily, through chambers, subcellars, cellars, and at last through a well-concealed door into a basement where he could hear, not far off, the sounds of people. He found a well-used stair and came up at the end of a short hall, the other end of which opened into the lobby of a public building. A public library. He stepped out into the street. He was in Red Dog, and only a block from the spaceport.

A perfect escape route. McCade stood in front of the library, watching the people pass on the beltway in front of him. He felt a sense of regret that fewer of the old Core members had been able to take advantage of the ancient tunnels, dug back when Seltique had first been colonized. Six thousand years ago mass transit had been underground. As the population had developed their world, beyond the level of most other neighboring worlds, they had abandoned the old tunnels, but had obviously not destroyed or closed them off. At various times, various groups must have made use of parts of them for one reason or another. But on the whole, they had been forgotten, especially after the embargo when the population of Seltique had begun to decline. This particular route, from the Fishermen Church to the library, was the only one McCade knew of. How far the system still extended, he did not know. Strange, that that little datum should have remained buried in his unconscious for so long.

He had other things on his mind now, more important than any ancient tunnels, whereever they went or whatever they might contain. Kelso was after him in earnest now. It made no difference what had happened to force the man's hand. It was enough that McCade was now marked, with a contract out on his life.

He thought back to the time he'd done some espionage work on Coldhorn. Then, too, he'd been a marked man, and had been in the awkward position where he could not afford to actually kill his enemy, or even disable him seriously. He knew that if he tried to kill Kelso, he would have the whole of the Separaitst League down on him, and his life wouldn't be worth a spent cartridge case. There had to be another way.

If there was, Red Dog was the place to find it. Though outwardly the district appeared to be like any other upper middle-class district on any other world, on Seltique it was the dregs. Here were the people who couldn't make it, the people who had failed, who'd never had it to begin with, the people who had been degraded from higher classes. If there was a black market anywhere in Loger, it would be here.

He knew what he needed. And though Red Dog appeared respectable, it was just like any other slum district. He'd been familiar with many, and he knew where to look.

He visited several taverns before he found the right one. To the eye, there was nothing to distinguish it. To the ear, it was just a bit louder, just a bit less delicate. To the mind, to one who had been in one, it was a dive, a hang-out of that element that most worlds try to deny that they have.

The bartender was human. McCade ordered a drink from him, sipped it, keyed his kidneys to take most of the alcohol out of his system, and ordered another. He waited for a moment when the bartender was unoccupied, then called him over.

"I've got a little problem," he said softly, "and I was wondering if you might possibly know of some way I could get in touch with somebody who could give me some advice."

The waiter said nothing, polished a glass, but his eyes said he was listening.

"It's a matter of a man's life," McCade went on, looking into his own drink. It was almost gone. He finished it off and put the glass out for a refill. The bartender poured him another but still said nothing.

"The truth is, I don't want to kill him," McCade said, his voice very low, very reasonable. "Don't ask me why; he deserves it. But it would go bad for me if he died. It would be nice if I could just put him out for a while; you know what I mean?"

The bartender kept looking at him, and his expression did not change. He knew.

"So I was wondering, you see, if there was any way, that wouldn't actually hurt the guy. I guess I'm pretty lame, but I've seen a little."

"No way," the bartender said.

McCade pulled out a packet of vouchers, held it under the counter, ripped one off, and put it down next to his glass. It was gold with black scrollings and maroon figures.

"Know what this is?" he asked.

The bartender's eyes said he did. That little bit of foil was worth the equivalent of fifty thousand dollars. His eyes said he knew that. His eyes said he wanted it, badly. And his mouth, which must have gone suddenly dry if one could judge by the way his tongue kept working, said he saw no way to get it. McCade slipped the voucher back into his pocket and flipped out a blue-green one instead.

"Every little bit helps," he said. This note was a come-down, only a hundred, but the bartender took it. McCade finished his drink and left. He'd hit the man hard, but had not left an enemy.

He tried several other places, but none of them suited his purposes. Then, while he was having a light supper, a dapper young woman slipped into the chair beside him.

"I hear you're looking around," she said.

"You could say that," McCade said, and went on eating.

"What's it worth for a good steer?"

As if by magic a blue-green voucher appeared on the table. The girl turned her head away and did not touch it. It lay there while McCade finished his steak, then was exchanged for a red one, worth five times as much. This time it disappeared.

"Hogey's," the girl said, and slipped away. McCade went on eating. When he finished he went over to the public comcon, punched the directory, found Hogey's, and left.

He took the long way there. He did not trust the girl. It was night in Red Dog in Sagger Month, and he didn't trust anybody.

He got to Hogey's the back way, by cutting between two buildings on the other side of the block and going across the tavern's back yard to a side door. He went inside casually, as if that were his normal means of access, and from his obscured position at the back of the tavern surveyed the room. Twice. There was nothing here to indicate a trap, so he went on in and sat down at a long table which curved around one side of the room and, with the sunken floor behind it, substituted for the bar.

The bartender came up for his order.

"A little chickie said I should come here," McCade said.

"Did she now?" the bartender returned. "Did she tell you why?"

"Something to do with putting a man to sleep, for a little while." A bit of red foil appeared between his fingers. The bartender wiped the table underneath and the red disappeared.

"I don't know anything about that," the man said, "but Phil Nestor might."

"That's quite encouraging," McCade said. "Is there any way I could make Mr. Nestor's acquaintance?"

"At this time of night he's at home."

"Will he know I'm coming?"

"You gotta be kidding."

McCade left. In another place he used the comcon directory and got the address. Nestor was only a couple of blocks away. He walked along the side of the belt, ignoring the stares of the people passing by. Music, always the music. It swung him gently now, and he let himself move with it, and whistled along.

The building, when he got to it, was the least elegant he had so far seen in Red Dog, and the lobby inside was no better than that of an average hotel. The foyer on the fifty-seventh floor was not much better, but when the door admitted him into the single apartment, he stepped into luxury that rivaled Kelso's. A voice came from a wall speaker.

"Put the gun on the door stand," it said. McCade complied with the order. Only then did Nestor show himself.

He was about McCade's age, but taller and thinner, and dressed in a style that made the most extravagant upper classes appear dowdy. He was handsome, in a hard sort of way, and his eyes never left McCade's face.

"You took your time," he said.

"I always do, fast or slow," McCade answered.

"I understand you're in the market for a sleeper."

"That's right. Just a little something to put a man down for three hours or so."

"You are aware, are you not, that any drugs or medication of any kind is totally prohibited by law, and possession thereof carries a penalty of degradation of two classes."

"To tell the truth, I was not aware, but I suspected something like that."

"If you get caught," Nestor said, looking at McCade's class badges, "you go down to nineteen. But if a twenty-one gets caught, they just kill him."

"Delightful system, isn't it?" McCade said. He took out his gold credit voucher and dropped it on a low table.

"Don't need it," Nestor said. "Look around you. I've got more credit than any two class-ones combined, except maybe Njaird and Corson."

"How about service?" McCade asked.

"Now that's something I can always use," Nestor answered. "What are you prepared to offer?"

"Anything that won't interfere with my own plans."

"That's generous. Very generous. Well, then suppose we sit down and talk about it." He made himself comfortable on a couch that it would have been difficult to do anything else on.

"I know the stuff you want," he said. "It's called 'sorbil anthrocain.' Can be taken orally, but by injection it acts instantly. A tiny amount goes a long way. Can be administered, for example, on the tip of a pin. Produces a coma resembling death, unless you have an EEG. Lasts for about two hours. Quick recovery, no side effects. Some good people got here instead of into the ground by using it on themselves."

"That's exactly what I was looking for," McCade said. "Shall we talk prices?"

"Surely. It's really very simple. You see, I don't have any. Never needed it. But an acquaintance of mine does, and all you have to do is get it from him. The thing that makes it so simple is that in order to get it, you'll have to kill him, which is the price. Neat?"

"Very." McCade leaned back. He didn't like it. He'd never killed except in self-defense before. He thought a moment about the priest. Maybe his morals *were* deteriorating. But outright murder was an awfully big step.

"Easy," Nestor said again. He got to his feet. "Shall we go?"

"Lead on, McFrench," McCade said, retrieved the voucher from the table, his gun from the stand, and followed Nestor out of the building and onto the street.

They took the beltways south, through Warwick and Riverside, into the nineteenth-class district of Valley. Near the center of the district they got off the belt at an open air coffee shop. It was still full of people, in spite of the late hour, and Nestor led him to a table.

"His name's Jonas," Nestor said. "He's about two meters, very heavy, black hair, and always has at least two mugs with him. He comes in here every night at about two-thirty and sits at that table." He pointed.

"Shouldn't be hard to spot."

"No. The hard part is that he keeps the stuff at home."

"That's tough. But I think I can swing it."

"Then I'll leave you here. Good luck." He stood and without another word turned and left. McCade ordered coffee and settled down to wait.

At precisely two-thirty, a large, heavy, black-haired man

with four, not two, mugs following him came in and sat at the table McCade was watching. The four bodyguards arranged themselves at other places nearby. McCade sat a half-hour longer, then got up from his place, and went over to the man. As soon as he started, the four guards took notice and watched him closely. He sat down at Jonas's table and looked the man square in the face.

"You're on the wrong beat, buddy," Jonas said.

"I don't think so," McCade answered. "I've got a proposition for you."

"You won't have any proposition for anybody if you don't beat it."

"How about Nestor?"

"You shitting me, buddy? Your ass is grass, man—you just died."

"Not if Nestor dies first."

"What do you mean?"

"That's the proposition. I understand you've been having some trouble getting at him."

"Go on."

"I also understand you have something I might find a use for."

"Go on."

"So I'll make an exchange. *I* can get at Nestor. And you can let me have a little sorbil anthrocain."

"You on the level?"

"Try me. You can't lose."

"*You* can. Okay." He signaled to one of his men, who came over and bent his head. Jonas whispered in the man's ear, and the man left the coffee house.

"Have a cuppa," Jonas said. McCade did, and they waited without talking. Twenty minutes later the guard came back, and nodded at Jonas.

"Okay," the big man said, "let's go." McCade, Jonas, and the four bodyguard-thugs left the coffee house together, the guards following and keeping an eye on their boss's companion.

"We're going to this place," Jonas said. "Nestor makes a pickup there every night. You bump him and the drug is yours."

"Suits," McCade said, and they rode on in silence back to Red Dog, to the extreme western edge of the district. They left the belt and walked a mile or so out into the bordering parkland.

"This is the place," Jonas said, stopping by a pile of rocks. "We can't wait; he'd spot us and not show. But if you can get to him—"

In high gear at eight times normal acceleration McCade moved, slashing his hand across Jonas's throat, then diving first at one guard then another, stiff fingers driving into solar plexi. In two seconds it was all over. Five dead men lay on the grass by the pile of rocks. McCade stood a moment, back in normal time, looking down at his handiwork. There was a lump in his stomach, and his chest and face felt tight.

"This is going too far," he muttered, and spat sour. "It had all better be worth it." He rubbed his hands repeatedly against his clothes, as if to wipe something off. Then he knelt by the guard who'd gone off on Jonas's orders, frisked him, and came up with a tiny phial, with a neatly typed label. "Sorbil Anthrocain," it read. He slipped it into his own pocket.

"An amazing piece of work," said Nestor's voice from the outcrop. "For a while there I thought you had crossed me."

"I could have," McCade said, bitterly. "It would have cost four fewer lives."

"What made you do it, then?"

"You were the lesser of the two evils."

"Hmm. Well, thank you, I guess, *Seventeenth Larson McCade.*"

"I was wondering when you'd check up on me."

"As soon as I left the coffee shop. It wasn't hard. You've cut quite a swath in the last two months. But I learned something more. I learned that less than half of you is what it appears to be. Even *my* sources can't get a complete line on you, McCade, and that's saying something." The voice still came from the shadows of the outcropping.

"I'll take that as a compliment," McCade said. "I have what I want now, and so do you. I wish I could say it's been—"

"Wait," Nestor said. "Wait a minute. You've done a real service for me tonight. An ampule of sleeper isn't really sufficient recompense."

"It's what I asked for."

"True, but it's not the end. You know that better than I. I have something else that might interest you."

"What's that?"

"Sterpreen."

McCade jerked. He could near Nestor softly chuckling somewhere out of sight in the rocks.

"What do you know about Sterpreen?" he asked, trying to keep his voice steady.

"Not much. Mostly that you want to find out who he was. Not many people ever knew that, but down in my neck of the woods, you still hear the name now and then. He was a guy, like me, who the old Planet Master found useful on occasion. I don't know what for."

"Was he connected with the Core in any way?"

"The Core? *Them*? No, I don't think so. At least, he lived thirty more years after the pogrom."

"What happened to his estate?"

"He had two estates. One, like mine, which got eaten up by others like him after he died, and his legal one, in Bellamy, which is still there. He had no heirs."

Without another word, McCade turned and went back to the belt and took it to the nearest tube, which he rode into the center of Bellamy, a tenth-class district to the north. He got off the tube and took another belt to the Capitol building of the district, found the Survey Office, and since no other people were in the building, let himself in and had the comcon there run through the records of ownership of seventy years ago. It took him a couple of tries, but at last he found it, an entry which read that a man named Davis Sterpreen had died intestate, and that his home had been closed off pending sale or the discovery of an heir. There was an address.

The music was so loud in his head that he was surprised the other people on the beltway couldn't hear it. His feet kept moving in time to the beat, and his face was stretched into a broad grin. He got to the long-vacant house and, ignoring the marks of seal set about the grounds, went up to the front door and went in.

The place hadn't been touched in three-quarters of a century. There was no office or study, but in the master bedroom McCade found a safe set into the floor under the head of the bed. The melodies in his brain were so strong that he could hardly open it, but he did, and inside found packets of drugs, papers that looked like blackmail evidence, and a yellow, legal-sized envelope. He tore it open.

This was it. This was the key to the Planet Master. It was a detailed description of a long and elaborate series of legal maneuvers. Each one was designed to sever the ties with the status system, while retaining all power and wealth previously acquired. But it wasn't all just law. Some of it, with a subtlety that astonished him, was a kind of psychic biofeedback kind of training. To run through the whole procedure would result in a changed mind, as well as legal status. The result would be a personality that could not take advantage of the powerful and anomalous position to the detriment of the city or the planet. By becoming a Planet Master, a person would of necessity become worthy of being a Planet Master.

He didn't even bother closing the safe. He left the house, and with the first gray light of morning touching the eastern sky, danced all the way home.

His dancing stopped when he reached his front door. Something was wrong. The door was open just a crack. In all his years traveling on many worlds, he had learned to never go off without closing up tight behind himself. Someone had been here in his absence. Maybe they were still here. He tensed himself up, but moving easy, opened the door and walked in.

Kyle, Lupus, and Finewalls sat sprawled about his living room, and in a corner, tied securely to a chair, was Valyn Dixon.

"Hello, sucker," Kyle said. "You've been playing too long."

"Are you okay, Valyn?" McCade asked, ignoring the thug.

"Yes," she said. "I'm not hurt. Losing a little circulation, though."

McCade started to go to her but Kyle and Lupus blocked his way.

"You're not very polite to your guests," Kyle said.

"On the contrary, to *guests* I'm very polite. Get out of my way."

"Shut up, McCade. You heard the lady, she's all right. You have to talk to us now."

"Breaking and entering is still a crime," McCade said, "and kidnapping too, for that matter."

"So what?" Lupus said. "Nobody's going to know. Are they, Finewalls?"

"*I'm* not going to tell them," the girl said.

"Who's talking about telling?" McCade asked. "I'm talking about being within my rights when I throw you out of here."

"You ain't throwing nobody nowhere," Kyle growled. McCade trod on his foot, and the young man doubled up, howling.

"Beg pardon," McCade said. "An accident, I assure you." He brushed past Lupus and started undoing Valyn's bonds.

"You'll pay," Kyle shouted, sitting on the edge of a chair, holding his foot.

"How?" McCade asked. "You're in my house, without

my invitation." He cut Valyn loose and she rubbed her wrists and ankles where the cords had cut. "If you kill me here there'll be no question of challenges or duels. It will be plain and simple murder. Private residences are off limits even in Sagger."

"Oh, yeah? Well listen to me, bub. You've got something coming to you. You killed Billy Sereg, you're living in his house, and you start warning me about the law?"

"For christ's sake, are we going into that again?" McCade swore. "You check on it, Twelfth Kyle. He challenged. He drew. I defended myself. In front of the Director of the Academy. What more do you want?" Valyn got to her feet and took a step toward McCade's study.

"You stay clear of there, sister," Finewalls warned, but McCade moved between the two women.

"Go ahead," he said to Valyn, keeping his eyes on the others.

"Come on out," Kyle shouted. "Come on out, you coward, and fight me in the street. I bet you haven't got the nerve."

"You may be right," McCade said, "because I'm staying here." Nevertheless he began to key himself up. In the study, hc could hear Valyn on the comcon, talking to somebody at local Academy offices.

"You'll meet me," Kyle swore, and picked up a chair and smashed it against the floor. McCade just cocked his hip and folded his arms.

"Come on," Kyle said to his friends. "Let's take this place apart." Lupus and Finewalls got up from their chairs and smashed them too. They ripped the drapes down, broke the windows, smashed the statuary, and broke up the furniture. McCade just watched and made sure that none of the flying fragments hit him or Valyn, who'd come back into the room.

"Come on," Kyle screamed. He had worked himself up into a frenzy. "Come on, McCade, you bastard. You're a coward, a freak, an ugly outsider. Fight me, McCade."

"I wouldn't touch you," McCade said softly as the police

arrived. Kyle spun, pulled his gun, but before he could aim, four Academy choppers blazed and tore his body to shreds. Into the deafening silence Senna Reddy walked, took one look at the scene, and sighed.

"He was due for that," she said. "Too bad he had to mess you up first."

"No matter," McCade said. "Can't you get these people out of here?"

"No problem at all," Reddy said. Four heavily armed police moved to the now very cowed Lupus and Finewalls and took them outside.

"What will happen to them?" Valyn asked.

"Loss of all rank, possibly a drop in class. Are you all right?"

"I'm fine, First Reddy, just a little sore."

"Let me see your hand." Reddy took the girl's arm and inspected the rope marks on her wrist. "I could get them for assault," she said.

"Don't bother," Valyn answered. "It's not worth it. They didn't really hurt me, and it was only so they could get at Larson."

"Yes, so I understand." From the back of the house came the sounds of the maintenance machines getting ready to come out and clean up the damage. "Seventeenth McCade," she went on, "I'd like to talk to you for a moment, if I may. Have you someplace slightly less disheveled?"

"Certainly, First Reddy. Will the dining room do? Most of the house is shut up."

"That will be fine," Reddy said.

McCade led the way, Valyn falling in behind. The envelope from Sterpreen's safe was heavy in his pocket, but it would have to wait.

"I've been keeping an eye on you, Seventeenth McCade," Reddy said when they had seated themselves at the tables and McCade had the coffee poured. "You're a troublemaker, you know."

"In what way?"

"Lots of ways. Like that man you killed up in Newisle."

"He challenged and drew," McCade said.

"I know. That's all right. But why didn't you claim your class point?"

"I had other things to do."

"You *always* have other things to do, Seventeenth McCade. That's what bothers me. You don't fit in here. You're always off somewhere where I can't find you. I begin to suspect your motives."

"You won't be the first," McCade said, "nor the last. But I told you before, I didn't want to become a part of this. I didn't have any choice."

"You could always leave."

"Toledo won't be back for over three months."

"I happen to know that you could call him here any time you wanted to."

"That's more than *I* know," McCade said. "So far as I know, I'm stuck here."

"By your choice."

"By necessity, Director. I wish I could tell you about it, but I can't."

"You know, McCade," Reddy said, leaning back in her chair, "you rcmind mc of somcthing."

"Oh, really? Nothing unpleasant, I hope."

"In a way. A display in the St. Clair museum." Valyn gasped. Reddy looked at her sharply.

"You know what she means, Valyn?" McCade asked.

"No. No, I don't."

"Well, I'd better be going," Reddy said. She looked at Valyn again, then back at McCade. "If I were you," she said, "I'd be very careful from now on. You skirt pretty close to the edge of the law yourself sometimes. Next time it might be you at the other end of those choppers."

"Now, Director," McCade said smiling, "you know me better than that."

"Yes," Reddy admitted, "I do. I wish I didn't. Stay out of trouble." She left.

McCade turned to Valyn, who was staring at him wide-eyed.

"What is it, Valyn?" he asked.

"Nothing."

"That museum exhibit she mentioned. It means something to you, doesn't it?"

"No, nothing at all."

"I'm too good a liar to be fooled by you," he said. "Tell me what it is."

"No. I won't."

"I'll find out anyway, you know."

"I know. Don't, please."

"I have to, Valyn. We've been all over this before."

"Isn't there anything I can say or do to make you change your mind about this?"

"I'm sorry, Valyn."

"So am I. What will you do now?"

"Sleep for a while. I've been up all night. I learned some very interesting things at the Fishermen Church, and they lead to other things. I'm beginning to see the end of it all."

"It's gone that far, then."

"It has. I think you had better go away, Valyn, somewhere out of sight, if you can. Things are going to get nasty from here on out, and if you get involved, you could get hurt."

"What could anybody do to me, even if they wanted to?"

"Use you as lever against me. When you leave here this morning, go away as if you were never coming back. And then don't. Stay away from me, Valyn. I've never been safe to be around, but I'm poison now, and soon it will be death to be seen with me."

"It doesn't make sense," Valyn whispered.

"Yes, it does, though not the kind you're used to. When I first got here, I thought this would be one place in the Orion Limb where the kind of brutality and selfishness I've seen all my life no longer existed. I should have known better. Seltique is no different from any other world. Just classier."

He touched her hand, and she let him. They sat there for a moment, and then he stood.

"You'd better go now," he said. "When this thing is over, if I survive it, I'll call you. If you haven't forgotten me by then, maybe we can give it another try."

She stood but would not meet his gaze. Without speaking she turned from him and walked from the dining room. A moment later he heard the front door close as she left.

He stood there in the empty house for a long moment, then deliberately he put thoughts of her out of his mind, sat down again, and took out the envelope. The three pages it contained were covered on both sides with fine printing. Painstakingly, he memorized the entire legal-psychological ritual. When he was sure he had it without error, he burned the pages. Then he went to his bed and slept until late afternoon. He awoke, inspected his repaired but somewhat bare living room, then fixed himself a huge meal. He dressed carefully in clothes that were snug, had nothing to flap or snag, and that were durable and unostentatious. He cleaned his gun, oiled it, loaded it, and tucked it away in an inside pocket. He stuffed a handful of extra cartridges into another pocket, turned off the house, and left.

St. Clair was a twelfth-class district on the eastern edge of Loger, and the museum was the biggest in the city. He entered the main hall and found himself in front of a huge display depicting the first landing on Seltique over six thousand years ago. Reading the sign beside the display, he learned that the landing ship in the center of the display was the actual vessel used by those explorers to come down from their orbiting starship. Space travel had changed quite a bit since then, he reflected. Whole spaceships were not much bigger than that landing craft, these days, and much more comfortable than the old huge, hulking starships had been.

He left the display and wandered aimlessly through the

halls. There were all the usual exhibits one expected to find in any big city museum. There were displays of the geography and geology of the planet and the immediate area, of plant life common and exotic, animal life extinct and extant—and imported, including a grouping of the black birds of Klooshkai's race. Two pair had been brought to Seltique five thousand years ago from a world McCade couldn't pronounce. He wondered idly whether they had come by choice, and whether they were as intelligent on their home world. But it was useless speculating.

There were other halls of natural history, kilometers of them, and he moved through them quickly. They were all fascinating, and more than once he found himself distracted by the displays. But this was not a sightseeing tour. He had a lot of ground to cover, and one particular display to find.

Another wing was devoted to technology, with articulated displays that demonstrated principles when buttons were pushed. He found this more interesting, but moved even more quickly here. It was unlikely that the display he sought would be among the engines, communications devices, levers, rocket drives, duplicating machines, and so on. Still, it was tempting to stop and push buttons and see how things worked.

He went through the halls of medicine quickly and the science exhibits almost as fast. Then he got to the wing where the history of the planet was depicted. Here, too, he was able to go from hall to hall with little more than a quick glance.

He did pause at the exhibits depicting the period of the embargo. There was much to learn here, but at last he tore himself away, and now he knew where to go. Without stopping again he found his way to the political history section of a hundred years ago. He examined most exhibits closely, and almost passed over the critical one.

It was a series of photographs, telling the story of the last year of the last Planet Master. And there, in the middle, was one in particular, the one Reddy must have been referring to.

It was a picture taken in a private home at a meeting of the Planet Master, the Number One of Loger, and the Directors of the Eight Brotherhoods. Ten men and women sat in chairs and couches in a large study, dominated by a huge desk, at which sat the man at whose home the meeting was being held. The caption named the men and women, and three of them, besides Merenthar, he knew from the list of Core members he had gotten from Norther's file. Of the ten faces, one he knew. One of these people McCade had seen before. Now he understood Reddy's remark.

As he looked at the picture something else about it caught his eye. A tarot deck, Subriente had said, but McCade had heard other things about the Book of Aradka on other worlds, and knew that the Book was not just a deck of cards. Similar, perhaps, but anything supposedly made by a legendary race of beings who had withdrawn from the galaxy millions of years ago was not going to be just a pack of playing cards, not if it had survived this long.

McCade looked at the picture, and the melody in his mind made his head swim. He knew what the Book was now. And he knew where it was. He didn't need the lists any more. He didn't need to translate the inventory or location codes. The Book of Aradka was the thing he was after, the thing that would ensure his absolute independence and freedom for the rest of his life. And it was right there, in that room in the picture.

His head bursting with inaudible sound, he slid away from the display, and letting his feet move the way they wanted to and ignoring the stares of the other museum visitors, he left the Halls of History, danced out into the Main Hall and past the display of the First Landing and down the steps to the street. The song rang in his brain, and he felt his whole body swaying and bending with the rhythm. Grinning broadly and immensely happy, he started to sing—and then four hands grabbed him roughly.

"Quite the little fool, aren't we?" the man on his left said.

"Kelso is tired of you mucking around in business that's none of your concern," the other said.

"Pardon me," McCade said, regaining his composure, "but do I understand that you are challenging me?" Around him people were stopping to watch. It was still Sagger, and they thought they knew what was going on, though two against one was a little unusual.

"You understand correctly," the man on his right said, and they reached for their guns.

Without even thinking, McCade shot out both hands and grabbed each man by the throat. The guns went off, and a slug whined as it ricochetted off into the air. McCade squeezed and the bodies in his hands convulsed momentarily, then went limp.

"Not now," he hissed through tight teeth as he let the bodies down onto the lawn. "Not now, you bastards, not when I'm so close." Ignoring the crowds, he turned and went away.

EPIKRATESIS

EPIKRATESIS

Once again McCade rode the beltway into third-class St. Germain. It was the middle of the next morning, and in spite of the Sagger he had to take the chance. Kelso had something he wanted, and the only way to get it was to see the man in person.

He was a registered fourteenth class now. His two kills of the night before had done him that much good. And his reputation had obviously spread, because although, as a lower-class person, he was fair game in St. Germain, nobody challenged him, and he moved unhindered past estates that rivaled those of the wealthiest of men elsewhere in the Cluster and the Orion Limb.

He reached the gate of Kelso's estate, and spoke his

name to the speaker. There was only an instant's hesitation before the gates opened, and then McCade was riding up Kelso's private belt to the house. He climbed the steps at the front door, which opened as he neared it, and a humanoid automaton greeted him and asked his business.

"I'd like to speak to Second Kelso, if you please," McCade said.

"Second Kelso is engaged in business right now, sir," the automaton answered. "Will you call back later in the day?"

"I will not," McCade said. "Tell Kelso that I want to speak with him now. He knows who I am."

"Yes, I do," came a voice from an inner room. McCade turned and saw a solidly built man in his fifties, standing in a doorway.

"Won't you come in?" Kelso invited, and stepped back. McCade nodded and entered the room, a very lavish den.

"Make yourself comfortable, Fourteenth McCade," Kelso said, sitting on a huge, overstuffed chair. "I can't tell you how happy I am to meet you at last. Though I must admit, you have cost me some unpleasant moments."

"I don't doubt it," McCade said, taking a less sumptuous chair. "But let's not kid around, Second Kelso. You're as happy to see me as you would be to find a dead fish in your bed."

"Very true, Fourteenth McCade, very true. But in a way, I am glad you're here. You've been on the loose too long, and it's time you got yourself out of circulation."

"What do you have against me, Second Kelso?"

"Oh, everything. You're an offworlder. That in itself is a threat to our world, to our way of life. Then you go around asking about the Core. Now that's really bad, McCade. The Core was a corrupt group of people who wanted to sell Seltique to the Samosar Cluster, who wanted to rape this beautiful world of ours for their own profit. I have devoted my life to tracking down relics of their activities and their organization, and eradicating them. You also went to the Pro-Galaxy Group. They're as bad as the Core, though nowhere near as dangerous. Still, it's about time something was done about them, too. All in all, McCade, you have been an infernal nuisance. I shall not be sorry to see you put safely out of the way."

"You may not find that too easy," McCade said. He had no fear of this man. He knew he could defend himself. His only fear was that he would have to kill him, and he didn't want to do that. He congratulated himself on his foresight in acquiring the ampule of sorbil anthrocain, though he had not as yet devised a means of administering it.

"You mean the way you killed my agents?" Kelso was saying. "Yes, I must admit that was well done. They were careless and paid the price. Perhaps it's just as well. If they had been successful, I would never have had this opportunity of talking with you. I intend to take every advantage of it, believe me."

"Oh, I do," McCade said. "And I, too, shall not let opportunity pass. But you're the host, sir. I'm at your service."

"I almost admire you, McCade. You're so cool. Nothing seems to ruffle you. How do you do it?"

"Childhood training. I was brought up to be an actor."

"I can believe it. Then the front you show does not reflect your true internal state."

"No, it never does. I am the king of fools, Kelso, an actor, a jester, a master liar. I am never what I seem."

"Bravo, McCade, brave speech. Too bad all that talent will go to waste. But surely you did not come to Seltique just to play games with us. Or did you?"

"Not at all. I had a purpose. I still have. And it is that purpose that brings me here this morning."

"Indeed. Well, I hope it is something that can be consummated quickly, McCade, because I intend to kill you very shortly."

"That would not be to your advantage."

"Oh, really? And why not?"

"I have something you want, Kelso."

"Now what could you, a mere fourteenth class, have that

I, a second class, could possibly want, McCade? You know, it surprises me. The arrogance of these lower classes, I mean. Who do they think they are? They play their games, and struggle for rank, and hope to increase their status by making kills and dueling and all that crap. What can they know of status? Only the first order knows anything of status, McCade. I was born second class. I come by my rank naturally. I *know* I'm among the best; I don't have to prove it."

"Haven't you ever wanted to be just one step higher?" McCade asked.

"First class? Oh, no. They're not that much better off. Besides, most of them don't do anything with themselves. I have more power, McCade, more influence, than half the first class put together."

"How about two steps higher, Kelso?"

"Two steps? You mean Planet Master? Well, yes, I have thought about that. But it would mean giving up so much. You're an outsider, McCade, and you don't understand this. A Planet Master has responsibility, he has a duty. True, he has power, but to get that power, he must give up *all* status, *all* rank and class, and all the prerogatives that go with it. Yes, I've thought of it, and so have many others, but as you may or may not know, one doesn't just apply for the job. There's a ritual, a key . . ."

"Yes?" McCade said softly. "Go on."

" . . . a key." Kelso hesitated. "That has been lost since the last Planet Master, Merenthar, was killed, in an unfortunate accident. Just what are you getting at, McCade?"

"It is a document, about three thousand words long," McCade said. Kelso snorted in disbelief.

"You don't know anything about it," he said.

"Don't I? Then who would?"

"Nobody! The key was lost!"

"Sterpreen knew," McCade said softly.

"How did you know that?"

"I have my ways."

"But Sterpreen has been dead for seventy years."

"But documents don't die."

"You mean Sterpreen actually had it, the key, the ritual for becoming Planet Master?"

"He did. But not any more."

"Where is it, McCade? So help me, I'll break every bone in your body."

"I destroyed it," McCade said. Kelso uttered an inarticulate howl. "But I memorized it first," McCade went on.

"My God. *You* have the key. You actually found it. People have been looking for that for a hundred years. How did you do it?"

"Professional secret. But as I said, the document no longer exists. I have the key, all right, but it's locked away inside my head. You can't get it by killing me, Kelso."

The older man slumped back in his chair, his eyes hot and wild. Once, twice, he started to get to his feet, but fell back again.

"So *that* was what you were after all this time," he said at last. "You want to be Planet Master."

McCade laughed.

"No, Kelso," he said, "not that. As you said, it involves too much responsibility, too much duty. I'm a free man. I always have been. I enjoy my independence too much to ever take on a job like that. I discovered the key only by accident, while looking for something else."

"I don't believe you," Kelso said. "Who would throw away an opportunity to be the absolute ruler of a whole planet?"

"What you don't understand," McCade said, "is that that is just the thing I'm trying to get away from. My family is big, Kelso, and out in the Cluster and the Orion Limb, they control an aggregate that equals ten planets. I didn't need to come here if all I wanted was power. I could have stayed home and gotten all I wanted, safely, from behind a desk."

"I can't understand that. What could anyone want more than power?"

"Freedom, Kelso, freedom. Ever since I was fifteen I've

been trying to get out from under the shadow of my family. But I'm too used to wealth and ease. If I cut myself off completely, I'd go broke in five years. And without money, Kelso, my freedom would be lost. I'd have to go back to them again, just to keep alive."

Kelso snorted. "You don't have any appreciation at all," he said.

"Maybe not, but I know what I want. *Not* to rule the Samosar Cluster, which so desperately needs leadership, or even one little planet, but just to go on living as I have been, with no cares, no responsibilities, no fear of doing without. Sounds selfish of me, doesn't it? It is. I know it. But that's the way it is."

"I don't see what that has to do with being Planet Master or your being here on Seltique."

"It's simple. Seltique is not unknown out in the Cluster. Lots of stories are told about it. Some are just stories, but some, I've learned, are absolutely true. One of those stories concerns a certain thing once owned by the Core. If I had that thing, I would be free for life. I could go wherever I wanted, whenever I wanted, and be beholden to no man."

"I begin to get the picture," Kelso said, "but you're wasting your time. Any of the things the Core ever had were either destroyed by us or hidden by them."

"I know that. But I found this thing, Kelso. I know where it is."

The other man remained silent for a long moment, gazing thoughtfully at McCade. "All right," he said at last. "What is it?"

"It's called the Book of Aradka."

"Never heard of it."

"Never? That's too bad. It's an ancient artifact, made some millions of years ago, the last remaining fragment of a race that has long since disappeared. Such a thing would be of no use to you here, Kelso. You couldn't use it for anything. You don't use money, and you carry on no commerce with other worlds, other than whatever it is Ben Toledo buys and sells. But for me, Kelso, think of it. It is in one hundred sixteen parts, and each part, out in the Limb, worth literally millions. I'm used to money, Kelso, but most of our family wealth is in ships, factories, developments and the like, not cash. If each of these pieces of the Book of Aradka brought three million, just think of what one hundred of them would bring. I could name my price. And then, Kelso, I would be, out there, just like you are here. Only there'd be nobody to compete with me."

"Yes, McCade, that I can understand. And you're right, this book of yours means nothing to me. This is my world, and I don't care about the rest. All that out there is a horror to me. On Seltique such a thing would be worthless."

"And so you see," McCade said, "we have nothing to fight about. I don't want to be Planet Master, you don't want the Book. I suggest we exchange."

"You're forgetting," Kelso said, "that I don't have your Book."

"No, but it's under your control, though you may not be aware of it. It's in a house, Kelso, that you have had sealed. I tried last night to get into it, but I couldn't even make it onto the grounds. It was very frustrating. Usually I can pick any lock, scale any wall. They haven't made a jail yet that can hold me, if I don't want to be held. But Seltique has progressed technologically, in some areas, beyond the rest of the Cluster and the Limb, and the seals you put on your houses, when you lock them up tight, are beyond my ability to break."

"So what do you want," Kelso asked, "the key to this house? And in exchange you'll give me the secret of the Planet Master?"

"That's right. If you give me the key so I can break the seal, I'll write out for you the whole formula. It's perfectly clear. And then I'll go and get the book, and go to Red Dog, and charter a ship from Phenolk P'talion to come out and get me. I'll go away and you'll never see me again, and you can become Planet Master and do anything you damn well please."

"I think, Fourteenth McCade, that we may be able to

strike a bargain." Kelso was smiling broadly now; not a pretty smile, but McCade didn't care. Kelso pressed a button on the arm of his chair.

"Bring us," he said when the automaton came in, "—Scotch, I believe?" McCade nodded. "And a pad of paper and a pen." The robot left. "Now then," Kelso went on, "which house is it that you would like to have unsealed?"

"The Scott chateau in Scott's Woods, Second Kelso."

"No!" Kelso bellowed. "No, no. By God, I should have known. That's one place you'll never get into, McCade."

"You surprise me," McCade said mildly, even though he *was* surprised. "Why in the world would you covet that place?"

"That's where most of the Core's documents were kept. And they're still there. I've searched that place a hundred times, and I can't find a thing, but it's all there, and if you're sharp enough to dig up the secret of the Planet Master, you'd dig all that stuff up too. No, McCade, not that."

"But I don't want that stuff," McCade protested. "I just want the one thing. If you like, you can come with me, and see that I take nothing more. If you like, I'll even help you look for these documents. But I must have the Book."

"You idiot. You don't really understand, do you? There's only one way I can legally break the seal on that house, and that is to assign it to an heir. I can go in there because I put the seal on it, but nobody else can."

"So break a rule. We've both done it before."

"It's not a matter of rules, McCade. That seal is a death lock, as you no doubt discovered last night. Anybody besides me going onto the grounds gets fried. I can't even take an assistant with me when I go there myself. I have to go there alone."

"So make me the heir. Then I'll take off the seal, take the Book, and leave. You can seal it again when I go."

"Impossible. Some laws are bigger than me, McCade. Once that chateau is out of my hands, I can never get it back. You don't know what I went through to get that seal on there in the first place."

"I can imagine," McCade said dryly, "but I don't care.

All I want is the Book of Aradka." The automaton came in just then, with a tray of drinks and a pad. Kelso snatched the pad and pen and threw them at McCade. The automaton set the drinks down on a table between the two men, then left.

"No way," Kelso said. "No way in the world am I going to give you the key to the Scott chateau. You'll have to find some other treasure to make yourself rich with."

"But I have my heart set on the Book," McCade said, and picked up one of the glasses. He sipped. It was good.

"Too bad," Kelso snarled.

"Well, then," McCade said, "I'm afraid I'll have to keep the Planet Master's secret to myself."

"You don't have it," Kelso snapped.

"Don't I? How about this? In order to become Planet Master, the candidate must comply with certain laws of resignation of status, in a form outlined only in the Planet Master's Secret. They involve certain public renunciations of status or desire for status, and also involve certain mental exercises which must be practiced to perfection and demonstrated to the satisfaction of the Directors of the Eight Brotherhoods and the highest-ranking member of each class and, if they exist, the previous Planet Master and the current Number One of Loger."

"Get out of here," Kelso yelled. "Get out of here. I'll get it from you, some way, some day, but now just get out. Do you hear me?"

McCade put down his glass and left.

The Scott chateau was located in the heart of Scott's Woods. It had been the first estate established in the district, and had remained in the Scott family for almost four thousand years. When Loger had begun to develop its status system, Scott's Woods had been the residence of the wealthiest people of the city, and had been designated first class. And the Scott family, after whom the district had been named, had contributed more than their share to the roll of Number

Ones of Loger.

McCade stood on the strip of grass separating the beltway from the estate proper and looked longingly in over the overgrown bushes and lawns at the huge house, climbing up the side of a hill like an outcropping of precious stones set in iron. There, so near that he could reach it in five minutes, was the thing he had wished for, searched for, fought for almost all his life. There was more to it than that, of course, but that didn't matter. At least he tried to convince himself it didn't.

At the edge of the estate, a pale green light flickered, almost invisible against the green of the foliage, so that he had to get up within ten centimeters of it to see it. And it was deadly. If he touched it he would fry. Occasionally insects, flying too close, snapped with a brief flare as they brushed against it. There was nowhere along the whole perimeter where even a gnat could get through. And the seal, after rising five meters into the air, arched over in an enclosing dome. There was no way in.

The chateau was double sealed. The whole building had been enclosed in a stasis field, a device usually not used except as emergency treatment in hospitals or on perishable goods for long shipping hauls, and then never of such a size. McCade could see the generator at the side of the chateau. The whole building opalesced faintly.

His life was in extreme peril, here and now. It was the height of the Sagger, and he was a lowly fourteen, who could be killed out of hand just for being here in the first-class district. Yet he had taken the chance, for the second time, just to make sure he hadn't missed something. But the chateau and its grounds were just as securely sealed as they had been before he had gone to see Kelso. His chest ached with longing.

At last he turned away and started back to the belt. It was then that he noticed the people out on the lawn of the estate across the way. He froze, then kicked himself and went on. They were too far away to see his class badges, but if he behaved oddly they would know him for a trespasser, and there would be sport—hunting the intruder through the woods and across the lawns. And they would win. He reached the belt, got on, and started away. The people out on the lawn looked up as he passed, then ignored him. He kept moving.

An hour later he got back to his place in Sands and fixed himself a light supper. He sat eating it in his study, staring idly at the walls. He was down. If Kelso wouldn't trade the chateau for the secret of the Planet Master, then he was stumped at last. There was nothing more he could do.

He needed a rest. Maybe if he took a few days off and tried to relax a solution would come to him. But he bored too easily. He couldn't sit around this empty house twiddling his toes. Maybe he should go out on the streets and participate in the Sagger. A challenger only got rank points, though a defender got class points. It took twenty rank points to make the class jump. He was fourteen-seven at the moment. He could slowly work his way up. After all, that was what Sagger was all about. That was what one was *supposed* to do. He reached for his gun and checked it, then slipped it in his pocket. He took a last sip of beer, and with a feeling of frustration and futility, went out the door. There was a flutter of wings, and Klooshkai settled on his shoulder.

"You look glum," the bird said. "Are you in trouble?"

Briefly, McCade told the bird about his near success and ultimate falure.

"That's too bad," the bird said. "Fortunately such desires do not exist for my species."

"What desires do you have?" McCade asked, grateful for the diversion.

"We are philosophers," the bird answered. "After all, without hands, what can we do but talk?"

"I hadn't thought of that, but it makes sense. Maybe you're lucky."

"I think we are, but there are times when even words won't satisfy us. Like now, for example. I've been horny for the longest time and every chick I approach says she has better feathers to pluck."

"So you're male then."

"Yes, didn't you notice? I guess it wouldn't make any difference to you. It does to me, though, I can assure you. What are you up to?"

"I was going out to see if I could pick a fight, but I've changed my mind."

"Going to boost your status a little, eh? That's a good idea, I suppose, though I don't approve of the killing part."

"I don't either, basically," McCade said. "I just wanted to let off some steam, and it was the first thing that came to mind."

"Well, don't put it away completely. Non-status conscious as I am, I still think you would do well to get a boost along those lines. If you could work your way up to where you could put some additional pressure on your friend Kelso, you might be able to salvage something out of this situation."

"You have a point there, but I just don't know how to go about doing it. Killing innocent people just isn't to my taste."

"Even though that was what you were setting out to do."

"I would have cooled down before I actually started anything."

"Are you sure? Anyway, do something. I just dropped by to say hello. A friend of mine's got me fixed up with this little bird he says is really friendly."

"I wish you luck."

"From my experience these last few weeks I'll need it. See you later." And with avigorous flapping the bird was gone. For a moment McCade wished he were as carefree. Then he got on the belt and headed for Lestrange.

Elex Norther was in his offices, and admitted McCade immediately. McCade had hesitated before actually going up to visit the man, remembering what he'd told Valyn about providing Kelso with a lever, but he decided that Norther was too high-class, held too important an office to be easily intimidated, even by Kelso.

"Come in, come in," Norther said happily. "I was just finishing up for the day. How have you been?"

"Up and down," McCade said, easing himself down into a chair in front of Norther's desk. "Things aren't exactly all going my way these days."

"Sorry to hear that. Is there anything I can do to help?"

"Not unless you can turn Kelso into a nice guy."

"Sorry, Larson, but if Kelso's your nemesis, there's nothing much I can do for you."

"I didn't think so. But that's not why I came up. I need some advice on another subject."

"Shoot."

"Don't—use that word, please," McCade said.

"Huh? Why not?"

"That's just what I was going to do when I left the house today, shoot up a bunch of people and rake in a few rank points."

"Ah, I see. Getting tired of being one of the great middle class?"

"That's not it exactly, but pretty close. I've got the idea that if I could improve my status, I could deal with Kelso a little more effectively. God, listen to me, yammering away about status like a native!"

"Don't worry about it," Norther said, chuckling, "nobody will notice. Status, hmmm? Well, that's really a job for a Patron, but since you're here I'll see what I can think up. You could do like you said, go out and kill people. Or, you could try to join one of the Brotherhoods. If they accept you, that would boost you a point."

"How long would that take?"

"About a year from the time you submit your application, if they accept you. Once in you can work your way up the hierarchy inside. Inside of twenty years you could climb all the way to second or third class without once having to pull a trigger."

"I'm afraid I don't have that much time," McCade said.

"Didn't think so. Well, if you went to any parties, you could find yourself a nice high-class girl and marry her. Valyn Dixon, for example. She's a nine. That would make you a nine too."

"Thanks, Elex, but that's really another subject entirely."

"Oh, is it? I'm sorry, it shouldn't be. But I keep forgetting you're an offworlder. Okay. How about this. There are always openings in the athletic branch of the Academy. You could become an athlete. You can climb quite high that way, I understand. If you're any good."

McCade didn't say anything, but just grimaced. He could do it, and he knew he'd be good, whatever he did, but it wasn't his style.

"Don't like it?"Norther asked.

"Not really. It's a possibility, though I never have been a sports fan, and again, there's the time factor. I don't know, Elex, maybe I don't need status after all."

"Everybody needs status except the Planet Master, and you aren't that. Besides, if you've got Kelso on your back you're going to need all the help you can get. That fellow can bring a lot of pressure to bear on you if he wants to. He's killed more than his share and ruined lots of others. He's been known to break a man from tenth class down to twentieth. He's a rough character."

"That part I know about," McCade said. "I had a run-in with him personally."

"And survived it? Where?"

"At his house."

"I don't believe it. This is Sagger. How did you get into St. Germain?"

"Gall. Sheer nerve. I tried to make a deal with him, but he went rabid. If he hadn't been so mad I don't think I would have gotten out of there. As it was, he had me already set up for a kill."

"You do like to live dangerously, don't you? You're never going to live long if you go on this way. Listen, if you're going to compete with Kelso you've *got* to have status, just to get in the ring with him. You've been lucky so far, but you can't count on it continuing. You'd better see a patron, Larson. Try Arvin Saranof. She knows you already, and I'm sure she'd be glad to help."

"Could she do me enough good, do you think?"

"I don't know. But that's her specialty, helping people gain status. But she won't do you any good if you get squashed first."

"Maybe you're right, Elex. I don't know. I'm not used to asking for help. I guess I'm too used to being on my own. But I've hit a dead end and I can't go any further. Something's got to be done."

"Then go home and make a professional appointment with Arvin. If she can't help you, she can steer you to someone who can."

"I might as well talk to her It certainly couldn't hurt."

"Absolutely not."

They chatted a while longer, and then McCade left. He hadn't felt this helpless in years, and the thought of going to *any*one for assistance didn't make him feel any better. For status, of all things.

It was a beautiful evening as he rode the beltway home. But then it always was. Out in the rest of the world it was turning autumn, but in the city it would always be early summer. After a while, he thought, that could get boring.

The light was fading from the sky and the first stars were beginning to come out when he left the belt in front of his house. There was a man waiting at the door.

"Good evening," McCade said as he walked up. "What can I do for you?"

"Are you Larson McCade?" the man asked as if he already knew.

"I am. What can I do for you?" he repeated.

"I'm from the Academy. I'm sorry to inform you that we have received an order to close your house."

"I don't understand. Kindly explain yourself."

The man sighed. "The Academy has received a complaint to the effect that you have come into possession of this house illegally, and has therefore put a closing order on it pending the outcome of the necessary investigation."

"But that's ridiculous. I inherited the house by default

from Billy Sereg, who assaulted me in Director Reddy's presence."

"I know that, sir," the policeman said, for that was what he was. "But the complaint has been duly filed, and the investigation must be held."

"Who made the complaint?"

"I can't tell you that. You will be duly informed at the hearing, which will commence after the investigation."

"And how long will *that* take?"

"Normally such an investigation should take no more than two weeks."

"I see. And abnormally, in this case, how long do you estimate it will take?"

"At least three months. Due to certain technicalities."

"That's very interesting. May I enter and remove my belongings?"

"Nothing may be removed from the house until it is determined just what was part of the original furnishings."

"So I'm kicked out in the cold."

"I'm sorry, sir."

McCade turned and stalked away. Kelso had already moved.

But if Kelso had done this, then he was more eager to get the secret of the Planet Master than McCade had thought. Maybe he had a chance after all.

But there was something else to do first. If it was Kelso who had put the closure on his house, it could only mean that Kelso thought there was something there among his papers that would give a clue to the Planet Master secret, or at least could be used as a lever against him. McCade had to make sure that nothing of any value got into his enemy's hands. He had to get into his house somehow, and remove or destroy all the results of his searches and inquiries.

He took the belt to the nearest public building, the local offices of the Cartel, the Brothers of Integrity, who directed

Loger's business and maintained conservation of its environment. He had no difficulty getting down to the basement and the cellars beneath. He stepped up his perceptions and his associative faculty and soon found the doors that led to the subcellars, and from there it was easy to locate the deep stairwell down to the ancient underground transport system. He had a perfect sense of direction and, once in the vast tunnels which honeycombed the ground beneath the city, took the passages that brought him as close as he could get to the area beneath his own house. There would be no regular access stair here, of course, but there might be something else.

There was. Two kilometers from the spot that, he judged, was directly beneath his house, a service stair left the subway, and went up a short way into a tangled system of sewers. These, too, were no longer in use. The city of Loger had long since stopped dumping its wastes into the environment. Now, like everywhere else, everything was reclaimed to be converted into materials that could be used again. But that development was relatively recent, and the sewers that had once serviced the city were extensive. They were dry, but they were pitch dark. He still had his little flash with him and that helped, but most of all he needed his sense of absolute direction, another product of his biotraining.

The sewers did not lead him back directly to his house, but he was able to get to within five hundred meters after several false turns and much wandering. At least, so he judged. Of course, he was still a long way down, but there was hope yet. Sewers are no good unless there is some means of getting the wastes into them. Somewhere, there had to be drains coming down from the surface or near it.

Irregularly spaced along the ceiling of the sewer were broad round holes which could be gotten to by means of rungs set into the sewer wall. He stopped under one of these and looked up. His sense of direction was good; he knew which way was north to within half a degree. But it was hard to judge just exactly how much distance he had covered underground, especially with all the twists and turns his route had taken. He knew just how far the Cartel Building was from his house, in a straight line, and he knew the length of his stride and had been subconsciously calculating since he'd found the access stairs. But there was considerable room for error. He could be off by half a kilometer or so.

There was nothing to do but try it. He put the flash away and in absolute darkness took a hold of the rungs and started climbing. His ears told him when he had entered the hole in the sewer ceiling, and they told him before his hands did when, after a climb to within twenty meters of the surface, the shaft bent and became horizontal. Stepping out onto the level floor, he took out his flash again, and by its dim light, examined the tunnel.

He was in a round tube some two and a half meters in diameter, which ran a short distance before forking. He took the left branch, and went on for perhaps sixty meters before he found the sloping tube, a meter and a half across, coming down from above and behind. He entered this on his hands and knees and went up. The slope was gentle, and the surface of the drain rough, so the climb was easy.

After a little way the slope leveled off, and smaller tubes joined the one he was in from the sides. He could only guess now. He did everything he knew how—which wasn't much—to make the best choice, picked a tube, and entered it.

It ran level for a little way, then began to curve upward, slowly at first, but at last going up at about forty degrees. Then abruptly he was out of it and standing, filthy and covered with ancient grime, on the floor of small chamber which was three meters long, two wide, and two and a half high. The roof was pierced with several holes and a hatch. He went to the wall beneath it, climbed the projecting bricks that served as a ladder up to it, and gently lifted it up.

He was in the cellar of some house, but which house he did not know. He climbed out of the tank, closed the hatch, and keying himself up, cautiously proceeded to find the stairs.

He had guessed right. He was in the basement of his own house.

The stairs let up to a service hall at one side of the house, in the portion he had closed off, but very near the kitchen. He stood listening at the head of the stairs for a long moment. He could hear people moving about in the back parts somewhere, but nothing from the front. Moving as quietly as a cat in velet slippers, he left the stair, crossed the hall, and entered his kitchen. There was nobody about and nobody in the dining room, living room or study though he could hear, outside his front door, the guard he'd spoken to earlier talking with a woman, probably another guard.

Entering his study, he saw that nothing had been disturbed. Quickly, he went to his files, and took out and destroyed in the waste disposal basket every computer printout, every note, every piece of paper. He paused now and then to memorize certain items, not that he really needed them, but because they might come in handy in his struggles with Kelso. But the books from the library and the list from the church he put in his attaché case, along with all his extra ammunition.

A footstep sounded outside the closed door. Quickly, he stepped to the wall beside it. The door opened and a woman in police uniform stepped through. Without thinking, he stiffened his hand and hit her on the neck at the base of the skull. There was a dry snap and she slumped. He barely had time to catch her before she fell. He laid her down on the floor and felt for signs of life, but there were none. He cursed himself. The last thing he needed was to kill a member of the Academy. Well, there was nothing he could do about it now. He picked her up, sat her in a chair, then made a dash to his bedroom, where he picked out a clean change of clothes which he wrapped in another shirt. Then he hurried back to the kitchen and crossed the service hall to the stair.

Back in the basement, he lifted up the hatch to the underground overflow tank, and went down. Then, still keeping his body at full key, he sped down the drains, through the sewers, and into the abandoned underground transport tunnels. He would pay later for keeping his body going at such a high pitch for so long, but time was critical now. He had to get away. He had to be somewhere else so that there would be no way anyone could connect him with the dead policewoman in his study.

Accelerating to five times normal speed, he raced through the subway to the access stairs that led up to the cellars below the Academy Building in Laking's. It took him a moment to find a custodial station where he could change his clothes and clean his face and hands. He dumped his old clothes and the extra shirt in which he had wrapped the new ones into a disposal chute, then went up and out of the cellars and made himself conspicuous among the people moving through the lobbies and hallways. He took a crowded elevator up to Director Reddy's offices, rather than an empty one. There he made a point of asking the human secretary for permission to see the Director.

Senna Reddy admitted him after only a short wait.

"I'm sorry, Fourteenth McCade," she said as he entered her private office and sat down.

"I came as quickly as I could, Director," McCade said. He set his attaché case down by his feet and leaned back. "Can you tell me what's going on?"

"Essentially, a formal complaint has been made, as my guard told you. He contacted me as soon as you left, and I've been expecting you. I warned you, Fourteenth McCade."

"Warned me, First Reddy? What did I do to deserve this kind of treatment?"

"I don't know. Ask Second Kelso."

"So he *was* the one?"

"Yes. I'm not supposed to tell you that, but under the circumstances . . . Well, dammit, *I'm* the witness, and I know you got that place as honestly as anyone ever could. I don't like having my statements questioned, even, or especially, by Second Kelso. But there's nothing I can do about it."

"The wheels of the law. Yes. I know. I understand, Director, and I certainly don't hold anything against you personally. You're one of the few people in this city I regard as a friend—whether you like that or not."

"Oh, really? What kind of company am I in?"

"Elex Norther. Valyn Dixon."

"Hmm. Very nce people, both of them, though I don't know Ninth Dixon too well. I'm not usually associated with that kind."

"You've expressed interest for my welfare, Director, however acidly. Nobody else cares. Not that I'm so important, except to myself, of course. It's just that, on this world, so few people do care about other people, at all. You three are more like the people I know out in the Cluster. That's all."

"I can accept that. Okay, Fourteenth McCade, we've been pleasant, and I appreciate your compliment, but that's not why you came here."

"Of course not. I want the closure lifted from my house."

"I can't do it. And I want to, Fourteenth McCade, because it angers me to have my word doubted. But the due process is explicit. There's nothing I can do."

"How about this investigation, Director? I understand it's going to take six times longer than usual. Why is that?"

"Kelso is why, again. Damn his eyes. He knows perfectly well that all I have to do is make a statement as witness that you inherited the house fairly, by default, and the whole thing would be over in an hour. Not even two weeks. But he has stipulated, in his complaint, that a thorough search must be done into the backgrounds of all parties concerned, Billy Sereg's, yours, even mine. That takes time, especially where you are concerned—"

"*That's* why," McCade said.

"Huh?"

"He doesn't want the notes in my study, he wants my background. And what better way than to have the Academy, which is completely equipped, even if not prepared, to initiate an off-planet search into my family history. That's it. Let's curse him in unison, shall we?"

"Are you sure about that?"

"Absolutely."

Reddy's face grew red and her mouth worked. She spluttered. "That ass!" she muttered, when she had better control of her voice. "I knew he was just using us, but I didn't know he was using us *that* way. Do you realize what such an investigation costs? And he's getting it free. When I get untangled from this I think I'm going to do a little pressuring myself. The Academy is not the weakest of the Brotherhoods."

"My sympathies, Director. You can appreciate how I feel, now. But I take it, then, that your hands are tied."

"Absolutely. I won't be able to do anything even on my own behalf, until the investigation is over."

"That's rough. I was hoping . . . But I'm still out in the cold. I could always go back to the Morphy Chessica, but I've gotten used to the soft life. Is there anything I can do to ease the pinch a little?"

"Not as a Fourteen. If you were a ten or higher you'd be in the second order and could file a claim for temporary housing in one of the uninherited villas."

"That would be nice; how do I jump my status?"

"No way that would be quick enough to suit you, unless you'd care to admit to some killings."

"What kind of killings?"

"We found some bodies in the park west of Red Dog a while ago. They look fair, but nobody has put in a claim for the points. Sound interesting?" Her eyes were on his, and she was not joking.

"Very," McCade said. "Yes, I can admit to them. There were five, weren't there?"

"There were. Killed clean, like I say, without a weapon. Each of them was armed, so it looks like they had taken you out there for some sport."

"Yes, it does look that way."

"If it weren't for the fact that one of the five was a man named Jonas, whom the Academy has been wanting to nail for a long time, I might be a little upset about the business and suspect that there might have been other reasons for you to have been out in the park with them, but under the circumstances, I don't really care too much. As I said, the case *looks* good, and all we need to close it is somebody to take the points."

"How far up would that take me?"

"Up to eleventh class."

"That would put me in Foxes, wouldn't it?"

"Yes. And they're the only other district besides Red Dog that provides regular temporary housing."

"Sounds good. What do I do?"

"Sign here." She handed him a form which he read quickly. It stated that, in the absence of witnesses, he admitted to the killings and swore that he had been defending himself. He signed.

"And that," Reddy said when he handed the paper back, "is all I think I can do for you."

"You've been a great help, believe me," McCade said. He made his goodbyes and left.

Back on the street he began to feel the effects of his exertion. He took a tube into Foxes, looked up the Housing Administration, a branch of the Cartel. He found a little bungalow of only eighteen rooms in the north end of the district and moved in.

The streets were all empty and all the beltways had stopped. Overhead the sky was a starless black, though the buildings around him were brightly lit. He wandered aimlessly, his mind in a haze, and wondered idly where everybody had gone and why the parks had all been turned into stores and hotels.

The road ran straight ahead of him, between towering white buildings that glowed strangely in the non-light. In the distance he could see the figure of a man, standing alone in the center of the road. McCade walked toward the man, and it seemed to take a long time to get there. He was tired, and all he really wanted to do was lie down and rest a while. But the man still waited, and something about him compelled McCade to continue walking.

At last he reached the man, and stopped a meter or so in front of him. There was nothing remarkable about him, unless it was his lack of any distinguishing features.

"Hello," McCade said. His voice sounded strained and far off. "What am I doing here?"

"Looking for your sister," the man answered in a voice with no timbre or depth.

"My sister? Why? Is she lost?"

"She is lost," the man answered in a voice that was more like the wind than a voice.

"But is she here?"

"In the city."

"But she can't be. She doesn't belong here. How did she get here? Toledo doesn't usually take passengers. Why did she come?"

But he was talking to himself. A chilly breeze blew around the corners of the old buildings and houses. And somewhere, out there in the city, was his sister. He had to find her, to help her. She couldn't go on alone. She needed his help, and leadership and guidance. What could he do?

He went up the dusty, deserted streets, calling her name. The only answers were echoes. There were no other people anywhere. He entered building after rickety building, but nowhere could he find a clue, or any trace of her. He worried. She was older than he, but had never been as independent, though she had always tried to pretend she was. She had spurned him long ago out of jealousy. But he didn't mind. He was still her brother, and now, when she needed him, he was only too glad to come to her rescue. If only he could find where she was. He went through residential areas and shopping centers. He combed the spaceport. He called and ran through concrete canyons. No answer anywhere. The sky overhead closed down.

Somewhere on the fringes of his mind he became aware of a vague threat. Somebody wanted to stop him. They didn't want him to find his sister. They wanted her to wander endlessly and forever in the deserted and crumbling city. But he couldn't permit that. He didn't want the responsibility, but who else was there? It was him or no one.

The threat became more tangible. There *were* other people out there, unfriendly people. They wanted to hurt him, to stop him. He had to work out a plan. If he wasn't careful they'd trap him.

There they were. Just a few blocks away. The breeze stiffened when he saw the first of them, and dust mixed with fog made all the air hazy. He could not make out their features, but they were all around him, moving in. He ran up an alley. If he could just get behind them.

But there were too many of them. Six, eleven, five, he didn't know the number, but it was too large. He stood at bay under a colonnaded portico, and they came at him from all sides, moving slowly through the blowing haze and mist. It was cold, and he shivered.

He had to get away. He had to find his sister. More than just her *life* was at stake. They were ringing him now, vague, indistinct figures, whose only discernabile feaures were threat and damnation.

"Stop," he called, but his voice was weak and thin. "You don't understand," he tried to say, but they would not listen, could not hear.

"I don't *want* to do it," he cried, but they just laughed at him evilly, and reached out clawing hands. He had no choice. He had to do it, though his heart cried within him. He told them his real name.

They were blocked. Their clutching hands had no strength. Their evil faces aroused no more fear. Their bodies were just thicknesses in the evaporating mists. He choked back a sob and looked up into the starry sky.

His sister. She was safe now. She was there, waiting for him. Exultation mingled with sadness in his heart, and he started out up the street to meet his sister.

He got the message two days later. Kelso wanted to meet him, but not at his home. The address was a service building in Beach Harbor. McCade took the beltways and made sure that no one was tailing him.

Even in a city like Loger, there had to be areas where goods were made, where machines were kept. Beach Harbor was the district, twenty-second class, where most of these were to be found. Highest-class district of the fifth and lowest order, it was also the largest district of Loger, and had the largest population. It sprawled in a great blotch around and to the south of the harbor which gave it its name and was filled with very busy people of all classes who had the responsibility of making sure that the city as a whole kept running.

The building McCade wanted would have looked good anywhere else. But here in the opulence and luxury of Loger, it was an eyesore—a great square vault of a building where the city's maintenance machines were stored. There was a constant if faint hum, and the first even slightly unpleasant smell McCade had ever noticed in his almost three months here. He circled the building twice, studying the layout of the surrounding landscape, the location and position of the neighboring buildings, the windows and doors and other access ways of the building itself. He did not trust Kelso and dared not just walk in cold. He wanted to be able to come out again.

When he was satisfied that he knew the outside of the building as well as he could, he went to the entrance Kelso had named and went in. He walked up a brightly lit corridor with many glass-paneled doors on either side and one solid wooden door at the end. This one he opened and stepped through onto a kind of balcony about three meters above the main floor of a large, high-ceilinged room, with stairs running down from either side of the balcony. The room itself was empty except for a table and two chairs near the far wall between two other doors. In one of the chairs sat a man. Kelso.

McCade took the right-hand stairs down from the balcony to the main floor and crossed it to the table. Kelso did not rise as he neared, but just sat there, smiling in a self-satisfied way.

"Sit down, McCade," Kelso said. "We have much to talk about."

"I had given you up as a hopeless case," McCade said, taking the empty chair.

"Really? That was hasty, McCade. I'm sorry if I inconvenienced you, but I'm sure you realize how much this means to me."

"Oh, I realize it, all right. I'm just sorry you don't show reciprocal understanding."

"You like big words, don't you, Eleventh McCade?"

"Certainly. I always have. If I ever say anything you don't understand, just say so and I'll be glad to explain."

"Very funny. For a man in your position, you're pretty cool."

"It doesn't pay to be any other way, Second Kelso. You should know that. Now what do you want to see me about?"

"The secret, McCade. The Planet Master secret. I want it."

"I had guessed as much."

"I mean to have it, McCade."

"Lots of luck."

"I went through all your papers back in Sands, such as there were. I found nothing. The files were empty. I guess you know that. What did you do with them all?"

"Destroyed them. I didn't need them any more, and I saw no reason why I should let you have the fruits of my labor. Put yourself in my position, Second Kelso. Wouldn't you have done the same?"

"Of course, but the thing that puzzles me is how you did it, how you managed to sneak in after the closure. You did kill that guard, didn't you?"

"How could I have, Kelso? I was on my way to Director Reddy's office. A man can't be in two places at once."

"Then how did you know when she was killed?"

"A bulletin came in when I was talking to Reddy. You can check up on that."

"I intend to. But first I want to talk to you about Planet Masters."

"Talk away."

"I want the secret, McCade."

"Like I said, lotsa luck."

"I mean to have it."

"Bully for you."

"You're going to give it to me, McCade."

"Do you really think so? Just like that? I've worked hard for that bit of information, and I mean to sell dear."

"So name your price."

"I already have. The key to the Scott chateau."

"And I already told you, no. Anything else, McCade, anything at all."

"Sorry, Kelso, but that's my price"

"I'm sorry too," Kelso said, and four men came out of the door behind McCade. He had just enough time to turn around, but not enough time to accelerate or hype his body, before something heavy hit him in the back of the head, knocking him from the chair. He fell to his hands and knees, and tried frantically to clear his head long enough so that he could charge up his neuromuscular system, but a kick in the side distracted him.

He looked up through bleary eyes and saw hands coming down for him. He struck out blindly and hit something, but he was hit harder, in the side of the head, and for a moment he went blind.

They were very professional. And very thorough. He didn't know what instruments they used and didn't care. He didn't bother to fight them, but spent what energy he could blocking the pain and keeping himself from getting sick. They worked him over for a long time, concentrating on his joints, which they beat repeatedly, and every now and then Kelso's voice would bellow in his ear, "The secret, tell me the secret."

He didn't know how long they worked on him. He was numb, from his own blocking, but he knew he was severely hurt. His mind floated in a vacancy almost as soothing as sleep, except for the anger he felt like a distant throb somewhere in the back of his fading consciousness. At last they stopped, and he felt his mouth being pried open and something liquid being poured down his throat. He didn't know what it was, because he was still blocking all incoming pain signals, but it had the effect of clearing his vision somewhat and waking him up a bit.

He was sitting in the chair again, supported on each side by one of Kelso's thugs. Kelso himself was somewhere else, but after a moment he came back from out of McCade's line of sight and sat in the other chair.

"You're a strong man, McCade," Kelso said. McCade didn't even try to answer.

"You took a lot of punishment," Kelso went on. "I can respect you for that, even though I think you're foolish to hold out so long. It won't do you any good, you know. Everybody has a breaking point."

"Not everybody," McCade mumbled, and was surprised that his speech was so clear. Evidently they hadn't hit him in the mouth.

"Yes," Kelso said, "everybody. Even you, McCade. You see, we've just begun. We haven't broken anything yet. We haven't cut anything off yet. We can keep on going, McCade, at slow intervals, until at last you're just a stump and a pain. But you'll talk long before then."

"Don't count on it," McCade said. He felt strangely at ease. "You can hurt me all you want, but pain won't get you anything. You can even kill me, but what good would that do you? It will all be lost then. I have the only copy of the rituals, and they're all in my mind.The original is gone. The secret exists only in my memory, Kelso, and you don't want to kill that."

"You're right, of course," Kelso said, "but you have no idea of the things that can be done to a man without killing him. After a little rest, I think we'll give you a sample."

"Go right ahead," McCade said, and now he felt himself grinning. "Do whatever you want. But I can outlast you, Kelso. There's nothing you can do that can make me tell you anything."

Kelso was frowning now. He didn't like the expression of McCade's face, or the calm assurance in his voice.

"You think not—" he started to say.

"I *know* not," McCade interrupted. "Listen to my heart." Kelso gestured, and one of his men put his ear against McCade's chest. He started, listened a moment longer, then stood up.

"It sounds like it's missing a few cogs," he said, his voice anxious.

"What do you mean?" Kelso snapped.

"It keeps on skipping. It's weak and there's a flutter. This guy's almost dead."

"God dammit," Kelso swore, his eyes wide and his mouth slack, "God dammit, the idiot's got a bum heart."

"Didn't used to," McCade said. "You must have done something to it."

"You idiots," Kelso shrieked at his men, "if this slob dies I'll see you all strung up!" He was panting, frantic.

"All right, McCade," he said at last in a dead voice. "You win. You can have the chateau. Write me out the formula."

"Sorry," McCade said, "I can't do that."

"Why not?"

"My hand won't work."

"Well, tell it to me then, and I'll write it down."

"Not on your life. Or mine. I'm not that kind of a fool, Kelso."

"But I tell you, I'll give you the key."

"Okay, for the sake of argument, let's pretend I believe you. But you must admit that, at the moment, I'm in no condition to look out for my own best interests or defend myself." Even as he spoke, a wave of blackness threatened to cover his mind and his head wobbled.

"Okay, okay," Kelso said, "I believe you. You're a sick man. Let's wait until you get better. But remember, we have a deal."

"Don't worry," McCade said thickly, "I won't forget." He felt himself slipping down toward unconsciousness and was only vaguely aware of being picked up and carried somewhere. A little later he felt himself being laid down on some hard surface, and then the waves of blackness rolled over him and he went under.

He had hazy impressions of people talking and then of being picked up again and placed on something softer. There was a sensation of movement which lasted for a while, and then it stopped. A little later light tried to force its way past his eyelids, and people were doing things to him. He was rolled over and the darkness came again.

He was aware only of the passage of time. He did not dream, and he did not hurt, but he could feel, inside himself, that there was much damage. It was healing, he knew, but there was a lot to be done. More time passed.

When he opened his eyes at last it was to see only a pale green ceiling, striped with light slanting in from windows on his left. He lay there motionless, collecting himself. His internal clock said four days had passed since the beating, and it was now early morning of the fifth day. Most of the damage he had suffered was healing well, but he was still weak, and had not the strength to even try and find out if he could move.

He heard a tapping at the window. He rolled his head toward it and saw Klooshkai outside on the sill. The bird squawked at him, but no sound came through the glass.

He twitched, the bird flew away, and McCade lapsed

back into semiconsciousness. A while later the door opened and a nurse entered. She came over to him, read the diagnostor above his head, then smiled down at him.

"Glad to see you coming around," she said. "How do you feel?"

"Under the circumstances, not bad."

"That's good. You took quite a beating. If it's any consolation to you, the Academy is investigating."

"Yes, that helps," he said and smiled feebly.

"If it hadn't been for that strong heart of yours," the nurse went on, "I don't think you'd have made it. But the doctors say you're the healthiest person they've ever had the pleasure to examine."

"Thank you," he said and smiled more broadly. The nurse smiled back, and left.

"You find the most bizarre ways of having fun," a throaty soprano said. McCade looked up in surprise and saw Klooshkai perched on a vase in the corner.

"How did you get in here?" he asked.

"It wasn't easy, but you can't keep a good bird down, as the saying goes. I'm glad to see you're still alive. Was it worth it?"

"I don't know yet. The deal has yet to be consumated."

"But you have what you were searching for."

"In theory, but Kelso is still in my way," he said, and he told the bird the situation, briefly.

"Are you sure you really want to do this?" Klooshkai asked when McCade had finished.

"I'd better be," McCade answered. "Don't think I haven't thought about this a lot."

"That you have, I know, but have you looked at all sides? Are you aware of all the possible consequences?"

"I think so. Why?"

"I'd just hate to see you go through all this mess, get your precious Book, and then find you didn't want it after all."

"I don't think that will happen," McCade said. He paused a moment. "Tell me," he said, "why should you care?"

"About what?"

"About whether I'm all right, whether I get the Book of Aradka, or what happens to me afterward."

"As to the first," the bird answered, "I care because you are one of the few humans who doesn't think of me as some kind of dumb animal. You talk to me, respect my intelligence. I'm grateful for that. Anybody who shows that much understanding is worth being concerned about.

"As to the second, I don't really care, except as it relates to the first. You're a unique person, Larson McCade. You do things nobody else would or could do. You see things that are invisible to other people. There's something in you that's worth saving. I don't know what your motives are or the real significance of what you're doing, but whatever it is, I hope you succeed, for your own sake if for no other.

"And as to what happens after, who can say? This world is on the edge of something. I've seen it coming for a long time. There are tensions in the city, and they can't be eased by more status hunting. And things are happening outside, too, if I can trust the newscasts from Phenolk P'talion. I don't understand what it all means. I'm just a bird with no hands, stranded on a world not my own, like you are. But I can think, Larson McCade, and I can see and hear, and something is happening. And you're in it."

"I work for myself, Klooshkai. I always have."

"I know, I know, but never in a vacuum. Well, I'm glad to see you'll be doing okay. I'd better get out of here before somebody finds me and uses me for shooting practice." He fluttered over to the door, clutched the knob with one claw, braced the other against the jamb, twisted, and pulled the door open.

"Be seeing you around," he said softly, then slipped through the door and was gone.

McCade lay back in the bed with a sigh. He hadn't been aware of sitting up. The bird intrigued him. Why should it care, in spite of what it had said? McCade had had considerable experience with non-human intelligent species. No one who did much traveling between the stars could avoid it. But he had never met a non-human with any kind of empathy for other than its own kind of people. It was not surprising. McCade couldn't feel for them, either. But Klooshkai was different. Were all the birds that way? Another useless speculation.

He dozed and was awakened when breakfast came. Afterward he slept some more, encouraging his body to grow back together. Lunch came and for the first time he was really hungry. He ate, then slept some more.When he woke again he thought it was supper, but it was Lupus and Finewalls.

"Well, well," Lupus said, "what have we here?"

"Looks like our friend's been playing with the big boys," Finewalls said.

"Pleasant company," McCade drawled. "What brings *you* here? Come to gloat?"

"Sort of," Lupus said. "We heard about your little 'accident' and just stopped by to see how bad off you were."

"We would have come sooner," Finewalls added, "but they wouldn't let you have visitors."

"Maybe I was just lucky," McCade said. "Can't think of anybody I'd like less to have gazing with disrespect on my poor unconscious body."

"Except maybe Kelso?" Lupus asked.

"Oh, he doesn't worry me. He wants me alive. Wish I could say the same for you two."

"Yeah, isn't that too bad? Well, Eleventh McCade, it seems your time has come. The front desk assured us you were in no shape to get up and move around, and we've come to take advantage of that fact."

"That's right," Finewalls said, smiling evilly. She took a long, thin dagger from her belt. "We're going to have some fun with you, Cadey old boy, and if that upsets old man Kelso, too bad for him."

"Think you can get away with it?" McCade asked. He was better off than the front desk knew, but to defend himself now would put a severe strain on his already depleted resources and would set him back quite a bit.

"Of course we'll get away with it," Lupus said, coming over and twitching the covers off McCade's naked body. "We came here to visit somebody else. We were never in your room at all." Finewalls reached for McCade's groin, and he summoned all his strength and went into overdrive. Reaching up, he grabbed Lupus's arm and flung him across the bed at Finewalls. Then he sprang up and before the two could disentangle themselves he stepped on Finewalls's back and, grabbing her hair, yanked. Her spine snapped. Lupus came up swinging, but McCade put his knee in the tough's solar plexus, then smashed him with the edge of his hand on the side of the neck.

He straightened up, shaking, and allowed his body to return to "normal."

He stood for a moment looking down at the two corpses, then staggered over to his bed. He fell into it and reached up with a shaking hand to press the button at its head. Almost at once a nurse came in, saw the bodies, and ran out again. She returned in a moment with two armed orderlies who bent over the crumpled forms while she came to McCade, straightened him out, and pulled the covers up over him again.

"They're both dead," one of the orderlies said.

"How did you do it?" the nurse asked, wonder and fear mingling in her face.

"Desperation," McCade gasped, and lost consciousness.

The door announced a caller, and McCade went to answer it personally. It was Arvin Saranof.

"Come in, First Saranof," he said. "Forgive the disorder, but I've not been myself lately."

"So I've heard," Saranof said. She came in, looked around the rather jumbled living room, removed a pile of books from a chair to the floor, and sat down. "How do you like Foxes?" she asked.

"Quite well, thank you. Closest thing on this world to the places I grew up in. A little wealthier, perhaps."

"I just came by to see how you were," Saranof went on. "Elex Norther mentioned some time ago that you might want my help in gaining status, but I don't think you really need me."

"Not if people keep on cooperating and give me the chances for defensive kills. It's not the way I'd prefer, but it is effective."

"To say the least. You started out at nineteen, and now you're a nine. Those two hoodlums in the hospital were just too much. I'm glad they gave you full credit."

"How could they else?" McCade asked. "It was obviously their assault, I was physically incapacitated. I'm just lucky to have survived."

"Luck had nothing to do with it. You know, I don't think I've heard of anyone gaining so much status in such a short time. Five classes in a lifetime is considered good. You've made ten classes in just over three months. You're a dangerous man, Larson."

"I wish my enemies realized it."

"But if they did," Saranof said dryly, "where would you gain your next class point?"

"Would you believe me if I told you I didn't care?"

"After what you've done so far? No, I would not. But it does occur to me that you are not, perhaps, very well equipped to take full advantage of your position. Usually, a person has time to adjust to his new class, learns the ways of it as he lives with it for a while, works his way up by slowly accumulating rank. But you have jumped too high too fast. You were not fully adjusted to your role as a nineteen. And as a nine you are a total loss. Why, you don't know the first thing about how to behave, what is expected of you. And you should move into a more suitable residence, in Riecheleaux, or Amaranth perhaps."

"Lots of higher classes live in Foxes."

"They do, but they do so with a thorough understanding of why they are here. But you, my young friend, know nothing about anything. You certainly don't need my help in gaining status, but you do need an education in what your status means. I'd like to see you become more familiar with your position in life. Will you let me help you?"

"Certainly, First Saranof. But I can't promise I'll be a good student."

"I know that. But you will try, won't you? All right then. I've come to take you to a show. The Studio is putting on an exhibit of some of their best works. The Studio is an important Brotherhood, in more ways than one."

"I appreciate that, First Saranof. When is the showing?"

"This afternoon. Will you come?"

"Good God, First Saranof, I'm hardly able to totter around the house. I only came home two days ago."

"Nonsense. You're in better health than I am. *I* know you're still recovering from your shock, but you're not the kind to play the invalid. It's a good show, and it's today only. Afterwards, they move everything over to a place in Red Dog."

"What will they do with it over there?"

"It's part of the Studio's contract with that space captain, Ben Toledo. He gets first pick of all the shows."

"So he's an art dealer. He never told me what his business was."

"Yes, he buys art from us and in return brings in microfilms, mostly journals and texts, I understand."

"So Seltique knows more about what's going on off world than it likes to admit. That's very interesting. What do the Sepratists think about this?"

"They don't like it much, I'm afraid, but they can't do anything about it. All the Brotherhoods, except possibly the Temple, support it."

"That's a hard coalition to beat. Well, all right, I don't suppose it will do me any harm. And I might pick up a little culture in the process."

She gave him time to change his clothes, suggesting that he wear his best but most subdued. After a few moments, he presented himself, she sighed in resignation, and they left.

Outside, beside the belt, was a long, low vehicle. A private car.

"So you're one of the lucky few," McCade said as they got in.

"It's a necessity of the job," Saranof explained. "I frequently have to transport a number of persons or objects, and a car is the only way to do it." The vehicle lifted up a few inches off the ground and, keeping to the grassy edge of the belt, started off.

"Where are we going?" McCade asked.

"Three Rivers, the fifth class. They won the competition for this year's show."

They drove on, chatting about inconsequentials. The car was fully automatic, of course, and needed no guidance, so they were free to relax and enjoy the ride.

The car purred into Three Rivers and stopped in front of a spired and glass-walled building surrounded by rolling lawns and small trees dense with fruit. McCade and Saranof left the car, which drove off to park itself somewhere, and went inside.

When he saw the first display, McCade understood why Toledo made the trip to Seltique and back. This was art of the highest quality, all of it. There were paintings in oils, watercolors, and fluorescents. Sculpture in steel, clay, bronze, stone, and plastic. There were mosaics, tiles, and pots of every form and color. He'd seen a few objects like these elsewhere, and knew that they brought fantastic prices. Toledo must be a very rich man, he thought. They spent two very pleasant hours going from exhibit to exhibit, and McCade felt a sense of envy that these people here should be able to produce such insipiring and moving pieces, while all he had produced so far was death.

"This is what Seltique is really all about," he said. "For this alone, your world has justified its existence."

"Why, thank you, Larson," Saranof said, surprised. "I didn't know you were an art fancier."

"I'm not. But you can't mistake the quality of this work."

"It's not much better than other shows have been."

"But then you're used to it. Out in the Cluster, this painting, or that sculpture, would be almost priceless."

"Really? I wasn't aware of that."

Derk Renseleau, the artist McCade had met at Saranof's party so long ago, was here with two of his sculptures, constructed of silver wires and iridescent crystal sheets. They were abstracts that caught the eyes and the mind and led the imagination into depths of fascination and wonder. Renseleau was one of the few artists with more than one piece represented.

One sculpture in particular fascinated him. It was a set piece, in translucent marble, of an old man in rags, worn out and exhausted after a hard life of physical labor, standing sadly over the body of a dead dog. It was only eighteen inches high, but each detail was perfectly wrought, and the artist's interpretation of sorrow over the loss of a loved pet was so well depicted that it completely avoided any sense of preciousness or sentimentality.

"This is excellent," McCade said softly. "Who did it?"

"Jon Dorn," Saranof said. "He's right over there." She gestured and McCade saw the shabby man he'd met in the gun shop in Emeraud.

"My God. You mean that oddball can carve something as fine as this?" He looked again at the figure of the old man and the dog. In spite of its deliberate emotionality, it worked.

"You like it?" a voice asked, and McCade looked up to see Dorn smiling hopefully at him.

"I do, very much."

"Jon Dorn," Saranof said, "is one of our finest sculptors." The artist grimaced, pleased in spite of himself.

"It brings me status," he said, "which I don't want. I've learned to limit myself to one piece a year."

"Why only one?" McCade asked.

"Each one gains him five rank points," Saranof answered. "He hates it, but he keeps on working."

"Artistic compulsion," McCade said, "but with reverse

penalties. Do you know, Jon, that out in the Cluster an artist must suffer starvation to keep working? Here you suffer status. It's ironic."

"It is, I guess," Dorn said. His face was haggard, and he did not look well.

"Does gaining status really hurt you so much?" McCade asked.

"Hard to believe, isn't it?" Dorn answered with a dry chuckle. "But yes, it does. Nobody here understands, McCade, but maybe you would. I do *not* want status. It's repellent to me. But I have to work; my art is my life, and it does no good to hide it in cellars. So no matter how hard I try to keep low, I'm continually raised to status levels I find ever more uncomfortable, ever more sickening."

"And no way out of the dilemma," Saranof said. "Well, Larson, if you'll excuse me, I see some people I really should talk to." She smiled at him and Dorn and moved off into the crowd. McCade saw her approach a small fat man, and then turned back to Dorn.

"It's too bad people just don't leave you alone," he said.

"They can't bother me forever," Dorn answered, and there was something in his voice that made McCade think of suicide.

"Come now," he said, "you have too much talent. You can't let it go to waste."

"Can't I?"

"No. It drives you to create, even though recognition hurts. Your art is far more important than your loathing of status. You know that. *I* know that. And millions of people on thousands of other worlds know that."

"Do you really think so?" Dorn asked dubiously, almost childishly.

"Yes. I do. You have the ability to perceive and understand emotion, and to capture it in a bit of stone. It's a rare and beautiful gift." He touched the small statue gently. "Here," he said, "we have the representation of an emotion I didn't think was felt on Seltique."

"You recognized it then? I wasn't sure—that is, I had no model for that, of course, so I had no way of knowing whether I was actually expressing the ideas I had. Nobody I know has ever expressed an emotion like that"—he gestured at the statue—"and it took me seven tries before I got it down. Some of those early models were really grotesque. I'm still not convinced this is right, but it's as close as I can come. I've just been trying to explain to these people here why the old man is so sad, and I'm afraid I'm not succeeding too well, since I don't really understand it myself. It's just something I feel."

"And they can't see it. It's a condemnation. It struck me forcibly. You may not understand what you feel, but your art expresses your feelings accurately."

"You impress me, Ninth McCade," Dorn said. "Are you unique, or are there other offworlders who can appreciate what I'm trying to say?"

"There are," McCade said. "Many. Believe me, there are millions."

"I don't know if I dare believe you. I've spent my whole life . . . I see there are certain points on which we cannot agree"—he touched McCade's badges of rank—"but perhaps you'd spare me a few moments, and talk with me about—well—things."

"I'd be glad to. I'd like to find some other topic than one's status to discuss."

"It makes me sick," Dorn agreed. "Literally and physically. I was not made to deal with that kind of thing. Shall we go outside?"

"Won't they miss you in here?"

"Not at all."

They left the building and wet out into a park that was adjoining. There they sat and for several hours discussed the significance of emotion and the artistic problems and principles of capturing it. McCade was way over his head most of the time, but Dorn understood him, however imprecisely he expressed himself.

At last the artist said he had to go.

"I have business elsewhere," he explained. "Some clod's demanding I fight him. And I must. He will die, I'll gain another point, and even as I live, I shall betray my own beliefs. But that is the trap I am caught in. But I want to thank you, Ninth McCade. You have given me more encouragement in these few hours than I have received for many long years. Maybe I shall not give up the fight just yet."

"Please don't," McCade said, truly sincere. "No matter what else happens, I shall look forward to seeing your next piece."

Dorn just nodded sadly, as sadly as his marble old man, and turned and walked away.

"Why can't that be cherished?" McCade asked the air.

"Because *all* men are fools," a throaty soprano said, and Klooshkai flapped down to settle on his shoulder.

"Hello, Klooshkai. You do get around."

"That's what birds are for. But I come bearing tidings, O great warrior. Thine enemy awaits thee, at that place from whence thou wast carried away, not so long since."

"He does? And how do you know?"

"A little man told me," the bird cackled, and flapped off into the sky.

At night the service building, unlike most of the rest of the city, was dark. As human beings seldom had any reason for being there, very little provision was made for their comfort. On the few occasions when maintenance personnel did have to visit, light and air conditioning was switched on in whatever section was desired at the front offices. At night, in the long hallways and rooms with their muttering machines the air was dead still, and the light level just enough so that a misplaced person wandering through would realize that he wasn't blind.

But that was enough for McCade. Besides, it made a big

impression on people when one entered a room out of what was, to them, absolute darkness.

He stood now in the door on the balcony, totally invisible in the black, looking into the room at the table and chairs near the far wall, with the one tiny but brilliant light making a small circle of white in the surrounding darkness. Kelso, too, had a sense of the dramatic and knew how to set a stage.

McCade smiled. One hand smoothed down his curly hair. The other fingered the loaded gun in his pocket. He did not want to kill Kelso, but he would have no compunction about gunning down any of his thugs that so much as happened to show a face.

The first faint strains of a new song drifted through the echoing chambers of his mind. It was rhythmic, like the pulse, and filled with major and seventh chords that, to his inner ear at least, made it forceful and heavy. The smile stayed on his face as he listened to this newest melody. It froze there, a soft, small, cynical smile, as of one who has seen and knows the perfidy he is about to approach, the futility of any hope for success. Yet the music played, distant and not yet completely formed, but his feet wanted to move to it. Too bad he wasn't a composer.

Kelso fidgeted nervously in his circle of light. Obviously he was expecting to see the reflection of a flash coming up the hall and to hear the sound of footfalls. It was ten minutes past the appointed meeting time, according to the message that had been placed on McCade's door in Foxes. But McCade was not late. He had been there for fifteen minutes, watching, letting the man wait, taking the psychological advantage that Kelso had hoped to get.

Kelso fidgeted again. "McCade?" he called out, his voice steady. "Are you there?"

"I'm here, Kelso," McCade answered, just loudly enough to be heard.

"Well, why didn't you say so? Come on down and we'll talk."

"I didn't like our last conversation," McCade said. "You have bad manners."

"Look, McCade, I'm sorry about that, but you have to realize my position."

"Everybody does, Kelso. Do you ever give a thought for anybody else? How about *my* position, for instance?" Soundlessly, invisibly, he descended from the balcony and moved to one side of the room. Kelso kept staring into the darkness at the door on the balcony.

"Okay," Kelso said. "I admit that your situation and mine are about the same. But we have things to discuss. Come down here where I can see you."

"You could see me any time you want," McCade said, and Kelso's head snapped around, "if you hadn't tried to be so melodramatic. This is your setup, not mine." He crossed the room to the other side, as silently as before.

"McCade," Kelso said, peering futilely through the black, "cut this nonsense. We don't have time for games. We made a deal, remember?"

"I remember," McCade said, and Kelso jumped. His nerves were getting the better of him. "But it hardly seems that the situation is at all equitable."

"What do you mean? Dammit, man, what are you doing out there?"

McCade arced toward the table, so that he approached it from the direction of the door. Kelso saw him when he was about four meters away, and jumped again.

"The price has gone up," McCade said, stopping just outside the circle of light from Kelso's lamp.

"Dammit, McCade, we made a deal. I give you the key to the Scott chateau, and you give me the Planet Master formula." He pulled himself together. Now that he could see his adversary, even though McCade stayed out of the light, he was no longer jittery.

"That deal," McCade said, "was made in good faith. But you wanted the formula for nothing. You took advantage of me, Kelso, and the price has gone up accordingly."

"So you got a few lumps—"

"And eight days in the hospital. I nearly died, Kelso. To

say nothing of my pride. You humiliated me. Do you expect me to let that just pass?"

"Look, McCade, I said I was sorry."

"Big deal. It's like I said. Do you want to talk terms, or shall I go home?"

"All right, McCade, tell me what you want."

"For the formula, the key to the chateau, as before. For the damage to my body and dignity, status points to make me second class, and the credit to go with it."

"Status points? What do you think I am?"

"A man who has more power and influence than half the first class put together."

Hit with his own words, Kelso sat stunned. McCade stepped forward until just his feet were in the circle of light on the floor. He heard a movement from the door to Kelso's left and, without hesitation, he shot. The flash of the gun showed just one man. A second later the sound of his falling body came out of the darkness.

The song in McCade's head was stronger now, more fully instrumented. But his body did not yield to its tempting rhythms.

"Very foolish," he said. "But you're no fool, Kelso. That's my role. You're just greedy. You're going to have to learn that that kind of behavior doesn't pay."

"Look who's talking about being greedy," Kelso cried. Beads of perspiration were forming on his forehead. "You can't just hand out status points like candy. Second class, man? I don't have that kind of influence. The credit, sure, I can get you all the credit you want, more than you could spend in a lifetime. But status is something that's beyond my ability to control. Why, if I could do that for you, I would have made myself first class long ago."

"Bullshit, Kelso. You like being second class. It gives you an advantage. It makes you look honest. And besides, you hate the first class. You wouldn't want to be associated with them. You can do it, Kelso. You just don't want the formula badly enough."

Kelso muttered an inarticulate oath.

"You're going too far, McCade," he said. "I warn you, if you push me, you'll get hurt."

"Not again, Kelso. Once was enough. You ever hear of pyroveldine? It's a poison, a very potent and fast-acting one. Taken internally, it penetrates the mucous membranes within a fraction of a second. It attacks the nervous system, destroying all the synapses. A complete short circuit."

"Yes, yes, McCade, I know all about it. Are you threatening me?"

"I have a capsule, Kelso. I'm prepared to bite it."

"My God, man, but the secret, the formula, if you kill yourself it will be lost forever."

"Strange how long it took for you to figure that out."

"But you can't be serious. You wouldn't kill yourself, McCade. It wouldn't be worth it."

McCade stepped forward into the light so that Kelso could see his face. The gun in his hand was pointed not at Kelso but at the door behind the big man. He smiled softly at his enemy, a gentle smile of absolute self-assurance.

"Don't you ever try to guess," he said softly, "what anything would be worth to me. My values are not the point under discussion. It's the price of the formula we are talking about, and therefore *your* values that we must learn. It is what it's worth to you that we have to determine. Because I hold a pat hand, Kelso. It's the key or death for me, and it's getting to the point where I'm beginning not to care which. A little more, and I might just die, just to spite you, Kelso. Think about that for a moment."

It was obvious that Kelso didn't like the idea. His jaw worked, his face went alternately red and white, and his hands clutched the arms of the chair so tightly that they cracked.

"Damn you," he croaked. "I'll see you burn for this. All right, McCade, you win. You can have the chateau, *and* the status and credit. Just write out that formula."

"Fair trade, Kelso. I write the formula when I see the key and the status points on that table. Not before."

"It will take time. Maybe two weeks."

"I can wait. Can you?"

"Get out of here, McCade," Kelso rasped. "I'll let you know. You just take real good care of yourself. Real good care."

McCade stepped backward slowly, keeping his eyes on Kelso and the gun on the door until he was completely enveloped in darkness again. Then, as silent as the darkness itself, he turned and left the room and the building. In his head the music thumped; syncopated and vibrant, it ran along the nerves of his body and made his face into a clown's mask of triumph. He stepped onto the beltway with a dancing motion and rode away through the brightly lit city, his whole body expressive of the emotion he was feeling.

He saw the two men get on the belt behind him. They mingled with the other people, but he knew they were there. And he didn't care. They could follow him all they wanted. They dared not touch him, and he wasn't going anyplace special.

He sang as he rode the beltway south and west into the district of Hadoth. The people he passed looked at him and smiled. He was so obviously happy, so full of good spirits that everybody around him became infected.

He danced away through Hadoth, around Scott's Woods, and into Aragon. His two tails followed, and he led them through the brightest parts of the district.

"Larson," someone said, and he turned. The music died in his head, and his feet stopped dancing. The smile left his face, and he rode on stiff and straight and dead inside.

"What's the matter, Larson?" Valyn Dixon asked. "Aren't you glad to see me?"

He looked over his shoulder at the two men following him, and even at that distance, he could see the slow smiles sprcad.

"I never wanted to see you less in my life," McCade said, turning again to Valyn. He felt a cold, soggy sinking in his stomach and a tightness across his chest, though all that he let show was a calm and cool severity.

"But you were so happy a moment ago," she said, "and it's been so long. I heard about that horrible beating you got, and I wanted to come to see you. What's wrong, Larson? Do you hate me that much? What have I done?"

"I don't hate you," he said. His voice was flat. "Quite the opposite, in fact. But I warned you, Valyn. I told you to stay away from me. When you saw me just now, you should have just gone by."

"But why? What harm could it possibly do?"

"Look behind me. Do you see those two men? The ones who are grinning? They're Kelso's men. They're following me. They were hoping that I'd do something, or meet someone, so that Kelso could get a lever on me, and not have to hold up his end of the bargain."

She turned and looked, and her expression became worried. "You made a bargain with Kelso?" she asked.

"I have," he said, and told her briefly. They rode on for a while in silence.

"So what do I do now, Valyn?" he asked. "He didn't know about you before. Now he does, and his problem is solved. He won't have to get me the status and credit. I don't care about that; it was just a punitive demand, to hurt him like he hurt me. He won't even have to give me the key to the chateau. All he has to do is pick you up, call me in, and make a new deal—your life for the Planet Master formula."

"Larson, I'm sorry. I didn't know."

"That doesn't help much, does it?" They were silent a while longer. The belt took them through Aragon, south into Red Dog.

"What do I do, Valyn?" he asked.

"I—I don't know." She was scared now. She knew Kelso's reputation well enough.

"I have only two choices," McCade said. "I can make the trade. I can give Kelso the formula in exchange for your life. I can give up my only hold over him and with it everything I've worked for these last few months, everything I've wanted for as long as I can remember. I can save you, and throw away all my work, my pain, forget my future, cancel everything. It's my life, more than my life that's at stake. My sanity, my self-respect. Everything I've ever done has been with the idea of one day getting the Book of Aradka. I can throw that all away."

"Or . . ."

"Or I can let him kill you." And that was that. "What do I do, Valyn?" But she had no answer.

"Put yourself in my place," he said, "if you can. Think about it. What would you do, save my life or yours and everything your life had ever been and ever hoped to be?"

Still she had no answer, and he could see in the lights of the spaceport as they passed that tears were rolling down her cheeks.

"You see how it is?" he asked, and his heart broke. He didn't want to do this. Hadn't he been looking for a girl like Valyn, too, all his life? But he hardened himself, shut all sense and feeling from his mind, and as he spoke, his voice was as calm and as even as if he were talking about the city or the night.

"I'm stuck, Valyn," he said. "I would have come to you when it was all over. If I had lived. But that's all changed now, and nothing can mend it. Whatever I do, my life will be broken. Why couldn't you just have walked away and waited a while longer?"

But she was openly crying now, and he couldn't help himself. He put his arm around her, pulled her to his side, and held her as the belt whisked them—and the two very happy men behind them—through Red Dog, across a corner of Warwick, and into Riverside.

"There is one other alternative," he said hesitantly. "I don't know if it will work. In fact I'm sure it won't. But it's worth trying, I think. There is danger if Kelso or his men ever get their hands on you. If we can keep them from getting to you, if we can keep you out of his reach, then I won't have that decision to make. But I can think of only one way to do that.

"You'll have to stay with me. I don't know if I can protect

you or not, but I can try. If you stay with me, and never leave my sight for a moment, they'll have a hard time getting to you. You know what I can do if I have to."

"But I have responsibilities," she said, "and plans."

"You won't be able to fulfill them in any event," McCade answered. "The minute you leave me, those men will move in and take you away. Can you see that?"

"Yes."

"Then what choice have we? You don't want me to make that decision, do you? I surely don't want to make it. It will hamper everything severely, to have to keep my eye on you, but at least I won't have lost the whole gamble."

"Okay," she said. Her voice was strained, and her face was not in the least pretty now. She was showing her fear and fatigue and bitter regret. His heart went out to her, but what else could he do? Inside, he was frozen. He dared not contemplate the future, not yet. To be so close, to have the key to his life tickling the palm of his hand, and then to have it snatched away . . .

They rode on in silence, and gradually the beltways swung them east, then north, and at last they were in Foxes, heading for his temporary home. He wished that they were going there under any other circumstances.

A sweetish odor began to wake him up, and he regained just enough consciousness to see, in the darkened bedroom, four men with gas masks, coming toward him and Valyn. He tried to get up, but he couldn't move. His whole body was paralyzed, and he could only watch as one of the men ripped the covers off the bed.

Valyn was bound first, wrapped in a sheet and then tied. He didn't know if she was awake or not. Her body was so limp that she might have been dead.

Then they turned to him and treated him the same way. The four men carried him and Valyn out of the house and put them into the back of a private vehicle. When they were all inside, the vehicle lifted up and sped off down the margin of the beltway. It was not yet morning.

Kelso had moved fast. It was less than three hours since they had come in from their long ride around Loger. Somehow, in that time, Kelso had been able to get the paralyzing gas and set up the whole stunt. As a kidnapping, it was perfect, and McCade hadn't had the chance to defend himself, let alone Valyn.

The car rode silently through the city. From where he lay, McCade could not see where they were going, what districts they were passing through—not that it really mattered, he thought. The drive took a lot longer than it should have to have taken them to any part of the city, so he supposed that they were just driving around to either pass time or get him lost.

The drug had begun to wear off when the car finally floated into an enclosed area, but he made himself stay limp when they pulled him from the car and carried him from the garage through a door, down a short flight of steps, and into a room half underground. But if they had hoped that he wouldn't know where he was, they had hoped in vain. He had been in this room before. It was the interrogation room in Kelso's house.

They sat Valyn down on a chair against a wall, and McCade in another a few feet from her. Across the room from him were two other doors, and in the middle the table and two chairs Kelso seemed to like to use so much. The four men went through one of the two doors and a moment later Kelso came out the other. He sat down at the table and gazed at his two prisoners for a long time in complete satisfaction.

"Well, McCade," he said at last. "We meet again. Only now, I think, we will finally get this thing taken care of. It's been too long unresolved, McCade. I can't wait any more. I know you're awake and can understand me. You can probably even move a little bit by now. Perhaps even speak. Isn't that so?"

"That's so," McCade said, making his voice thicker than it had to be. Inside, he was tuning his body, making his blood work to collect the gas from his system, making his liver filter it out as fast as it could. He was halfway to normal, but it wouldn't do to let Kelso know that.

"Now, then," Kelso said. "I suggest we get down to business. Very convenient of you to provide me with just the tool I needed, wouldn't you say? I don't suppose you're very enthusiastic about it, however. Kind of blows your whole position, doesn't it?"

"We don't know that yet," McCade said.

"Oh, but we do. I have you now, McCade, make no mistake. I dictate terms, you listen."

"That doesn't mean I have to accept your terms."

Kelso got up from the table, came over to McCade, and smashed him across the face. Then he hesitated. "Oh, I'm sorry," he said mockingly. "I'd forgotten that kind of thing doesn't bother you." Then he went over to Valyn and gave her a resounding slap. "But that does, perhaps," he said. McCade said nothing.

"It's all very simple," Kelso said, going back to his chair and making himself comfortable. "Since you value your own body and life so little, we'll just have to start bargaining all over again with something that means a little more to you. You understand? Now, there will, obviously, be no increase in status for you, no extensive credit. Neither will there be any key to any chateau, not Scott's chateau, not Billy Sereg's house, not anything. There will be just one thing—this girl's life. I wish I had known about her sooner. It would have made things so much simpler. Don't you agree?"

Still, McCade kept his silence. His body was almost completely free of the drug now, and he twitched experimentally, to see if he could loosen his bonds, but there was no give, no slack. He was held tight and could not break the cords.

"Work away," Kelso said. "Struggle all you want. I don't think it will do you any good. I'll still have my way.

"Now here is what's going to happen. And believe me, it *will* happen. You are going to dictate to me the full text of the Planet Master formula. Just to make sure, you will dictate it twice. I have a recorder, and I will take it all down. Then I will compare the two recordings, word for word. I'll know if you've left anything out. I can tell if you change anything around. And then, when I'm sure that I have the formula, complete and accurate, I will let you and your girl friend go. But not before then."

"And if I don't give you the formula?" McCade asked. His brain was pounding. He had to think of some way out of this. He couldn't give Kelso the formula. Nor could he let him kill Valyn. He wished he did have a capsule of pyroveldine he could bite. Then it would be all over, and Kelso be damned. But no such luck. He had to do something. Or else he would be forced to make the choice. And much as he disliked it, he knew what that choice would be.

"If you don't give me the formula," Kelso said slowly and flatly, "I will have the young lady taken into the other room and shot."

"You wouldn't dare," Valyn hissed, her voice thin with shock.

"Awake, my dear? How charming. And why wouldn't I dare?"

"How would you explain the body? Murder is a crime, Kelso. They'd get you."

"No they wouldn't. I have already arranged for the necessity. I have another gentleman, somewhere else, who will conveniently be accused of the deed. And he won't be able to deny it. In the course of his doing away with you, he shall be killed himself. No problems, no questions. But I do not anticipate having to make use of this other man. I'm sure Mr. McCade will not force my hand. I feel he thinks too much of you to let you die."

"Don't be too sure," McCade said.

"Oh, come now, McCade, what is more important, a silly book or a person's life?"

"You answer that, Kelso."

"Why, a life, of course, is much more important than any book, however valuable, however much money it might be worth."

"More important than a formula, by any chance?"

"By no chance, McCade."

"So you threaten to kill an innocent girl, just to become Planet Master. I don't think you really understand the system of values you pretend to be using. One life more or less won't deter me from the Book of Aradka. One life? Why, Kelso, I've already killed fourteen to get that Book. Now what do you think?"

"I think you're insane."

"I know you are. You want to play hard, Kelso. That's a game I've been playing all my life."

"You're a fool, McCade."

"That I am, and like the fool I step off the cliff with the dog-tiger at my heels, and yet I always survive."

"Larson," Valyn said. He looked at her. Her face was white and drawn, her eyes wide and red, her mouth slack.

"I'm sorry, Valyn," he said, and wanted to scream, to cry out, but he kept himself icy.

"I know," she said. "It's my fault. You'll beat him, Larson. I know you will."

He could not answer. He felt his heart thudding. He wanted to say something, anything, but no words came. He tried to think, to come up with some plan, some delaying tactic, but the ice around his brain wouldn't let him. He shuddered. She saw it, knew what it meant, and tried to smile at him.

"Come on, McCade," Kelso said. "Make up your mind. I don't have all day."

"I told you my mind," McCade said.

"Very well, then." Kelso's face was grim. Things weren't going his way after all. He pressed a button on the side of the table, and two of his thugs came in from the back room.

"Take her out," he said, "and kill her when I ring."

The two men came over to Valyn, picked her up roughly, and dragged her toward the door. She did not struggle. She did not beg. She did not look back. They took her through the door and out of sight, but they left the door open.

"This is it, McCade," Kelso said.

He was frozen. He thought about the Book of Aradka, his lifelong quest, his dream of absolute independence. He thought about Valyn, of returning to his family, of trying somehow to live with himself if she died—or if he failed.

But after all, didn't she represent the second most important quest in his life? And if he gave Kelso the formula, all was not over. It would take longer, it would be harder, but—

A bell rang, a shot thundered, a choking gasp, a thud. It was too late.

Outwardly he retained his calm, but inwardly he raged and screamed and cried and clutched at a memory and a wish, and for a moment his mind was black with madness. Slowly, the agony receded, and he regained control of himself. His voice was as steady as a glacier when he spoke, and as hard and emotionless and cold.

"A little hasty, there," he said. "You almost had me, Kelso. Just three seconds more, and you would have won. Too bad."

Kelso's face went white, and McCade could hear his teeth grating.

"And what are you going to do now, Kelso?" McCade asked. His blood was pounding in his ears like a drum, and he wanted to vomit. "You used your lever, but it broke. What now?"

"I can't believe you," Kelso hissed. The corners of his mouth were flecked with foam. "You can't be real. You sit there trussed up like a pig, your lover's just been shot, and you don't give a damn."

"Oh, I give a damn, all right, quite a lot of them. But not for your satisfaction, Kelso. Shall we begin negotiations again?"

"I'll eat you, McCade, I'll roast you, so help me God I'll have you strung out all over the city, I'll—"

"Nasty, nasty," McCade interrupted. "Mustn't lose your temper. It's bad for your health."

"Damn, damn, damn," Kelso swore. "All right, you bloody bastard. All right. What do you want?"

"Untie me, Kelso. And bring me some clothes."

His hands shaking, his teeth clenched and bared, his eyes hot points, Kelso touched the button on the table a third time. One man came from the back room, looked inquiringly at his boss, and saw that things were not right.

"Untie him," Kelso grated. "Bring him some clothes."

The man was surprised and looked worried, but he left the room and came back a moment later with some of McCade's own things.

McCade stood from the chair, flung the wrapping sheet from him, and without modesty or embarrassment dressed slowly, precisely, as he always did. But in his head, the Death and Damnation March from Sorenko's *Hellfire* suite throbbed through his brain. When he was fully dressed, he kicked the cords from near his feet, and sat down again. On his mouth was a small smile. His eyelids drooped slightly, and he sat in a relaxed slouch.

"Let's go through it again," he said softly. His voice, like winter wind off a glacier, cut through the air. "You know what I want, Kelso."

"You'll get it," the man said. The veins in his head stuck out, and a pulse beat irregularly in his throat. "The key, the status, the credit. It's all yours."

"I'm sorry to say, however," McCade said, "that the price has gone up again." Kelso just gaped.

"It's your own fault," McCade went on. "At the beginning, it was so cheap. The formula for the Planet Master, in exchange for a thing you didn't even want. But you were greedy, Kelso. You tried to grab without fulfilling your end of the bargain. You jacked up the price on yourself, but that wasn't enough. You didn't learn, and you did it again. The girl is going to cost you, Kelso. She's going to cost you a lot."

But Kelso's eyes were glazed. He sat limply in his chair, not seeing, not hearing.

"The formula, Kelso," McCade said. "Don't you want the formula?"

"Yes," Kelso said weakly.

"Are you willing to pay for it this time?"

"Yes," Kelso said again. "What do you want?"

"Why the rush, Kelso? Surely another day won't matter to you." The man looked up blankly at him. "I mean," McCade went on, "I'm going to have to think about this for a little while now, aren't I? You don't think I came here prepared with a handy price list? I must think about it, Kelso, and then I'll let you know. Tomorrow, Kelso."

"Whatever you say," Kelso whispered.

McCade stood there a moment longer, then turned and left the room, the garage, and the house. As he rode the beltway back to Foxes, his eyes streamed, and the dirge in his brain thundered on and on and on . . .

Without quite realizing how he got there he found himself walking into his house in Foxes. He felt exhausted, though a check on the time told him it had been only an hour since he'd left Kelso's place. His head was tight, as if stuffed with soggy cotton and then strapped with wire. His steps were unsteady, and his hands shook.

He had never suffered in this way before. He had always been able to control himself, every aspect of his body and his mind. That was what his long years of biotraining were all about.

But even the best training in the Samosar Cluster—or even the Orion Limb—cannot anticipate every trauma. He had been so close, so close to losing his quest, to saving Valyn. And the psychic shock was workng on him, unsettling him, tearing away at the foundations of his stability.

He went from room to room, looking for something.

He couldn't find it. He wasn't sure what it was. He seemed to be lost in a maze of corridors and stairs that narrowed on him, and pressed him in.

He went to the kitchen, but he wasn't hungry. The thought of food nauseated him. But there was something, somewhere. He had to find it. He couldn't remember what it was. He wished he could think.

Valyn was out there somewhere, her spirit if not her body. She had gone to her doom; she had accepted her fate. Had she loved him that much, then? The thought of it agonized him, but there was no going back up that road. The past was done, and only the empty future remained.

He stood by the bed, with its covers on the floor and its missing sheets. What he wanted was not here. There was only sorrow and grief, and he had enough of that to last him the rest of his life.

The walls of the corridors pressed in and closed behind him. He could only go forward. Something awaited him ahead. Something tried to tell him what it was, but he could not understand, could not hear.

Her death must not be allowed to go in vain. In this city where taking a life was the way one gained status, this one life, at least, would count for more. He could not let her down. He had to be as great as she. But there was something *he had to do*. What was it? Where was it? It wasn't in the library. Only gibberish there, no sense. He felt himself panting, openmouthed, and he tried to regain control of himself. He had come here for a purpose, a reason. But something in the back of his head whispered, "the only thing to fear is a pack of fools." Now what in hell did *that* mean?

He wandered into the living room again, and began to become aware of his surroundings. He was home. He had come here with a purpose. Because he was going to get the key to the Scott chateau from Kelso, and he was going to get the Book of Aradka, and he was going to take it and with it he was going to open up Seltique and—

"No!" he cried, and the vision faded. What had it been

all about anyway? He was in his study now, standing before his desk. Without thinking, his hand opened a drawer, and took out the phial of sorbil anthrocain. Clutching it tightly, he went to a little room at the back of the house. It was a store room, and he had looked in it only idly once before. But there, on a shelf, was a little gun. It worked on compressed air and shot little tufted needles. It was only a toy for target practice. Its maximum range was only twenty meters. But the clip held almost a hundred of the little needles. He disengaged the clip, and dipped the tip of each needle into the phial. Then he put the gun back together, made sure its air cartridge was fully charged, slipped it into his pocket, and left the house.

His mind was clear again. He knew exactly what he was going to do. No songs echoed in the hollow of his skull. Only one crystal clear, cold thought. The Book of Aradka.

He rode the tube to Whitefriar, and the belt to Kelso's house. Once, when a first class confronted him, he shot, and the woman crumpled in a heap. The gun made no sound. He knelt over her body. She seemed to be dead, but he could detect the faintest electrofield still radiating from her brain and nervous system. She would recover in two hours, to wonder what had happened. He left her where she lay and went on.

He entered the grounds around Kelso's house and moved quickly and cautiously over the lawns, avoiding all the alarms and booby traps. He worked his way around to the wing where the interrogation room was and bent low to look in the windows.

The room was empty. The table and the chairs still stood where they had been, the sheet and ropes that had bound him still lay on the floor. He moved to the windows of the room where Valyn had been taken, and looked in.

She lay there, on a cot. But she was dressed now, and he could see her breathing. She was still alive. A thrill shot through him, but another, colder thought followed hard after, and he made himself stay calm. He touched the window. He opened it. Silently, he squirmed through and dropped to the floor just two meters from where she lay.

She opened her eyes, looked up at him in surprise, and started to rise. He held out his hand and stopped her.

"I made it this far," he said, "and I'll make it the rest of the way. You said I'd win, and I will."

"They told me you'd killed yourself," she said wonderingly.

"Did they? Well, let's prove them liars, shall we? Will you come with me?"

"Yes, I will."

"Then let's go. Kelso still has the key. But not for long."

They left the interrogation room and went into the house proper. Quickly McCade led her through rooms, halls, corridors, into the main wing. On the second floor was Kelso's study.

As they climbed the stairs a woman came out of a room behind them. McCade shot once, and she fell. Valyn stifled a scream.

"It's only a sleeper," McCade whispered. "She'll wake in two hours." Valyn looked at him with large eyes. "Really," he added, then went on up the stairs.

One of Kelso's thugs was lounging in the hall, and McCade dropped him. They moved on down the hall to the door McCade wanted and went through. Two more bodyguards sat there, and McCade fired twice. The men slumped in their chairs with only the slightest rustle. Silently, like a whisper of a wish, McCade left Valyn at the outer door and crossed the anteroom to the door of Kelso's study. He put his hand to the latch and cautiously, so cautiously, eased the door open.

Kelso sat at his desk, his back to the door, sorting through some papers, riffling his drawers, muttering to himself. McCade sharpened his ears and listened closely.

Kelso was complaining about all the trouble he'd gone to to get the status bonds and credit checks. He rambled on about what he wanted to do to McCade. He fretted over what else McCade was going to ask of him. He planned his revenge when he finally became Planet Master. And something else, too soft for even McCade to hear.

Then he got up from his desk, went to a picture on the wall, pushed it aside, and opened the safe revealed there. He took out a tray of flashing jewelry, then pressed his thumb into a depression in the floor of the safe. There was the softest of snicks, and a panel below the safe fell open. Behind it was a little aperture, and inside was—

The key. McCade shot. Kelso dropped, and McCade ran into the room. He reached into the sub-safe and took out the key. It was a flat rod, square in section, about twenty centimeters long. It iridesced slightly.

He turned then to the desk and grabbed up the status bonds and credit checks. He didn't need these any more, not if he had the key, but he stuffed them in his pocket anyway.

"I was going to take your life in exchange for Valyn's," he said to the unconscious body, "but I don't have to do that any more. Instead, I'll just keep the Planet Master formula."

He looked up and saw Valyn standing tensely in the doorway.

"He'll be all right," he said. "Believe me, he's okay."

"I believe you," she said. "It's just . . ."

"I know. It's all right. But we're not at the end of this yet. Not quite. I still have to unlock the chateau, turn off the stasis field on the house, and get the Book of Aradka."

"May I come with you?"

"Yes," he said gently, then smiled. A happy little tune began to wriggle in the back of his brain. "By all means," he said, "please come."

ANALEPSIS

ANALEPSIS

It was not very far from Kelso's house to Scott's Woods to the southwest. Only an angle of Westbridge lay between, so they took the beltways. Valyn was very subdued as they rode away from Kelso's house. "It's been a long fight for you, hasn't it?" she said. "Very long," he answered. "I can't remember when it started. Something my great-grandfather told me when I was a child, I think. He had lots of stories, and some of them were about the Book of Aradka. Ever since I could remember I've wanted it, and as I grew up I learned more about it. I began to appreciate what it really was, as much as any person could. Nobody knows what the Book *really* is. That it was a tool of the Aradka is certain, and that, at one time at least, it was a very powerful tool, is also known. But its purposes or functions are a complete mystery. Though it was held by the Core, it was never subjected to any examination that I ever knew of. But even if it is only one hundred sixteen pieces of dead metal, it's a phenomenal artifact, the only remaining one of a species of beings about which we know nothing except that at one time they populated the galaxy, and then went away."

"And it will be yours now," Valyn said.

"Yes, Ninth Kelso," McCade said. "It will." She looked at him, not really very surprised.

"When did you find out?" she asked.

"When I saw you alive in the interrogation room. At first I exulted. He hadn't killed you after all. Then I wondered why. A casual life meant nothing to Kelso. What made you so different, so special that he would go through with that elaborate hoax? I thought about the difference in your ages, and realized you could easily be his daughter. Am I right?"

"Yes. Larson, can you believe that I never once told him anything about you?" He nodded slowly.

"I thought, for a while, that you had, but don't ask me why, I couldn't really believe that you had betrayed me. I don't know why you shouldn't have. Maybe it was because, even before you knew who I was, you disowned him."

"You mean my name? Yes, I hated him. He was a vile man. He killed my mother. Not directly, but in little ways. It was years ago that I left his house, took a cut in status, and changed my name. I didn't want to be associated with him in any way. The things he did to people appalled me. I didn't want anybody to know we were related. They did, of course, but after a while they began to forget. I hadn't even seen him in years, until this morning."

"Did you know he would spare you?"

"No, not for sure. But at that point, I didn't really care. What he was doing to you and to me made me want to die anyway."

"I'm not much better than he is," McCade said.

"Yes you are, infinitely better. You don't hurt people for fun. If I met you now, knowing what I do about you, I'd probably avoid you like some kind of bug. But that's not true, because I can see behind you a little bit. I can understand, a little, why you are the way you are. You have an excuse, I think. My father has none."

"You make me think maybe there's hope for me yet," McCade said.

"I think there is," she answered. "I wish it could be me."

He was silent a moment. "You don't owe me anything," he said at last. "On the contrary, I owe you much. I'm going to go on, Valyn. I have to. But you don't have to go with me."

"I think that would be best," she said, as they got off the belt at the edge of Scott's Woods. "I think I would have gone with you anywhere, even away from Seltique. But you were so hard back there. You didn't even blink. You just let me go off to my death and didn't say one word. I can't live with the memory of that."

He stood looking at her for a long moment, and wanted to cry out, clutch her to him, but instead he just turned toward Scott's Woods.

"I almost did," he said at last. "I almost cashed it all in. But your father was impatient, and rang the bell before I had the chance to speak." He looked at her again, then got on the belt, and rode into Scott's Woods, leaving her standing there. He did not look back.

He did not fear Scott's Woods now. He stripped off the badges of his class and threw them away. If anybody tried to stop him, a needle from his toy gun would defend him.

He needed no status any more. The Book was only a few kilometers away, and he had the key to the Scott chateau in his pocket.

He neared the estate and stepped from the belt to the margin in front of the gate. The pale green field crackled occasionally as some small insect flew into it. He took the key from his pocket and put one end into the hole in the gatepost. There was no click as the electromagnetic circuits closed. The field just disappeared. He stepped through and walked across the overgrown lawn toward the great house.

Near the door stood a post with a sphere at the top, about as big as a fist, with an aperture in it just big enough for a man's thumb. The music in his head swelled to a crescendo and he put his thumb in the lock. The stasis field switched off.

Kelso had been able to enter the house because he had put the seal on it. But no one else could unless that person's gene structure showed him to be an heir of the estate—which McCade's gene structure did. He entered the house.

He stood in the great hall, unlit, vast, dusty in spite of the stasis field. His heart pounded, and he was short of breath. How many times had he heard about this hall from his great-grandfather, the refugee without a name, who had been the younger Scott before he had fled the wrath of the Separatist League a century ago? And now, by putting his thumb in the lock and registering his relation to the man who had been the leader of the Core, the Number One of Loger, the owner of this house in direct descent through four thousand years, his great-great-grandfather, Larson McCade came into his inheritance. At the Academy, the disposition of the legacy would finally be recorded. Scott of Scott's Woods had come home at last, and once again, Loger had a Number One.

There was a squawk, and Klooshkai flew in through the still open door, and landed on his shoulder.

"I told you things were happening," the bird said.

"You know too much," McCade replied, not unkindly. "How did you know I was here?"

"From half a thousand meters up, a bird can see for an awfully long way," Klooshkai answered. "And, being used to spotting tasty bugs from that altitude, it's no difficulty at all for me to pick one particular man out of the crowd. I was going to come visit you anyway, when I noticed you having an unhappiness with the girl, so I thought I'd wait for a more propitious moment."

"I still say you know too much."

McCade moved slowly through the house. He went from room to room, and even in the dark they were all familiar to him. How many times had his great-grandfather described that study, this hall, those sculptures, that ceiling? Over and over again. The old man had had nothing left but his memories, and young Larson had been an avid listener.

He toured the whole house once, excitement riding high in him, the music in his mind triumphant, happy, exultant. The rhythms flowed as he went through bedrooms, game rooms, ballrooms. He was home.

At the end of the tour he returned to the great hall. Off on one side was the chamber of state, where his great-great-grandfather, the Number One of Loger, had conducted his business, received his callers, performed his function as leader of the city and where, if McCade stayed, he too would live and work. That was not his plan—he had other things in mind—but still the thought was compelling. He had saved this room for last, because it was in here that the Book of Aradka had been hidden. He stepped up slowly to the great, high, double doors that separated the Chamber of State from the great hall. He swung them wide and stepped into the room he had seen in the photograph in the museum.

There was the desk where his great-great-grandfather had sat, the chairs where the Directors of the Eight Brotherhoods had rested, and the place set aside for the Planet Master. The room had been changed a little since that picture had been taken, but not much.

He went up to the desk. The front of it was divided into a pattern of rectangles. Each rectangle, about eight by fifteen centimeters was ornamented, with a geometric pattern that somehow still conveyed the idea of animals, people, objects, places, and concepts. There were one hundred sixteen such panels. McCade stuck his fingernail under the edge of one and pried. It came off. The first part of the Book of Aradka lay in his hand.

"Very clever," Klooshkai said. "So obvious, no one ever found it."

"Do you know what this is?" McCade asked.

"No, I don't, but I can feel it. It is full of power."

One by one, McCade pried all the panels loose from the front of the desk. He gathered them together and squared them up neatly. They made a thick deck. He went around to the chair behind the desk, sat down, and sorted through the thin metal cards, one by one.

And then he felt it, too, a surge of energy coming from the cards. The Book of Aradka was not a dead artifact. It still functioned. He felt the energy flow through him, and suddenly he was afraid

"You have come into a great heritage," Klooshkai, still on his shoulder, said. "Greater, I think, than even you imagined."

"Yes," McCade said. "I dreamed of this. It frightens me."

The cards sifted through his fingers. He felt them. Not solid sheets of metal, each was in fact a miniature computer. But that was the wrong word. Each was a repository of knowledge. No, say rather power. But that was still wrong.

"A tool," Klooshkai whispered. "A tool. And when the Aradka outgrew their need to play with the laws of the universe, they cast it aside."

"I still say you know too much," McCade muttered.

"But can't you feel it?" the bird asked. "It's all there. The Book carries its own story."

"My mind is not as sharp in these matters as yours," McCade said.

"Perhaps not, but unlike my mind, yours can be honed. I can feel it, and it has already begun."

The cards slithered and slipped, and the Book of Aradka spoke to McCade. And then a shadow crossed the gloom of the Chamber of State, and McCade looked up.

"Come in, Kelso," McCade said.

"I want the formula," Kelso said, hard and angry.

"Certainly," McCade said. "Please sit down."

"We made a deal, and I'm going to hold you to it."

"In spite of the number of times you tried to back out yourself? Sit down, Kelso, it will take me a moment to write it out."

"Do you hear me, McCade? I want it."

"I'll give it to you."

"You'll . . . and my daughter, McCade. What have you done to her?"

"I left her at the edge of the district. I don't know where she is. Maybe she went home."

"If you've hurt her—"

"Sit *down*, Kelso." The man sat. "Now be still while I write this out." He took paper and a pen from a drawer in the desk and, writing quickly, copied down the Planet Master formula. When he finished he handed it to his enemy. Kelso scanned the pages.

"This is it," he cried, "by God, it *is*. I've got you now, McCade. It won't take long to put this into effect. Then I'll be the Planet Master, and you'll be nothing." He got drunkenly to his feet and, clutching his precious pages, staggered from the chamber and the house.

"Was that wise?" Klooshkai asked.

"It won't hurt," McCade answered. "He'll never live to take advantage of it. In order to become Planet Master, he has to undergo a series of psychological changes. They will kill him."

"Are you sure?"

McCade handled the leaves of the Book. Three fell out onto the desk.

"I'm sure," he said. "It's in the cards. The Book knows. It gives me the power, and I can feel him, even now. He will die, Klooshkai."

"And what happens then?"

"The office goes to the next in line, if anyone qualifies."

He paused. "I've won, Klooshkai," he said. "I've won." The energies generated by the Book of Aradka enveloped him. It was his, now, and his long quest had come to an end.

"But who will succeed him?" Klooshkai asked. But it wasn't really a question. "Who is the most qualified, Larson McCade?"

"I am," McCade whispered. The Book spoke to him. He had won, and in his hand was the tool that would break Seltique from its solitude, that would save the Samosar Cluster from stagnation, that would provide unity and leadership for the planet, the Cluster, the Orion Limb, and the Galaxy as a whole. In his hands.

The shadows deepened in the great room, but McCade, Number One of Loger and next Planet Master of Seltique, could see the Book of Aradka by its own light. On his shoulder, Klooshkai settled down more securely, and started to sing some song of his own, about a lost and wandering person finding his home at last and taking up the responsibilities he had inherited.

"But I wanted freedom," McCade said. "I don't want to rule this planet. I don't want to save the galaxy. I just want to go away and live my life."

"Heavy, heavy lies the crown, Master," Klooshkai said.

"Oh, dear God," McCade said, feeling the weight of mastery settle down upon him. "I didn't want this. I didn't want this."